One House Over

Published by Kensington Publishing Corp.

One House Over

MARY MONROE

www.kensingtonbooks.com

DAFINA BOOKS are published by

Kensington Publishing Corp.
119 West 40th Street
New York, NY 10018

All Kensington titles, imprints, and distributed lines are available at special quantity discounts for bulk purchases for sales promotion, premiums, fund-raising, educational, or institutional use. Special book excerpts or customized printings can also be created to fit specific needs. For details, write or phone the office of the Kensington Special Sales Manager: Attn. Special Sales Department. Kensington Publishing Corp, 119 West 40th Street, New York, NY 10018. Phone: 1-800-221-2647.

The DAFINA logo is a trademark of Kensington Publishing Corp.

ISBN-13: 978-1-4967-2452-6
ISBN-10: 1-4967-2452-6
First Kensington Hardcover Edition: April 2018
First Kensington Trade Edition: March 2019
First Kensington Mass Market Edition: March 2021

ISBN-13: 978-1-4967-1613-2 (e-book)
ISBN-10: 1-4967-1613-2 (e-book)

10 9 8 7 6 5 4 3

Printed in the United States of America

Acknowledgments

I am so blessed to be a member of the Kensington Books family. Selena James is an awesome editor and a great friend. Thank you, Selena! Thanks to Steven Zacharius, Adam Zacharius, Karen Auerbach, Lulu Martinez, the wonderful crew in the sales department, and everyone else at Kensington for working so hard for me.

Thanks to Lauretta Pierce for maintaining my website and sharing so many wonderful stories with me.

Thanks to the fabulous book clubs, bookstores, libraries, my readers, and the magazine and radio interviewers for supporting me for so many years.

I have one of the best literary agents on the planet, Andrew Stuart. Thank you, Andrew, for representing me with so much vigor.

The Neighbors
Book 1

Chapter 1

Joyce

June 1934

OTHER THAN MY PARENTS, I WAS THE ONLY OTHER person at the supper table Sunday evening. But there was enough food for twice as many people. We'd spent the first five minutes raving about Mama's fried chicken, how much we had enjoyed Reverend Jessup's sermon a few hours ago, and other mundane things. When Daddy cleared his throat and looked at me with his jaw twitching, I knew the conversation was about to turn toward my spinsterhood.

"I hired a new stock boy the other day and I told him all about you. He is just itching to get acquainted. This one is a real nice, young, single man," Daddy said, looking at me from the corner of his eye.

I froze because I knew where this conversation was going: my "old maid" status. The last "real nice, young, single man" Daddy had hired to work in our store and tried to dump off on me was a fifty-five-year-old, tobacco-chewing, widowed grandfather named Buddy Armstrong. There had been several others before him. Each one had grandkids and health problems. Daddy was eighty-two, so to him anybody under sixty was "young." He and Mama had tried to have children for thirty years before she gave birth to me thirty years ago, when she was forty-eight. But I hadn't waited this long to settle for a husband who'd probably become disabled or die of old age before he could give me the children I desperately wanted.

I was tempted to stay quiet and keep my eyes on the ads for scarves in the new Sears and Roebuck catalog that I had set next to my plate. But I knew that if I didn't say something on the subject within the next few seconds, Daddy would harp on it until I did. Mama would join in, and they wouldn't stop until they'd run out of things to say. And then they would start all over again. I took a deep breath and braced myself. "Daddy, I work as a teacher's aide. What do I have in common with a *stock boy*?"

Daddy raised both of his thick gray eyebrows and looked at me like I was speaking a foreign language. "Humph! Y'all both single! That's what y'all got in common!" he growled.

"I can find somebody on my own!" I boomed. I never raised my voice unless I was really upset, like I was now.

Daddy shook his head. "Since you thirty now and still ain't got no husband—or even a boyfriend—it don't look like you having much luck finding somebody on your own, girl."

"Mac is right, Joyce. It's high time for you to start socializing again. It's a shame the way you letting life pass you by," Mama threw in. They were both looking at me so hard, it made me more uncomfortable than I already was. I squirmed in my seat and cleared my throat.

"Anyway, he said he can't wait to meet you. He is so worldly and sharp, he'll be a good person for you to conversate with."

"I hope you didn't say 'conversate' in front of this new guy. That's a word somebody made up," I scolded. "The correct word is *converse*."

Daddy gave me a pensive look and scratched his neck. "Hmmm. Well, *somebody* 'made up' all the words in every language, eh?"

"Well, yeah, but—"

"What difference do it make which one I used as long as he knew what I meant?"

"Yes, but—"

"Then I'll say conversate if I want to, and you can say converse. It's still English, and this is the only language I know—and it's too complicated for me to be trying to speak it correct this late in the game. Shoot." My Daddy. He was a real piece of work. He winked at me before he bit off a huge chunk of cornbread and started chewing so hard his ears wiggled. He swallowed and started talking again with his eyes narrowed. "I got a notion to invite him to eat supper with us one evening. He is a strapping man, so he'd appreciate a good home-cooked meal. I even told him how good you can cook, Joyce. . . ."

My parents had become obsessed with helping me find a husband. My love life—or lack of a love life—was a frequent subject in our house. One night I dreamed that they'd lined up men in our front yard and made me pa-

rade back and forth in front of them so they could inspect
me. But even in a dream nobody wanted to marry me.

"What's wrong with this one? Other than him being
just a stock boy?" I mumbled as I rolled my eyes.

"Why come you think something is wrong with him?"
Daddy laughed but so far, nobody had said something
funny enough to make me laugh. If anything, I wanted to
cry.

"Because he wants to meet *me*," I said with my voice
cracking. My self-esteem had sunk so low, and I felt so
unworthy, I didn't know if I'd want a man who would settle for me. "He's probably homelier and sicklier than
Buddy Armstrong." I did laugh this time.

"I met him and I sure didn't see nothing wrong with
him," Mama piped in. She drank some lemonade and let
out a mild burp before she continued. "He ain't nowhere
near homely."

"Or sickly," Daddy added with a snort.

"And he's right sporty and handsome!" Mama sounded
like a giddy schoolgirl. I was surprised to see such a hopeful look on her face. Despite all the wrinkles, liver spots,
and about fifty pounds of extra weight, she was still attractive. She had big brown eyes and a smile that made
her moon face look years younger. Unlike Daddy, who
had only half of his teeth left, she still had all of hers.
They were so nice and white, people often asked if they
were real. She was the same pecan shade of brown as me
and Daddy. But I had his small, sad black eyes and narrow face. He'd been completely bald since he was fifty
and last week on my thirtieth birthday he'd predicted that
if I had any hair left by the time I turned forty, it would
probably all be gray. I'd found my first few strands of

gray hair the next morning. "I know you'll like this one," Mama assured me with a wink. She reared back in her wobbly chair and raked her thick fingers through her thin gray hair. "You ain't getting no younger, so you ain't got much time left," she reminded.

"So you keep telling me," I snapped.

Mama sucked on her teeth and gave me a dismissive wave. "He got slaphappy when we told him about you. I bet he been beating the women off with a stick all his life."

Mama's taste in potential husbands for me was just as pathetic as Daddy's. But her last comment really got my attention because it sounded like a contradiction. "Why would a 'sporty and handsome' man get 'slaphappy' about meeting a new woman—especially if he's already beating them off with a stick?" I wanted to know.

Daddy gave me an annoyed look. "Don't worry about a little detail like that. And don't look a gift horse in the mouth. You ain't been out on a date since last year, and I know that must be painful. Shoot. When I was young, and before I married your mama, I never went longer than a week without courting somebody. At the rate you going, you ain't never going to get married."

I'd celebrated my thirtieth birthday eight days ago, but I felt more like a woman three times my age. Most of the adult females I knew were already married. My twenty-five-year-old cousin Louise had been married and divorced twice and was already engaged again. "I guess marriage wasn't meant for me," I whined. I suddenly lost my appetite, so I pushed my plate to the side.

"You ain't even touched them pinto beans on your plate, and you ate only half of your supper yesterday,"

Mama complained. "How do you expect to get a man if you ain't got enough meat on your bones? You already look like a lamppost, and you know colored men like thick women. Besides, a gal six feet tall like you need to eat twice as much as a shorter woman so there's enough food to fill out all your places."

"It ain't about how much I weigh," I said defensively. "Last year I weighed twenty pounds more than I do now, and it didn't make a difference. But . . . I wish I could shrink down to a normal height." I laughed, but I was serious. For a colored woman, being too tall was almost as bad as being too dark and homely. I wasn't as dark or homely as some of the women I knew, but I was the tallest and the only one my age still single.

"Well, look at it this way, baby girl. You ain't no Kewpie doll and you may be too lanky for anybody to want to marry you, but at least you got your health. A lot of women don't even have that." Daddy squeezed my hand and smiled. "And you real smart."

I was thankful that I was healthy and smart, but those things didn't do a damn thing for my overactive sex drive. If a man didn't make love to me soon, I was going to go crazy. And the way I'd been fantasizing about going up to a stranger in a beer garden or on the street and asking him to go to bed with me, maybe I had already lost my mind. "Can I be excused? I have a headache," I muttered, rubbing the back of my head.

"You said the same thing when we was having supper yesterday," Mama reminded.

"I had a headache then, too," I moaned. I rose up out of my chair so fast, I almost knocked it over. With my head hanging low, I shuffled around the corner and down the hall to my bedroom. I'd been born in the same room, and the way my life was going, I had a feeling I'd die in it too.

Branson was a typical small town in the southern part of Alabama. It was known for its cotton and sugarcane fields and beautiful scenery. Fruit and pecan trees, and flowers of every type and color decorated most of the residents' front and back yards. But things were just as gloomy here as the rest of the South.

Our little city had only about twenty thousand people and most of them were white. Two of our four banks had crashed right after the Great Depression started almost five years ago. But a few people had been smart enough to pull their money out just in time. Our post office shared the same building with the police department across the street from our segregated cemetery.

Jim Crow, the rigid system that the white folks had created to establish a different set of rules for them and us, was strictly enforced. Basically, what it meant was that white people could do whatever they wanted, and we couldn't eat where they ate, sleep or socialize with them, or even sass them. Anybody crazy enough to violate the rules could expect anything from a severe beating to dying at the hands of a lynch mob. A lot of our neighbors and friends worked for wealthy white folks in the best neighborhoods, but all of the colored residents lived on the south side. And it was segregated too. The poor people lived in the lower section near the swamps and the dirt roads. The ones with decent incomes, like my family, lived in the upper section.

The quiet, well-tended street we lived on was lined with magnolia and dogwood trees on both sides. Each house had a neat lawn, and some had picket fences. The brown-shingled house with tar paper roofing and a wraparound front porch we owned had three bedrooms. The walls were thin, so when Mama and Daddy started talking again after I'd bolted from the supper table, I could hear them. And, I didn't like what they were saying.

"Poor Joyce. I just ball up inside when I think about how fast our baby is going to waste. I'm going to keep praying for her to find somebody before it's too late," Mama grumbled. "With her strong back she'd be a good workhorse and keep a clean house and do whatever else she'll need to do to keep a husband happy. And I'd hate to see them breeding hips she got on her never turn out no babies." Mama let out a loud, painful-sounding groan. "What's even worse is, I would hate to leave this world knowing she was going to grow old alone."

"I'm going to keep praying for her to get married too. But that might be asking for too much. I done almost put a notion like that out of my mind. This late in the game, the most we can expect is to fix her up with somebody who'll court her for a while, so she can have a little fun before she get too much older," Daddy grunted. "Maybe we ain't been praying hard enough, huh?"

"We been praying hard enough, but that ain't the problem," Mama snapped.

"Oh? Then what is it?"

"The problem is this girl is too doggone picky!" Mama shouted.

"Sure enough," Daddy agreed.

I couldn't believe my ears! My parents were trying to fix me up with a stock boy, not a businessman, and they thought I was being too picky. I wanted to laugh and cry at the same time. A lot of ridiculous things had been said to and about me. Being "too picky" was one of the worst because it couldn't have been further from the truth.

I had no idea how my folks had come to such an off-the-wall conclusion. I couldn't imagine what made them think I was too picky. I'd given up my virginity when I was fourteen to Marvin Galardy, the homeliest boy in the neighborhood. And that was only because he was the only one interested in having sex with me at the time.

I was so deep in thought, I didn't hear Daddy knocking on my door, so he let himself in. "You done gone deaf, too?" he grumbled.

"I didn't hear you," I mumbled, sitting up on my bed.

"You going to the evening church service with us? We'll be leaving in a few minutes."

"Not this time, Daddy. My head is still aching, so I think I just need to lie here and take it easy." I rubbed the side of my head.

"And it's going to keep on hurting if you don't take some pills."

"I'll take some before I go to sleep."

Daddy turned to leave, and then he snapped his fingers. "I forgot the real reason I came in here. Mother's going to Mobile tomorrow morning with Maxine Fisher to do some shopping and she'll be gone most of the day. If you ain't got no plans for lunch tomorrow and that headache is gone, I'll swing by the school around noon to pick you up and we can go to Mosella's. Monday is the only day peach cobbler is on the menu, and I been dying for some."

"You don't have to drive all the way from the store to pick me up. That's out of your way. One of the other aides has an appointment with her doctor in the same block, so I can ride with her and have her drop me off at the store. I need to pick up a few items anyway."

"That'll work," Daddy said, rubbing his chest. "I'll see you around noon then?"

"Okay, Daddy."

It was still light outside, but I went to bed anyway. Each day I slept more than I needed and wished I could sleep even more. At least then I wouldn't have to talk to people and walk around with a fake smile on my face.

Chapter 2
Odell

I WAS SO ANXIOUS TO GET BACK TO WORK, I COULDN'T wait for tomorrow to come. I'd only been on my new job at MacPherson's for a week. It was a dyed-in-the-wool country convenience store with benches inside for people to sit on when they needed to take a break from their shopping. Regular customers could expect a complimentary pig foot or some lip-smacking pork rinds on certain days. I could already tell that this was the best job I ever had. It was a nice family-friendly business, and I was really looking forward to the experience, especially since I'd be working for colored folks. Mr. MacPherson didn't pay me that much to start, but as long as it covered my rent I didn't care. I was a born hustler, so I knew I'd find ways to cover my other expenses once I got a toehold on my new situation. Stocking shelves was much better than dragging along on farms and other odd jobs I'd done all my life. The small building where MacPherson's was located sat on a corner next to a bait shop. There was a sign printed in all capital letters in the front window that said: WE SELL EVERYTHING FROM APRONS TO MENS' PINSTRIPE SUITS. But they never had more than six or seven of each item in stock at a time. When inventory got low, the MacPhersons immediately replenished everything and gave their customers discounts when they had to wait on a certain item. The customers were happy because this kind of service kept them from having to make the eight-mile trip to nearby Butler where there was a Piggly Wiggly market and much bigger department stores.

People kept complaining about the Great Depression we was going through, but it didn't even faze me. Like almost every other colored person, I couldn't tell the difference because we'd been going through a "depression" all our lives. Some of the white folks who used to have enough money to shop at the better stores started shopping at MacPherson's. On my first day, me and Mr. Mac-Pherson had to help a nervous blond woman haul a box of canned goods, some cleaning products, produce, toys, and even a few clothes to her car. The whole time she'd belly-ached to him about what a disgrace it was to her family that they had to shop where all the colored people shopped, something she'd never done before. In the next breath, she complimented him on how "happy-go-lucky" he was for a colored man, and because of that he was "a credit to his race."

One of the things I noticed right away was how loosey-goosey the MacPhersons ran their business. Like a lot of folks, they didn't trust banks, especially since so many people had lost every cent and all the property they owned when the banks failed. One of the richest white families I used to pick cotton for had ended up flat broke and had to move to a tent city campground with other displaced families.

Preston "Mac" MacPherson and his wife, Millie, only kept enough in their checking account to cover their employees' checks and to pay their business expenses. I'd found that out from Buddy Armstrong, the tubby, fish-eyed head cashier and the nosiest, grumpiest, and biggest blabbermouth elderly man I'd ever met. The other cashier, a pint-sized, plain-featured, widowed great-grandmother named Sadie Mae Glutz was almost as bad as Buddy.

On my first day, they'd started running off at the mouth before the first morning break, telling me all kinds of personal things about people I had never met. Buddy and Sadie was good entertainment, so I pretended to be interested in their gossip and even egged them on. The MacPhersons were their favorite target. Even though it was supposed to be a company "secret," they wasted no time telling me that Mr. MacPherson kept most of his money locked up in his house. At the end of each day he'd pluck all the cash out of the two cash registers and stuff it into a brown paper bag.

"I hope that information don't get to the wrong person. I'd hate to hear about some joker busting into that house robbing such a nice elderly couple," I said.

"You ain't got to worry about nothing like that. Mac keeps a shotgun in the house," Buddy assured me.

"I hope he never has to use it," I chuckled.

"He done already done that," Sadie added. Before I could ask when and why, she continued. "A couple of years ago, some fool tried to steal Mac's car out of his driveway. Mac ran out just in time to stop that jackass."

"Did he kill him?" I asked, looking from Sadie to Buddy.

"Naw. He shot at him, but he missed," Buddy answered. "And that sucker took off in such a hurry, he ran clean out of his shoes. Then he had the nerve to try to steal another man's car in the same neighborhood. He wasn't so lucky that time. I was one of the pallbearers at his funeral."

"I'm glad Mr. MacPherson didn't kill that thief. He is such a nice man, I'd hate for him to get involved with the law," I stated.

"Thank you. Him and Millie got enough problems already. Especially trying to marry off that gal of theirs." Sadie shook her head and clucked her thick tongue. "She grown and still living at home. And she look like the kind of woman no man in his right mind would tangle with. She a whole head taller than me and probably twice as strong. If I seen her fighting a bear, I'd help the bear. Wouldn't you do the same thing, Buddy?"

"Sure enough." Buddy chuckled for a few seconds, and then he started yip-yapping about Joyce some more. "And she got the nerve to flirt with me almost every time I see her, with her *mugly* self."

"'Mugly'? What's that?" I asked.

"Oh, that's just a nicer way of calling somebody ugly. Anyway, she been messing with me ever since I started working here last September, grinning and sashaying in front of me like a shake dancer. But I would never get involved with a woman with feet bigger than mine. First time I make her mad, she'd stomp a hole in me."

This was the first time I'd heard about Joyce, and it wouldn't be the last. Every time things got slow on my first day, Buddy and Sadie would wander over to where I was stacking or reorganizing merchandise and start conversating and laughing about the MacPhersons' pitiful daughter.

"Y'all got me so curious now, I can't wait to meet this beast," I admitted, laughing along with them.

"You'll see exactly what we mean when you do meet her," Sadie told me.

"Why don't y'all like her? Is she mean-spirited, too?"

Buddy and Sadie gasped at the same time. "No, she ain't no mean person at all, and we do like her," Sadie claimed. "We talk about all the folks we know like this. But Joyce is such an oddball; we talk about her a little more than we do everybody else."

"I hope you'll like her too," Buddy threw in. "She ain't got many friends, so she need all the ones she can get."

By the end of the day, I had heard so many unflattering things about the MacPhersons' big-boned "old maid" daughter, it seemed like I'd known her for years. I felt so sorry for her. The next day when Mr. MacPherson bragged about how smart and nice and caring his only child was and how much he loved her, I told him I couldn't wait to meet her. I'd only said it to make him feel good, because I wanted to make sure I did everything possible for him to keep me on the payroll. I had heard that the stock boys before me had never lasted more than a few weeks. A couple had just up and quit, but the MacPhersons had fired all the others. I hoped that I'd get to stay a lot longer, or at least until I found a better job.

I had just enough money to last until I got my first paycheck. Mr. MacPherson had promised that if he was pleased with my work and I got to work on time, he'd eventually give me more responsibilities and more money. He really liked me and even told me I reminded him of himself when he was my age. I told him that if I looked half as good as he did when I got to be his age, I'd be happy. That made him blush and grin, and it made me realize that complimenting a man like him could win me a lot of points. It was true that I had a lot going for me in the looks department. But I never took it for granted. People had been telling me I was cute since I was a baby. My curly black hair, smooth Brazil nut brown skin, slanted black eyes, and juicy lips got me a lot of attention. One of the main things the women liked about me and complimented me on all the time was my height, which was six feet four.

Some women believed that old wives' tale that tall men had long sticks between their legs. I couldn't speak for other tall men, but I had enough manly meat between my thighs to keep the women I went to bed with sure enough happy. I wasn't just tall; I had a body like a prize-fighter. Years of backbreaking farm labor had rewarded me with some muscles that wouldn't quit. Women couldn't keep their hands off me. When I was younger, I used to have to sneak out back doors in bars just to throw them off my trail. I was thirty-one now, so I still had a few good years left to find a wife and have children before my jism got too weak. I was between ladies now, and because my last two breakups had been so bad, I was in no hurry to get involved with another woman anytime soon. I changed my tune Monday afternoon when I met Mr. Mac-Pherson's daughter.

Chapter 3
Odell

I HAD JUST FINISHED STACKING THE CANNED GOODS SHELVES in the grocery section aisle when I noticed Mr. MacPherson and a tall young woman walking toward me. She resembled Mac and was almost as tall as he was. He was leading her by her hand. I could tell by the way she was blinking and smiling that she was shy. That was probably the only detail about her that Buddy and Sadie hadn't told me. I liked shy women. They were easy to control.

"Odell, I want you to meet my baby," Mr. MacPherson said, grinning from ear to ear. When they got in front of me, he let go of Joyce's hand. I noticed how she sighed with relief and moved a couple of steps away from her daddy. My guess was that this poor creature let her parents control every move she made.

"This is your daughter?" I said, smiling so hard my jaws ached. I was impressed because Joyce was nothing like I expected. From the way Buddy and Sadie had described her, I had pictured a mule-faced giraffe in my mind. Shoot! She didn't look nothing like that! She wasn't even close to being as "mugly" as they'd made her out to be. Joyce was no beauty queen, but she was attractive in her own way. She had a cute narrow face and nice black eyes with long thick lashes. I preferred women with real long hair. Joyce's only came just below her ears, but it looked good on her.

If I had met her in a jook joint or on the street, I would never have approached her because she wasn't my type. But then I got to thinking about one of the things Buddy and Sadie had told me about her. According to them two busybodies, Mr. MacPherson and his wife were desperate for Joyce to get married and have a few children. That piece of information had really got my attention and even more so now that I was meeting her in person. And since she didn't have no brothers or sisters, she'd inherit everything when Mama and Daddy kicked the bucket. If that wasn't enough incentive for her to be my type now, I didn't know what was. I couldn't think of nothing better than me stumbling into an unmarried woman that had so much to offer a man who'd been down on his luck as long as I had. All I had to worry about was getting her to like me.

"Joyce, this is Odell," Mr. MacPherson introduced. He was beaming like a lighthouse. "What's your last name again, Odell?"

"It's Watson, Mr. MacPherson," I answered real quick.

"Boy, didn't I tell you to call me Mac and my wife Millie?" Mr. MacPherson said in a gruff tone. "We like to be real informal around here," he added.

"Okay, Mac," I said, grinning. I looked at Joyce again and gave her the biggest smile I could manage. "I've heard so much about you, I couldn't wait to meet you," I told her, extending my hand. She had such a tight smile on her face, I didn't know what to make of it. I hoped my good looks didn't intimidate her. One ordinary-looking woman that I'd tried to get my hands on last month told me—with the same kind of tight smile on her face that was on Joyce's—that she didn't want to get involved with a man that was prettier than her. Was the itty-bitty smile on Joyce's face a sign that she felt the same way? I hoped it wouldn't take long to find out.

"Hello, Odell. I'm glad to meet you. Daddy just mentioned you to me yesterday," she muttered. I could tell by the way her hand was trembling when I shook it that she was nervous. She seemed so sweet and ladylike, I actually *liked* her already!

"Mr.—oops, I mean, Mac, I been working for you since last week. You ought to be ashamed of yourself for hiding this beautiful girl from me all this time," I teased. I was good at a lot of things. One was using the right words when I wanted to impress somebody. Suddenly there was a huge smile on Joyce's face. Her eyes got kind of moist, and her body seemed to relax. I could tell that I'd just impressed the hell out of her.

"Heh, heh, heh," Mac laughed. "She ain't been hiding. She got a full-time job, so she don't get over to the store too often." He paused and let out a loud sigh. "She don't like to come here too often no more on account of we used to make her work the cash register after school when she was a teenager. And she came kicking and screaming." Mac squeezed Joyce's shoulder. I could see how much he loved his daughter. He looked at her like she was made out of gold. "She wanted to sit at home and read books instead. Now she don't come up in here until

she need a few items, or unless she coming to meet me or
her mama for lunch." He snorted and with a dry look on
his face, he said, "Would you believe this gal ain't been
on a date since last year? October to be exact."

"Mac, I know you lying!" I accused. I folded my arms
and blinked at Joyce.

"No, I ain't lying. Honest to God," Mac insisted. "Ask
her and she'll tell you herself."

Poor Joyce. She looked like she wanted to crawl away
and hide behind the racks where they hung the pinstripe
suits a few feet from the shelves I'd just stacked. I felt
even sorrier for her now and was willing to say anything
that would make her feel better. I slapped my hands on
my hips and said in the sternest tone I could push out of
my mouth, "I'm going to do something about that, starting with supper at a nice restaurant this evening."

She gasped, and her eyes got as big as saucers.
"M-me?" she stuttered in a voice so low I had to lean forward to hear her.

"Yeah, you!" Mac snapped. "What's wrong with you,
girl? Me and you the only other folks standing here, and
Odell sure ain't talking about taking me out to supper."
Mac rolled his eyes and wiped sweat off his forehead. I
was about to start sweating too, because I had no idea
what I was getting myself into. If things worked out good
between me and Joyce, that would be fine. If they didn't,
it could put me in an awkward position with her parents
and jeopardize my job security. It would be bad enough
for me to lose my job because Mac and Millie didn't like
my work. But it'd be much worse if they let me go because things didn't work out between me and their daughter. I was tempted to back off, but since I had already
invited her to go out with me this evening, it was too late.

"Odell, you can see that this girl ain't too sharp when it come to conversating with men, which is probably why she ain't got one. You'll like her once you get to know her. She ain't the best woman in the world, but she ain't the worst."

"Daddy, you stop that!" Joyce ordered, gently tapping the side of Mac's jowly face. I was glad to hear her using a firmer tone. Maybe she didn't let her parents control every move she made after all. She cleared her throat and blinked at me some more. "What time do you want to go out, Odell?"

"She'll be ready at six o'clock sharp," Mac blurted out. "You got a car?"

"Not yet, sir. I plan to get one as soon as I can afford to."

"Hmmm. Then you know how to drive?"

"Yes, sir. I been driving since I was sixteen," I said proudly.

"Then y'all can go out in my car." Mac glanced at the big clock on the wall above the door and gulped. "Lord a'mighty! Look how late it is! Come on, girl. We better shake a leg if we going to lunch, so I can get you back to your work on time."

"It was nice meeting you, Odell. I'll see you at six o'clock sharp," Joyce cooed, walking behind her daddy like a faithful puppy all the way out the door.

Buddy and Sadie gazed at me with their eyes so bugged out, you would have thought I'd just parted the Red Sea. I didn't feel like hearing any more of their crude comments or answering any nosy questions. I ducked out the back door, so I could be by myself for a few minutes. I needed to think about what I was getting myself into with my employer's daughter. It didn't take long for me to convince myself that I'd made a wise move.

Ten minutes later when I went back inside, Buddy and Sadie had several people to wait on, so I didn't have to worry about them bothering me for a while. By three p.m. Mac hadn't returned, so I figured he'd gone home early. With the big boss man no longer on the premises, and no customers in the store, Buddy slipped into his busybody mode again. He waltzed over to where I was straightening out the racks that held the women's blouses.

"Well, now," he croaked. "Look like you and Joyce done hit it off real good."

I gave him the most irritated look I could conjure up. "We did. She seems like a real nice lady and I hope I get to know her better."

"Why?"

I did a double-take. "That's a mighty odd question. Especially coming from you."

"I'm just trying to figure out what you seen in her that the other men don't see."

I folded my arms and said in the strongest voice my mouth could manage, "I seen a real sweet woman and I like her. She was nothing like I expected."

"Is that right? Hmmm. I do declare, I'm sure enough surprised," Buddy cocked his head and squinted. "After all me and Sadie Mae told you about that gal, I don't know what you was expecting."

"Well, it don't matter. I still like Joyce. Now if you don't mind, I'd like to finish my work, so I can go home and get ready for my date with her."

Buddy raised his arms and shook his patchy gray-haired, peanut-shaped head. "All right then. I was just trying to help."

"Do me a favor and don't 'help' me no more."

"Say what?"

"If you got anything else you want to tell me about Joyce, keep it to yourself. I'd really appreciate that."

"Oh. Okay then." Buddy bit his bottom lip and cleared his throat. "I'll tell Sadie the same thing if you want me to."

"Tell her exactly what I told you."

"Uh-huh. Um . . . I guess I should get back to work in case Mac come back. If he do, I hope he in a good mood, so he'll let me take off early today. I need to get home, so I can rinse out my good shirt and iron it dry. I got a date with a lady this evening myself."

"That's good, Buddy. I hope you'll have a good time." I ended the conversation with a smile and a pat on Buddy's shoulder and he returned to his cash register. That was the last time he or Sadie ever said anything to me about Joyce.

I didn't own no watch. I looked up at the wall clock every few minutes to keep track of the time. When I got off at five, I'd have just enough time to go to the flophouse where I rented a room and get ready.

Chapter 4
Joyce

*I*T WAS HARD FOR ME TO BELIEVE THAT A HANDSOME MAN like Odell could fix his juicy lips to call me beautiful. I was not blind, so I knew what I looked like. No matter how much I spruced myself up, I was only average-looking at best. One of the drawers in my bedroom chifforobe contained a big supply of nut-brown face powder, rouge, black eyebrow pencils, straightening combs, marcel curlers, and every hair pomade ever made. Even with all those props, I had never felt beautiful until now.

Odell liked me enough to invite me to have supper with him, but I still didn't think our date was going to lead to anything serious. If sex was all he wanted, that was fine with me.

I prayed that Daddy hadn't put him up to asking me out. In a way, he had, by telling Odell I hadn't been on a date since last year! I couldn't imagine what Odell must have thought when he heard that. There was just no telling what else Daddy had told him about me. I could just hear him blabbing about how I sat around the house every night with my head in a magazine or a book. But it was true. When I didn't feel like reading and went out somewhere by myself, I got jealous when I saw other women with their boyfriends or husbands.

Odell seemed like the kind of man who liked to see people happy, so he probably thought it would please Daddy if he took me out. I didn't want to think that was the case, but I couldn't help myself. After giving it a little more thought, I decided I didn't really care what his real reason was. I was just happy that I was going out with him.

After I had checked my make-up and hair for the third or fourth time, I sat on my bed and stared at the wall. I didn't like to spend too much time feeling sorry for myself, so I was relieved when Mama interrupted my thoughts when she knocked on my door ten minutes after I'd locked myself in.

"You all right in there?" she yelled.

"Yes, ma'am." I sounded so tired I probably should have been getting some rest instead of getting ready to go on a date.

"Odell just got here."

"Oh. He's right on time," I mumbled, and glanced at the clock on my nightstand. I didn't know what else he was, but at least he was punctual—which was more than I could say about any other colored person, including myself. I'd arrived at my own high school graduation so late, they had already passed out the diplomas by the time I got there.

I didn't want to keep Odell waiting because I was

scared Daddy or Mama might say something that would scare him off. I laughed at the thought of that happening. I didn't know what I was thinking! First of all, he worked eight hours a day five days a week with them. There was just no telling how many stupid things they'd probably already said to him about me. But he still wanted to take me out, so maybe he didn't care what they'd told him. Or maybe he was after my money. Just thinking about him being a fortune hunter made my chest tighten. If that was what he was after, he would be disappointed. Other than my paycheck, I didn't have any of my own yet. I would inherit the store and everything else Mama and Daddy left behind when they died, but they could live another five or ten years for all I knew. I figured that a man after money wouldn't want to wait around that long to get it. Besides, the other men I'd been involved with had known that I'd inherit a small fortune someday but they hadn't asked me to marry them. Anyway, a man like Odell could get any woman he wanted. Other than trying to please my parents, I couldn't think of any other reason why he'd want to spend time with a clumsy ox like me unless he really did like me; or, unless he was crazy.

Mama pounded on the door again. "If you don't get your tail out here and go out with this man, I'll go." She laughed. "I told Odell you'd probably be late for your own funeral. You sure took your time coming out of my womb."

I laughed too. "Mama, you behave yourself now. Tell Odell, I'll be ready in a minute. I just need to put on a little more make-up." I wanted to look extra nice, more for myself than Odell. I felt better when I looked good.

"Let me in!" Mama hollered, and pounded some more at the same time. I opened the door, and she clomped in with her hands on her hips. "I don't know why you lock this door in the first place when ain't nobody up in here but us. We don't even lock the doors to the house."

"I like my privacy, Mama."

"Privacy? What do you need privacy for? All you do in this room is read and sleep."

The last time I'd left my door unlocked, Mama had barged in while I was stretched out in my bed trying to pleasure myself with my finger, with no success. I had pulled the covers up over me in the nick of time. I didn't even want to think about what she would have said or done if she had caught me touching myself. As far as she was concerned, sex was only acceptable when it was between two married people. She made that clear every time the subject came up in my presence. "Unmarried folks and sex don't mix, and it's a deadly sin." That was what she'd said when Sadie told us about an unmarried woman who had come to the store to buy some salve to treat scabs on her private parts—which Mama called the appropriate punishment for fooling around. Regardless of what she or anybody else thought about sex outside of marriage, I wanted to get as much as I could. But pleasuring a woman was a man's job. My feeble attempt at self-gratification had not turned out the way I thought it would, so I never tried it again. I prayed that Odell would at least end my long dry spell. I'd glanced at his crotch right after Daddy had introduced us. It looked like he had the necessary equipment to get the job done right.

Mama looked around my room, frowning. I was a neat person, so everything was in place. Well, almost everything. There were a few magazines and the latest Sears and Roebuck catalog on the floor next to some chicken bones on a plate. She shook her head when she saw a stack of Gothic romance novels on my dresser that I had recently ordered from a mail-order company in New Jersey. "Lord have mercy. I can't for the life of me figure out why you spend so much money on reading material."

"So I can learn more about life," I muttered.

"Learn more about life? If you ain't figured life out by now, you never will. Besides, everything you need to know is in the Bible. If you read it more often, you wouldn't need to be wasting money on all them books. Did you wash up real good? We don't want Odell to think you ain't clean."

"Mama, I took a bath right after I got home this evening. Don't you remember how you fussed up a storm about me using up all the hot water?"

"You wash under your arms? A long, tall, strapping gal like you can get right musty in the armpits if you sweat."

"I'm old enough to know how to take a bath." I rolled my neck and eyes at the same time as I plopped back down on my bed.

Mama stood in front of me with her arms folded, looking me up and down. "Well, just to be on the safe side and make sure you don't get too ripe, you can rub some of my rose sachet up under your arms too." Odell must have really made a big impression on her because she never let me use any of her sachet. "Put a dab of baking soda behind your ears and on the back of your neck. That'll keep you from sweating too much."

When I shuffled into the living room a minute later, the first thing Odell said to me was, "You look even more beautiful than you did this afternoon."

Either he was crazy after all, or my ears were playing tricks on me.

Chapter 5
Odell

*D*URING THE RIDE TO THE RESTAURANT, I LEARNED A lot about Joyce. She chatted away like a myna bird. It didn't take long for me to realize that she was not shy like she had seemed when I met her. She even seemed more confident and relaxed now.

I could already tell that she was a fairly intelligent woman because she spoke like one. Since she read books, listened to the radio every day, and worked in a school with folks that had even gone to college, she didn't use as much bad grammar as me, and most of the other folks I knew.

Since she seemed to enjoy conversating so much, I wasn't going to say too much about myself until I had to. And I'd be particular about what information I shared. I only told people what I wanted them to know and never anything that would make me look even slightly bad, lazy, or trifling in any way. When people asked if I had kids, I always said no. But the truth of the matter was, I didn't know for sure. I'd started having sex when I was thirteen, so it was possible that I had a few kids out there somewhere. One girl accused me of getting her pregnant when I was fourteen and she was thirteen. She moved to Detroit to live with her grandma while she was still pregnant, and I never heard from her again. The only other time was ten years ago when a woman I'd slept with just once claimed she was pregnant by me. She died in a car wreck a week later. I thought about them two a lot, especially in the last few years. The older I got, the more I wanted to know what it was like to be a daddy.

Right after me and Joyce slid into one of the back booths at Mosella's we started discussing politics, the church, and our jobs. I read the newspapers a few times a week and listened to the radio often enough, so I could hold my own when it came to certain subjects. "Do you think President Roosevelt is doing a good job?" It was one of the first questions she asked.

I hunched my shoulders. "He could be, but it don't mean nothing to us colored folks. Everybody ought to know by now that whatever goes on in the White House is set up to help *white* folks. Just like the Jim Crow laws. We ended up in America by default, so it'll never really be our home."

I couldn't tell from the deadpan expression on Joyce's face what she was thinking. "Well, I'm sorry to hear you feel that way, Odell. I was born in America, so it's the only home I know."

"You got a point there and I'm sorry I said what I said. Me and you is just as American as Roosevelt. Did you vote for him?"

"No. When I tried to register, the white folks I had to deal with treated me so mean and evil, I gave up and came back home."

"I ain't surprised. Some of my friends got threatened when they tried to register, so I didn't even try."

"Do you think colored people will ever be treated like human beings in this country?"

I nodded. "Yeah, but probably not in our lifetime. In the meantime, all we got is one another. I think that as long as we work together and look out for other colored folks, and don't piss off the wrong white folks, we'll make more progress." I paused and cocked my head to the side and gave Joyce a serious look. I didn't want the night to end, because I was enjoying her company. She made me feel so comfortable and gave me so much hope; I *had* to make her my woman. "You have the most beautiful eyes."

She did a double-take and blinked real hard, which told me she was not used to getting compliments. "You think so?"

"Sure enough. They remind me of marbles. I can't thank you enough for allowing me to spend time with you. You made my day."

"You made mine, too." Her voice was so low I could barely hear her. I couldn't tell if the look in her eyes was sadness or desperation. Probably a little of both. Well, I was going to fix all that—if she'd let me get far enough into her dreary life. She dropped her head and stared at the top of the table.

"You shy, ain't you?" I accused.

She looked up and shook her head. "Who, me? Uh-uh. I don't think so." Her voice cracked over each word. "I'm just a little nervous."

"You don't have to be shy or nervous with me. I want you to let loose and enjoy yourself."

Mosella's service was always as slow as molasses, even when there was no crowd. It could take up to a whole hour to get served, another fifteen to twenty minutes to get the check, and a half hour more for the server to bring you your change. People complained all the time, but nothing ever changed. This restaurant was still the most popular colored-owned place to eat. For the first time, I was glad that the service was so slow. It would give me more time to conversate with Joyce. If I was going to get my future off the ground, I needed to get busy and start picking her brain. I hoped she'd give me enough information so I'd know where to go next with my plan to make her fall in love with me. I wasn't about to turn my back on all the benefits I could enjoy by being her man.

I was impressed when she told me she had finished high school and completed a six-month education training program, whatever the hell that was. She seemed proud of the fact that she had decided in her junior year of high school she didn't want to keep working in her parents' store after graduation, like she had been doing since she was thirteen.

"I don't mind working at all. I love my folks to death, but working in the store with them breathing down my neck was not what I wanted to do for the rest of my life. I tried a few other jobs after I finished high school, but when they offered me a position as a teacher's aide at the same elementary school I went to, I jumped on it and I love what I do."

"What is a teacher's aide's job?" I asked.

"I help Miss Kirksey, the fourth-grade teacher I've

been working with since I started, plan the daily activities. I'm more patient than she is, so I give the kids the individual attention they need. And, you know how rowdy kids in elementary school can be. I help keep the troublemakers under control."

"It sounds like a good job, but it must be a lot of hard work, too. That can be a heavy burden."

"It is, but I love kids so much I think of it as more of a blessing than a burden. And they pay me a decent salary."

"I wish I could have stayed in school long enough to graduate."

"Why didn't you?"

"My mama brung in half of the household money, so when she died, I had to drop out of school in eighth grade and get a job so I could help Daddy pay the bills."

"Do you have any brothers and sisters?"

"Both older and long gone. They took off while I was still in my teens. My sister, Maybelline, live in Birmingham with her husband and their retarded adult son. They got their hands full taking care of him and struggling with low-paying jobs just to get by, so she never helped out. My brother, Donnie, live in Birmingham too. He shine shoes in a hotel lobby. Him and his wife got six kids, so he sure can't do nothing to help Daddy. My siblings never got along with Daddy to begin with, so once they left home, they never looked back. Maybelline send him a Christmas card with a letter included every year. But she ain't been back to visit but four or five times since she left home, oh, twelve or thirteen years ago. Donnie ain't been back but twice and he left home a year before Maybelline did."

"What happened to your mama?"

"Tuberculosis killed her when I was ten. Daddy married my stepmother Ellamae a year later. That woman is a bitch on wheels. Two days after I turned sixteen, I threw some clothes in a bag and left that house running. I already had a job picking cotton, but I struggled for a long time before things got better. I go visit my daddy at least once or twice a week just to make sure Ellamae ain't mistreating him. She's another reason my brother and sister don't come around no more."

"Where does your daddy and his wife live?" Joyce was real interested in what I was telling her, but it was painful for me to relive my past, so I hoped we'd move onto a different subject soon.

"Out on Route One down in the boondocks near the cane and cotton fields. In the same miserable shack I grew up in." I cleared my throat to keep from groaning.

"Is he happy?"

I hunched my shoulders. "Well, he ain't dead, and after all he's been through, he should be happy he still alive. So, to answer your question: He's happy. He wasn't the best daddy in the world when I was growing up, but I love him to death, and I'm going to do all I can to make his last years better on him."

"That's nice of you to be so concerned about your daddy. Is he the reason you never married?"

I scratched my chin and gave Joyce the most sincere and intense look I could come up with. "No. I'm not married yet because I'm still looking for the right woman. . . ."

She blinked, tapped her fingers on the table a few times, and cleared her throat. She was smart, but I was smarter. I had got her number two minutes after I met her. I could tell that she was fishing for the same kind of information about me that I was fishing for about her. She was probably as anxious to lock us into a serious relationship as I was. "My daddy drives me up the wall sometimes, but I don't mind. I enjoy spending time with him. I don't know what I'm going to do when he dies."

"I can understand you wanting to be with your daddy as much as possible, but everybody should strike out on their own once they reach a certain age. If you don't mind me asking, if you got such a good job, how come you still live at home?" From the tight look on Joyce's face now, I could tell I'd asked a question that made her feel uncomfortable. "I'm sorry." I held up my hand and tried to look apologetic. "You ain't got to answer that. That ain't my business."

"I don't mind answering it." She stopped talking long enough to take a long, deep breath. "I tried sharing a room with another girl a few years ago and it almost ended in a bloodbath."

"Was she hard to get along with?"

"That and everything else, which was a surprise to me. I'd known her since tenth grade, and she seemed like the kind of person who'd make a good roommate. Well, I was wrong. She never had her share of the rent on time, and she kept the place looking like a pigsty. Her boyfriends were in and out all hours of the day and night. Every time I complained, she accused me of being jealous on account of I had one date for every five she had. I moved out and tried living by myself. It was okay for a few months until I got tired of coming home to an empty room and not having anybody to talk to."

"I see. That's one thing me and you got in common."

"Oh?"

"I don't like being lonely either."

I must have struck a nerve because Joyce's mouth dropped open. She looked me in the eye and told me in a firm tone, "I'm alone, but I'm not lonely. I have a few friends that I do things with, but I like to do a lot of things by myself, too."

I wanted to laugh. Only a "lonely" person would say something so pitiful. I didn't think it would benefit me much by dwelling on this subject, so I shifted gears. "You don't know how lucky you are to have a good job. Times is harder than they used to be for colored people these days. We have to take whatever we can get, whether we like it or not. You ain't got to worry about nothing like that."

"What do you mean?"

"If you ever get tired of the job at that schoolhouse, you still got your folks' business to fall back on. You lucky."

Joyce nodded. "I guess I am pretty lucky. But work is about the only thing I'm lucky in. . . ."

Chapter 6
Odell

JOYCE'S CLAIM THAT SHE WASN'T LONELY WAS NOTHING but a bunch of happy horse manure. I knew a lonely woman when I saw one. "What do you mean by that?" I had already made up my mind that I was going to take this woman, so I had to play my part to the hilt. I was going to be everything she wanted a man to be.

She took her time answering my question. "If I could be lucky in love, I'd be all right," she said with a faraway look in her sad eyes. Even with all the face powder she had on, I could still see the dark circles up under her eyes. Either she stayed up late reading every night, or she spent a lot of time crying. I had a feeling it was both.

"I know what you mean. I ain't had much luck with love myself."

Her eyes got big. "Say what? Why would a man that

looks like you need luck when it comes to love? Are you serious?"

I nodded. "I'm as serious as a heart attack. Looks ain't everything. Most of the women I done been with looking for a lot more than I have to offer. I got kinfolks so trifling I'm too ashamed to tell people I'm related to them. I dropped out of school in the middle of the eighth grade, so I ain't even got no education to fall back on. Folks like me, and Lord knows there's too many of us these days, we take what we can get. Most women want a man that's got a decent job." It probably wasn't even necessary, but I decided to add to my last comment anyway. "Like the job I got now. God is good. . . ."

"Hmmm. I can't tell you how happy I am that you came along when you did. My mama and daddy were getting desperate to find somebody to replace that last stock boy they had to fire. That lazy rascal could never get to work on time and when he did, he did only half of what he was supposed to do. Daddy has enough to keep him busy with the orders and dealing with the vendors and supervising his employees, but he's been doing his job too long. He does too much lifting and stocking and other things, and he's too old to keep it up. I tell him all the time that he needs to retire and let a younger person take over. Mama's not much help. She hangs out at the store almost every day but she spends most of her time in the office knitting or putting together new recipes. Up until you came along, they had a knack for hiring all kinds of creepy people. I know you must realize how strange Buddy and Sadie are."

I laughed. "Oooh yeah. I had them figured out a hour after I met them. It's been a long time since I met people who like to yip-yap as much as them two."

"If they ever say anything nasty about me, don't believe them. Sadie is a nice old lady, but she likes to be all up in other people's business. A couple of months ago, she told a woman from my church that I had turned funny. The very next day, that woman told me what she'd said."

"Funny how?"

Joyce swallowed hard and gave me a disgusted look. "Sadie likes to jump to conclusions. One day she asked me when I was going to get married. I told her I probably never would and that I didn't care because men didn't mean that much to me anymore. She took it and ran with it. Next thing I knew, she got it in her head that I was a bull-dagger."

"Sadie thought you wanted to start fooling around with women?"

"Uh-huh. And all because of that one little comment I made about not being into men anymore!"

"I don't know about you, but if somebody accused me of being funny, I'd set them straight."

"I did. First I told her that it wasn't true. Looking back on it now, I wish I had told her that the reason I wasn't into men was because they had stopped being into me. That might have set her straight and stopped her from telling other people the same thing—but she'd probably done that already. I told her if she ever said something like that about me again, or any other nasty thing, I'd make Daddy and Mama fire her. She's been real sweet to me ever since, but knowing her and Buddy, I'm probably still one of their favorite subjects to mean-mouth."

"Sadie's problem with you is jealousy. And I can understand why. You still have your whole life ahead of you, you got brains, a job to die for, and you look so much better than her. Her life is miserable and empty, and she's old and homely. And Buddy"—I snickered and rolled my eyes—"poor Buddy. A blind man could see his crush on you. But even with a list of instructions, he wouldn't know what to do with a woman like you."

"What do you mean?"

"For one thing, he's old enough to be your daddy. For another thing, you are way out of his league. I still can't believe I'm sitting here with you now. . . ."

I hoped that Joyce would stop widening her eyes every time I said something that complimented her, because I didn't want her eyeballs to roll out.

"I feel the same way," she said, almost in a whisper. A few awkward seconds of silence passed before she spoke again. "Um . . . Daddy told me you used to work for Aunt Mattie, that whorehouse woman. How did you end up in a place like that?"

"Well, at the time I didn't have nothing. I had a few bucks saved from my last job on a sugarcane farm, so I was able to pay my rent for a few weeks. When that ran out, I had to move. You wouldn't believe how many different folks' couches I slept on. When that ran out, I spent a week sleeping in one of my old bosses' barn. Aunt Mattie was the only person who'd give me a job." I stopped talking long enough to let my words sink in and from the pitiful look on Joyce's face, I could tell that I was getting to her. "I ain't proud of working in no whorehouse, but I did what I had to do. Believe me, it wasn't no picnic."

Joyce shuddered. "I'd rather shovel shit than work in that business. I can't for the life of me understand how some women can sell their bodies. A girl I went to school with works for Aunt Mattie. But she was the kind of girl who was giving it away for free to anybody that asked for it anyhow. I guess she got smart enough to start making money. What kind of work did you do for Aunt Mattie?" There was a tense look on her face.

"Oh, this and that. The usual handyman stuff. When something broke, I fixed it. When Aunt Mattie needed something hauled from one spot to another one, or a chifforobe busted up, I done it." I stopped talking for a few moments and laughed. "That Aunt Mattie. She's a real piece of work. She ain't all work and no play, though. Once or twice a week, she shuts the house down for a few hours. And then she and her girls go to the jook joints and bootleg houses to party and scout out new tricks to lure to the house. On them nights, I'd have to do some sweeping and dusting, and any other housekeeping chores that needed to be done. She even made me take a rag and sop the cum up off the floor when a trick shot his load too soon. If all that wasn't done right, Aunt Mattie would dock my pay."

The tense look was no longer on Joyce's face. Now she looked like she wanted to laugh. "Goodness gracious! It sounds like Aunt Mattie kept you busy."

She seemed to be enjoying my story, so I decided to keep talking. "Sure enough. On top of all the other stuff I did, I ran errands for her and her girls. Aunt Mattie is a good businesswoman. She'd send me to pick up high-grade liquor that she sold only to the white tricks. The colored tricks could only drink the homemade shit."

Joyce shook her head. "Even in whorehouses, white folks got the upper hand. Why did you quit that job?"

"Politics."

"Huh?"

"Or maybe I should say it was a family thing." Joyce looked confused. "When Aunt Mattie's godson Grady got out of the army, he needed a job." I let my shoulders droop and started fidgeting in my seat. "She had to let me go so she could hire him." I had told Mac and everybody else the same story. I prayed that he and Joyce would never find out that I'd been fired for trying to pick the pockets of one of the regular tricks.

"That's a damn shame. Well, you'll never have to worry about something like that happening now. I don't want to work in the store and everybody knows it. My relatives are probably as trifling as yours. And that's one thing my mama and daddy don't tolerate. But most of our folks live in Mobile and Birmingham and only come around when they want something, so there is no chance of Daddy or Mama firing you to give one of them your job." Another few awkward seconds of silence passed. "You . . . uh . . . ever been close to being married?" she asked with a little bit of hesitation.

Joyce's question caught me off guard, but I didn't waste no time answering it. "Nope. But I'm more than ready to settle down. . . ."

I ain't never seen a person's face light up so fast. This poor woman was screaming for attention, and I planned to give her all I could. "Me too. I'm itching to get married and have children."

I was so glad that our waitress finally brung our food before I had time to say anything else on the subject of marriage. The interruption would give me a few moments to reorganize my thoughts. I wanted to continue saying the things I knew Joyce wanted to hear.

Chapter 7

Joyce

MOSELLA'S WAS LOCATED ON ONE OF THE BUSIEST streets in the colored part of town. It was owned and operated by Mosella Cramden, a heavyset woman in her seventies with a sharp tongue and a lazy eye. She was one of my mother's closest friends and one of the nicest people I knew. Like my parents, she did all she could to help people get through the Depression by letting some of her regular customers eat meals on credit when they didn't have any money. She even passed out free sandwiches on the street four or five times every month. The small dull-brown building had once been a colored funeral parlor until ten years ago when a mentally disturbed man broke in and strangled the undertaker. People swore that the place was haunted by the spirits of the dead undertaker and some of the people he had prepared for burial. I'd never seen a ghost on the premises, but a lot of people claimed that they had. Every item on the menu was so good, some people would come in twice in the same day. There was a big boxy black phonograph and a stack of records on top of a milk crate near the door. If you wanted to listen to some music, you had to drop a nickel in the Mason jar on the floor next to it, and Mosella would let you pick out the five tunes. That record player never stopped playing.

I was enjoying Odell's company and listening to a record by a new singer named Billie Holiday, not to mention Mosella's fried pork chops and collard greens that we were smacking on. But I was anxious for this dinner date to end. I was getting tired of other patrons staring at us, and it was making me uncomfortable. I knew most of these lookie-loos' business and they knew mine. They were probably just as surprised to see me out in public with such a handsome man as I was.

I didn't know what was happening to me. My heart was beating so hard, it felt like it was trying to escape.

"Joyce, I'm really enjoying your company," he told me, looking at me like he wanted to lick my face.

I lifted a napkin and wiped off my lips and chin. Another thing about the food at Mosella's was that it was so messy, by the time you finished a meal it looked like you'd been swimming in a bowl of grease. "Um . . . thank you," I croaked. I cleared my throat and added, "I'm enjoying yours, too."

Of all the men I'd known, Odell was the only one who seemed to be sincere. He had no reason to lie to me, so I believed everything he said. But when I heard what he said next, I froze. "I don't want to sound like some of them jackasses that'll say everything they think a woman might want to hear, but . . ." I held my breath when he stopped talking and stared at his plate. When he looked back up at me, there were tears in his eyes. "Do you believe in love at first sight?" His question almost made me fall out of my seat. Except for my daddy and the preachers I knew, love was a word no other man had ever said in my presence.

I gulped. "I guess I do. It happens all the time in some of the books I read. Why? Do you?"

He nodded. "Sure enough, baby doll."

Baby doll? No man had ever called me such a cute name. "Oh, okay." I shrugged. "Are you telling me that 'love at first sight' happened to you before?"

"Something like that." Odell coughed and cleared his throat and gave me a serious look. "It ain't never happened to me . . . until today." He reared back in his seat and scratched the side of his head as he gazed into my burning eyes. I wasn't just nervous now; I was in a state of shock. "Before I go on, tell me if you think I'm moving too fast." There was a pleading look on his face.

This man was too good to be true! After all the sorry experiences I'd had with men, here was one telling me to my face that he was in love with me. "No! You ain't moving too fast!" I really wanted to tell him he was not moving fast enough.

"Maybe I should stop while I'm ahead. The last thing I need to hear is that you . . . um . . . want a different type of man. I mean, a beautiful woman like you could probably get a rich businessman."

"I don't want no rich businessman," I said, speaking so fast I almost bit the tip of my tongue. "All I want is a decent Christian man. And one who won't run off when he gets restless and leave me to raise a bunch of kids by myself like so many women I know." I closed my eyes for a couple of seconds and massaged my temples. When I opened them, Odell gave me a big smile.

"Where do you want to go from here?" he asked, squeezing my hand.

"Do the people who own the boardinghouse where you live allow you to have women in your room after dark?"

"Nope. Some of the men do it anyway. But the land-lady is blind in one eye and can't hear too good. She wouldn't know if the house was on fire. Why?"

"We can go to your room after we leave here if you want," I said with a sniff.

He laughed. "What I meant was, where do you want this relationship to go? But we can go to my room if you want to."

This time I laughed. "Like I said, we can go to your room. When we get there, we can talk more about where I want this relationship to go."

Odell squeezed my hand some more, told me how beautiful I was again, and commented on how he couldn't believe I was still single. Mama had been telling me since I was a little girl that anything worth having was worth waiting for. I hadn't believed her until now.

Odell was definitely worth the wait. Now I was glad no other man had asked me to marry him. But even after all he'd said, I still didn't want to get my hopes up too high. I recalled an ex-lover who had told me he'd been looking for a woman like me all his life. He borrowed five dollars from me on our second date, and I never heard from him again. That had really hurt, and it took me a while to get over it.

When our waitress brought the check and dropped it in

front of Odell, I immediately opened my purse and pulled out my wallet. "How much is my portion?"

He gasped and slapped my hand so hard I dropped my wallet. "What's wrong with you, girl? Put that wallet back in your purse. Don't be making me look like no fool up in here," he scolded.

"Oh. I didn't know you were treating me," I muttered. "I've been here and to other restaurants with men and almost every time I had to pay for my meal. I didn't think this date would be any different." Odell tickled the palm of my hand before he squeezed it again. And then he gave me the kind of look no other man had ever given me. He gazed into my eyes for about five seconds. Then he gave me such a warm smile, I thought I was going to melt.

"You'll never have to worry about that with me," he told me.

Chapter 8
Odell

I DIDN'T LIKE WHAT JOYCE JUST TOLD ME. IT MADE ME mad. I KNEW a lot of trifling men, but I didn't know any who would take a woman to one of the most expensive restaurants in town and make her pay.

"That's a sad thing to hear but it's funny, too. You must be joking," I said, giving her a pitiful look.

She shook her head. "I'm not joking. The last man I came here with claimed he'd forgot to bring his wallet. I had to pay for both our meals and the nickel tip. Then he borrowed a quarter to get some gas, and he never paid me back."

My jaw dropped so low, I was surprised it wasn't touching the table. "What kind of *niggers* have you been fooling around with, Joyce?" When I realized what I'd just said, I held up my hands and gave her the most apologetic look I could manage. One thing I didn't like to do was use offensive words in front of a lady. Especially one that the white folks hurled at us like rocks. "Excuse my language. And don't think for a minute that I use that word on a regular basis because I don't. The pecker-woods use it enough, but they don't mean the same thing we do when we say it. But I call things the way I see them. Only a nigger would take a beautiful, intelligent woman like you on a date and expect her to pay for it."

"Oh," she said again. For her to have such a decent education, she didn't use a lot of big words like other educated people I knew.

"That ain't never going to happen with me." I squeezed her hand one more time. For such a tall woman, she had small, soft, dainty hands.

"Oh," was all she had to say this time, too. "Excuse me while I go to the toilet."

Joyce was in worse shape than I thought. I really had my work cut out for me. But I didn't mind. I'd been working hard all my life, especially when it came to women. While she was gone, my mind wandered back to people and events I didn't like to think about too often.

When I was a youngblood, I loved women so much I juggled as many as I could at the same time. That was only because I had never been able to find just one who could meet all my needs. About ten years ago, I'd latched on to a young lady who was so good in bed, I had to see her every single day. But she couldn't cook worth a damn. My spare at the time, a stout woman old enough to be my mama, could cook up a storm. I used to show up at her house two or three times a week just in time for supper. My spare behind her was the kind of woman your mama would want you to marry. She was cute and smart and in the church. She didn't drink or go to jook joints, or nag me. But the best thing she could do in bed was sleep. Making love to her was like flopping around with a plank. She was just that stiff. But I'd really liked that girl, so we'd dated for a whole year. She had a good job working in a garment factory and was real generous with her money. If she hadn't took off with some railroad sucker, I would have asked her to marry me. The other two women I had been seeing at the same time eventually dumped me, and that's when I started roaming from one woman's bed to another. But that eventually got old. Now I had a itching to get married and raise a family.

It had been a week since I got fired from Aunt Mattie's place. Working as a bouncer/handyman in a whorehouse had been hard, but I'd enjoyed it. I'd never tell Joyce that, though. I wanted her to feel sorry for me, and I didn't think she would if she knew how much fun I had had working in a whorehouse. The women who worked for Aunt Mattie liked my looks, so free pussy on the sly had been a nice bonus. And I got free alcohol when Aunt Mattie wasn't breathing down my neck. She had let me share a pallet on the floor of her pantry with Rufus, the mulatto that played the piano during business hours. That old bitch was so greedy she made us pay two dollars a week for room and board. But I'd never complained because she'd let us have our meals for free. Almost every day by midnight, Aunt Mattie would be so drunk she couldn't tell her head from her feet, and we'd have to carry her to her bedroom. And then me and Rufus and the whores would do whatever we wanted.

I'd had a good thing going until I got greedy. I was sorry I had been careless enough to get caught going through the pockets of one of Aunt Mattie's regulars. When she fired my dumb ass on the spot, I slunk out of that place like a shamed hound dog with all my belongings in brown paper bags. I moved into Miss Mabel's boardinghouse—which was one step above a glorified flophouse—a few blocks away that same night.

I had seen the STOCK BOY WANTED sign in MacPherson's window a couple of days before Aunt Mattie fired me and was glad to see it still there the day after I'd moved into the boardinghouse. I'd immediately looked into it. As soon as I told Joyce's gullible daddy that I'd been "laid off" and was about to be homeless, he hired me.

He'd sat looking like a giant blob in a squeaky swivel chair at an unorganized, wobbly metal desk. His wife had stood over his shoulder with her thick arms folded in a small, cluttered room in the back of the store that they called an office (it was supposed to be a storeroom). She didn't say nothing until after I'd accepted the job. "Most of the boys that stock our shelves still in school, so they'll work for almost nothing," she pointed out.

"Ma'am, I'll mop the floors and haul out the trash, too, if you want me to. I just need a job and I don't care what you pay me. No matter what it is, it'll be more than what I got." There was a pleading tone in my voice and a desperate look on my face.

"We can't pay too much. I'm sure you know times is still real hard. Would thirty cent a hour suit you?" Mac asked with a look on his beefy face I couldn't interpret.

"Yes, sir! That'll suit me!" I had not expected that much to start because the few stock boys I knew made only twenty cent an hour and some made even less.

"Good. We need you to start straightaway," Millie told me. "Come on and let's go get you a smock, and we expect you to wear it the whole time during business hours." She unfolded her arms and waved me toward the door.

I was pleased as punch to have a new job stocking shelves. I had just been talking off the top of my head about me mopping floors and hauling trash, too, but when they told me that those two chores was also part of my responsibilities, I didn't care.

Just thinking about how easy it had been to win Joyce's parents over had given me a lot of confidence in my ability to talk a good game. I knew that if I told Joyce what she wanted to hear, I'd have her deep down in my hip pocket. But I had to move faster because I wanted to get her sewed up real soon.

When she got back from the toilet, the top button on her blouse was unfastened. I was not surprised because the blouse she had on looked like it was a size too small anyway. Her bosom looked like it was about to bust out, and I was enjoying the view. My mama told me once that when I was a baby, I'd loved being breastfed so much it had took her two years to wean me. If I got my mouth on Joyce's titties, it would take even longer for her to wean me. I had to hold my breath to keep from laughing at my own joke.

"Odell, did something funny happen while I was gone?" she asked, plopping back down in her seat.

"No. Why?"

"You looked like you was about to laugh."

"Oh, I just thought of something funny Buddy told me yesterday."

Joyce rolled her eyes and shook her head. "That Buddy. He ain't got a lick of class. I wish he would spend more time being serious about his job than cracking jokes." She picked up her napkin and started fanning her face. "I know they've already added up our check, but if you don't mind, can I have some dessert? Mosella makes a mean blackberry pie. I forgot it was on the menu for today."

"No, I don't mind at all. That sounds real good to me, and I wouldn't mind having some myself." I beckoned for our waitress.

After we ate our pie and scarfed down a few scoops of Mosella's homemade peach ice cream, Joyce wanted to hear some music, so she trotted over to the Mason jar and dropped in a nickel. She took her good old time choosing the five records she wanted to hear. After that, she left the table to go use the bathroom again. She was gone so long I thought maybe she had got nervous about going to my place and had chickened out and snuck out the back door. Or maybe she was just stalling because she wasn't sure if she really wanted to be alone with me.

"Joyce, it's getting late. If I don't get back to the boardinghouse before nine o'clock, they lock the front door and I won't be able to get in," I told her when she returned.

"You forgot to bring your key?"

"I ain't got one. The landlady only give keys to tenants after they been boarding three months."

"Oh! Then we'd better get going," she said, looking frazzled. "You should have told me sooner."

"I didn't want to rush you." I paused so I could regroup my thoughts. "Um . . . I just need to make sure you really want to go home with me tonight. This is our first date and all."

"Odell, I really do want to go to your room with you *tonight*." Every time Joyce smiled, she looked even better to me.

I paid for our dessert, gave our waitress a generous dime tip, and we left. When I turned onto the street where the run-down boardinghouse I lived in was located and parked in front of it, she touched my arm. "Is *this* where you live?" she asked with a mild frown on her face. "I thought the city had condemned this place."

"Uh-huh. It ain't much, but it's all I can afford right now. You told me it was okay to come here. You changed your mind?"

"It's all right. I can't think of no other place I'd rather be." She leaned over and gave me a quick kiss on the lips. After a little pause, she kissed me again. This time she wrapped her arms around my neck. I pulled her into my arms and held on to her like she was some kind of life jacket. In a way, she was. I was convinced that I was headed in the right direction. If I stayed on course, my troubles would soon be over. "I just hope I don't disappoint you," she whispered in my ear.

"I feel the same way," I whispered back.

For Joyce to be such a meek and prim and proper woman, she was a ball of fire in bed. I wouldn't have cared if she'd been as passionate as a dead fish because after I'd made her squeal like a pig, I knew then that I had the key to her heart. And I was going to hold on to it with both hands.

Chapter 9
Joyce

I HAD HAD SEX A LOT OF TIMES SINCE I WAS FOURTEEN. But none of my exes had ever made love to me properly, so I'd never enjoyed it that much. I had no idea what a climax felt like because I'd never had one. From what a couple of my female associates had told me, it was the most wonderful experience in the world. What I had enjoyed was being so close to a man's body. The physical connection and seeing the way their eyes rolled back in their heads when they climaxed had been enough for me. I had accepted the fact that that was the only ecstasy I'd ever get out of sex.

Tonight, Odell showed me what all the fuss was about. When he made me have my very first climax, I almost humped him off that rollaway bed in his closet-size room. I thought I'd died and gone to heaven. Every inch of my body was tingling.

"Baby, take it easy," he laughed after I had calmed down. He rolled off me and sat up on the side of the bed with his back to me. I couldn't believe the damage I had done to his back. I had clawed and scratched him so much, I'd broken off three of my fingernails. I was happy to see that my wild-woman behavior didn't seem to bother him. He got back in the bed and started stroking the side of my face and nibbling on my ear. "Ain't you never had no good loving before?"

I was almost out of breath, so it took a few seconds for me to answer. "No. I . . . I didn't know what good loving was really like." My mouth was dry and my voice hoarse from all the hollering I'd done.

"Now you do," he chuckled. "And once we get used each other's bodies, it'll be even better."

And it did get even better. By our fifth date in less than a week, which was a record for me, I didn't think I could live without Odell. I enjoyed everything we did together. He took me fishing, blackberry picking, picnics, and on long drives. Sometimes we just stayed in his room listening to his radio and making love. We'd been back to Mosella's several times since our first night there together. Each time the waitresses and waiters, other customers, and even Mosella herself, raised their eyebrows or gave us curious glances. I knew they were all trying to figure out what was going on, especially since Odell was the *only* man they'd ever seen me with more than a couple of times.

When he told me he wanted me to meet his daddy, I knew our relationship was something special.

Odell's daddy, Lonnie, and his wife, Ellamae, lived on a dirt road at the bottom of a hill in a run-down three-bedroom house on the outskirts of town. It was about a quarter of a mile from one of the same sugarcane fields where he and most of his family used to work. When we pulled up in the front yard, a three-legged hound dog hobbled up to the car and started sniffing at my door. "Odell, I'm scared of dogs. Make him go away," I wailed.

"Shoo, shoo, Duke!" Odell yelled and honked the horn. The dog howled and backed away, so I opened my door and piled out. When my feet hit the ground, Duke trotted up to me and started sniffing my leg. Drool was trickling off his lips, so it was a good thing I had decided to wear pants. I also had on the same low-cut blouse I'd worn on my first date with Odell because he liked it so much. I'd recently ordered three more just like it, but in different colors. "Don't worry. Duke don't bite and he ain't got no fleas," Odell laughed. And then he rushed around to my side and grabbed my hand. After taking a deep breath, he led me up onto a rickety front porch with a rocking chair on one side and a foot tub filled to the rim with soapy water on the other. "Daddy's mind comes and goes, so I guess he done got a little senile, but it ain't nothing to be concerned about. He still got a good disposition. My stepmama had a slight stroke two years ago, and it had a bad effect on her brain. She ain't too hospitable, and never was much in the first place. These days there's enough bad blood between me and her to flood the Dead Sea. Once you meet her, you'll see what I mean, and you probably won't want to stay longer than a few minutes. But if you want to leave sooner, just look at me and blink three times to let me know and we'll haul ass straightaway."

"Odell, be nice now. I'd like to stay long enough to get acquainted with your daddy and your stepmama," I insisted.

When we got inside, I understood why he thought I wouldn't want to stay long. A heavyset, elderly woman in a ratty gray housecoat and a plaid bandanna tied around her head stood in the middle of the floor with her hands on her hips. Her dusty bare feet looked like bear claws. There was such an annoyed look on her plain, round, reddish-brown face, I thought she was in pain.

The first words out of Odell's stepmother's mouth made me want to run back out the door. "I just mopped this floor! Look at all that sand y'all done tracked up in here!" she snarled. She looked me up and down and frowned when she got to my feet. Now that I had a man who was so tall that I had to look up at him, I had purchased my first pair of high heels. They were comfortable and looked good on my long feet. But the way Ellamae was staring at them, I wished I had worn a pair of shoes that wouldn't have drawn so much attention.

"Uh, hello, Ellamae," Odell greeted in a gentle tone. "I'm sorry about tracking up the floor. Next time I'll make sure we wipe our feet before we come in." He stopped talking and glanced from me to Ellamae. "I want you to meet Joyce MacPherson, my new lady friend."

I reached over to shake Ellamae's hand. "It's nice to meet you, ma'am." I forced myself to smile even though she looked mad enough to bite off a snake's head.

She ignored my hand. Instead, she reared back on her knotty bowed legs, looked over my shoulder, and shaded her eyes with her hand and stared at the car. "That jalopy y'all rolled up in belong to you, Joyce?" she asked, looking me up and down some more with her eyes narrowed.

"No, ma'am. It belongs to my daddy. He lets us borrow it when we go out so we won't have to walk or take the bus," I replied.

"How old is you?" For such a grumpy old woman, she had a pleasant, young-sounding voice.

Just as I was about to respond, Odell answered for me. "She's thirty, a year younger than me."

Ellamae folded her arms. Her eyes were still on me. "Thirty? Humph. Well, I do declare. I never would have guessed that. You look a heap older than that."

"That's because I'm so tall," I said, grinning. "When I was a little girl, I was so much taller than the kids I played with, some people thought I was a lot older than I really was."

Ellamae turned to Odell with an impatient look on her face. "Your daddy ain't here," she barked. "And I hope y'all don't plan on staying for supper on account of I didn't cook enough for four."

"We already have plans for supper. I came at the spur of the moment because I was anxious for you and Daddy to meet Joyce."

Right after Odell stopped talking, a back door slammed. An elderly dark-skinned man, who was even taller than Odell and just as handsome, shuffled in holding a bucket of blackberries. He was barefooted too. He set the bucket on the floor and wiped his hands on his overalls. "Ellamae, I didn't know we had company coming," he grunted.

"I didn't know neither," she growled.

"Who is these people? I ain't never seen them before," Lonnie grumbled, pulling a pair of glasses with taped frames out of his shirt pocket.

"It's me, Daddy," Odell said in a loud tone. He walked toward his father heaving heavy sighs all the way.

"Me who?" Lonnie put his glasses on and stared at his son. "Mighty Moses! It's my baby boy!" The way his eyes suddenly lit up, you would have thought Odell really was

Moses. He started grinning and patting Odell's shoulder. "Boy, I'm so glad you came. We killed a hog yesterday, so there's a pile of chitlins and hog maws that need to be cleaned, and the rest of the meat need to be hung up in the smokehouse. After we do that, I got a itching to go fishing."

I could tell from the look on Odell's face that he was embarrassed. I was sure that he would not have brought me to this place today if he had known we'd be asked to clean a butchered hog! "We can't do none of that this time, and I can't take you fishing today, Daddy. I just stopped by for a few minutes to introduce y'all to Joyce."

Lonnie squinted and gazed at me. "Hmmm. It's been a long time since Odell brung a lady to the house, so you must be special!" he gushed as he shook my hand.

"She is special, Daddy," Odell confirmed, smiling at me.

"I'm glad she ain't as fat, black, and ugly as that last one you dragged out here." Lonnie shrugged and scratched his head, and turned to face me. "Joyce, you hungry? Ellamae baked a great big possum last night and there's plenty left over."

Odell answered for me. "No, thanks. We got a bunch of things to do when we leave here. I'll come take you fishing one day next week and we'll stay for supper."

"Y'all can't stay long enough to drink a Dr. Pepper?" I could tell from the glum expression on Lonnie's face and his dry tone that he was disappointed.

Odell looked at me, and I blinked three times like he'd told me to do if I wanted to leave. He immediately opened the screen door and held it open. "No, we can't stay that long, Daddy."

"Hurry up and close that damn door before you let them

flies and gnats in! We ran out of bug spray last week!"
Ellamae shrieked.

We literally ran back to the car. "I told you that you
probably wouldn't want to stay long," Odell laughed as
he started up the motor.

"You were right about that," I chuckled. "Your daddy
seems like a real nice man, and I can't wait to get to know
him better. But I don't think I'll want to spend too much
time around his wife."

"And you won't have to. I want to keep you all to myself for as long as I can," he declared before he hauled off
and kissed me.

I didn't think things could get any better between us,
but I hoped they would.

A week after our visit to Odell's daddy's house, I decided that if he didn't propose by the end of the month,
I'd do it. If he turned me down, I wouldn't be too broken
up. At least I'd have some wonderful memories.

When June ended and he still hadn't proposed, I got
real nervous. I decided not to propose because after I'd
given it a little more thought, I was afraid something that
serious might scare him off. And that was one thing I
didn't want to deal with anytime soon.

Odell loved working in our store and Mama and
Daddy adored him. I was glad to know that I was seeing a
man my folks approved of. Six weeks after he'd come
into our lives, Daddy bought a newer model of the same
ancient Ford Model T he'd been driving for years and
sold his old one to Odell for fifty dollars, which he had to
pay only a dollar a week until it was paid in full. It was
the first car that Odell ever owned, so he was even happier. He was on such good terms with Mama and Daddy,
he even came to the house when I wasn't home. It made

my heart sing to come home from work or a long shopping trip and see the three of them on the living room
couch.

Odell was very good with his hands, and not just in the
bedroom. He fixed things around the house that Daddy
had been neglecting, and he was always eager to chauf-
feur Mama and her friends around when Daddy didn't
feel like driving.

If he wasn't leading up to a marriage proposal, I couldn't
imagine any other reason for him to be doing so much for
me and my folks. He had told me several times that he
loved me. But I still didn't feel too secure. I wanted a real
commitment from him. I didn't know what else I could
do to lock him in so that he'd be more permanent. The answer came to me five weeks after our first date when I realized I was pregnant.

Odell came to the house several times a week, but it
had already been three days since our last date and I hadn't
seen or heard from him. By the fourth day, I had run out
of patience. I left work early that Friday and walked the
two miles from my work to the store.

"Hey, baby. I was just thinking about you," he said
when he saw me. I had entered through the back door so I
could bypass Buddy and Sadie. Mama and Daddy spent
most of their time in the office when they were on the
premises, so I wasn't worried about bumping into them
before I talked to Odell. He was in the aisle closest to the
door. He slid a box that contained corsets off to the side
and rushed up to me and kissed my cheek. "Ain't you
working today?"

"I left early because I wasn't feeling well," I told him
in a dry tone.

He gave me a concerned look. "Oh? Is everything all right? You do look a little tired and flushed."

"Can I talk to you for a few minutes?"

"Yeah, sugar. What about?"

I took a quick glance around first. Other than a few customers in line to pay for their purchases, Buddy was the only other employee I could see. "Where are Sadie and Mama and Daddy?"

"Sadie left to go take a toilet break. Your mama and daddy can't be too far away. All three just walked by me a few minutes ago." Odell let out a raspy breath and looked toward the back door. "Do you need to see your mama or your daddy? I'm sure they can't be too far. Probably out back getting some fresh air. You didn't see them when—"

I didn't give Odell time to finish his sentence. His eyes almost popped out when I blurted out the words, "I'm in trouble."

"Oh?" He scratched his chin, and then he started shifting his weight from one foot to the other. "This trouble have anything to do with me?"

"It's got everything to do with you. . . ."

He sucked in some air and looked at me from the corner of his eye. "Joyce, what's going on? You don't look too happy. And exactly what is it you need to talk to me about?" He swallowed hard, and a worried look suddenly crossed his face. "Did you . . . did you . . . come to tell me you done met another man and don't want to be bothered with me no more? Is that it?" Tears pooled in Odell's eyes, and he started blinking.

I leaned closer to him and whispered in his ear, "I'm pregnant."

Chapter 10
Odell

*I*F JOYCE HAD PULLED A GUN ON ME, I COULDN'T HAVE been more stunned. A baby was going to have a big impact on our relationship. But I didn't know if it would be a good one, or a bad one. "What did you just say?" I asked dumbly. I had heard her the first time, but I needed to be sure I had heard right.

"I'm going to have a baby."

"My Lord!" I croaked. In my mind, I could see Mac loading up his shotgun. It wasn't easy, but I was able to keep the fear out of my tone and body language. I stood up straight and spoke in the most serious tone I could manage. "You been to a doctor yet?"

Joyce shook her head. "I don't need no doctor to tell me what I already know. I knew something was wrong last week when I started throwing up every morning."

I raked my fingers through my hair and looked around to make sure nobody was close enough to hear what we was discussing. Especially Mac! Since she was so close to her mama and daddy, I didn't know what kind of influence their reaction to her condition would have on her. They were old-fashioned, churchgoing people, and they associated with some of the snootiest, most self-righteous people in town. The funny thing about that was, some of the same men in Mac and Millie's circle of friends spent a lot of time and money in Aunt Mattie's whorehouse. I'd seen them there with my own eyes before I got fired. But since Joyce was the MacPhersons' only child and they doted on her, I knew they only wanted her to have the best things in life. Having a baby before she got married was not one of them things.

I had to think fast and not say something that might upset Joyce more than she already was. "Baby, we in this together," I acknowledged in a firm tone. She looked relieved, at least for now. "Did you tell anybody else yet?"

"The only person that knows so far is Miss Kirksey, the teacher I work with. I didn't tell her, but she figured it out on her own. She's had six kids and knows all the pregnancy signs."

"Good. Let's keep this to ourselves for now. I don't think we need to worry about the Kirksey woman blabbing before we figure out what to do about this problem."

Joyce gasped and looked like she was about to have a panic attack. But she continued speaking in a calm manner. "Problem? You think this is a problem?"

"Well, we didn't plan it. When people get involved like us, things happen. But everybody makes mistakes."

A threatening look suddenly crossed her face. She

looked mad enough to cut my throat. "Odell, you need to make up your mind. First you said we had a problem. Now you're telling me we made a mistake. If you think I'm a problem *and* a mistake, you need to let me know now so I can go on about my business and forget about you."

This time I gasped. "What's wrong with you, girl? Don't you be twisting my words. I ain't said you was no problem or a mistake."

"I'm not deaf. I know what I heard."

"Okay, let me start over. First off, I'm sorry if what I said upset you. I didn't mean to. I care too much about you. But we have a serious situation on our hands, and I just want to know how you going to handle it."

Joyce's eyes got big. "What do you mean? Shouldn't you be asking me how *we* are going to handle this 'situation'? I didn't get pregnant by myself!" she hissed like a snake. This was the first time I seen her get mad.

I pulled her into my arms. "Joyce, there ain't but one thing for us to do and that is to get married." I held my breath, hoping I'd said what she wanted to hear.

She looked so surprised, you would have thought I'd just threatened to kill her. *"You want to marry me?"* Her voice was so weak and raspy now, she didn't even sound like herself.

I wasn't sure what words to say next, so I just started grinning and nodding. "I know I ain't in your league, but I love you, and I want to spend the rest of my life with you. And the sooner we get married the better."

"Are you sure about that?"

"Damn right, I'm sure. Why wouldn't I be?"

"I never expected you to . . ." Joyce stopped talking

and cleared her throat. "Um . . . I'm not fresh and haven't been since I was fourteen. I've been to bed with a bunch of other men."

"You ain't been with nobody but me since last year," I reminded. "Or was your daddy exaggerating about that?"

"No, he wasn't."

"Then what's your point?"

"I was surprised you didn't ask me if I knew for sure you were the father."

"Well, since I know you ain't been with nobody else *since last year*, why would I think another man got you pregnant?" I stood up straighter and puffed out my chest. "Joyce, if you snuck out with another man and that's his baby, I love you so much I'd even be willing to claim it as my own and help you raise it."

Next thing I knew, she was crying like a baby. I held her even tighter. Her body was as stiff as a pine tree. "I . . . I can't believe what I'm hearing," she boo-hooed.

"Well, you better believe it because I meant everything I just said. The first time l laid eyes on you, I knew you was the only woman for me."

"But you don't even know me that well, and I don't know much about you."

"Look, I know enough about you. What do you not know about me that you want to know?"

"I need to know that if we get married, you won't ever leave me."

"Why would I leave? I just told you that you was the only woman for me and that I want to spend the rest of my life with you."

"You say that now, but some men do change after a while."

"Joyce, I will change in some ways over time. That's the law of nature, so I can't do nothing about that. But one thing that won't change is my love for you. If you marry me, I will never leave you. The main thing I'm worried about is you changing on me. For all I know, you might be the one to up and run off someday."

"No, I won't! I can't think of anything bad enough you could do that would make me leave you."

Chapter 11
Joyce

*O*DELL WANTED TO BE PRESENT WHEN I TOLD MAMA and Daddy I was pregnant and that he wanted to marry me. But I insisted on telling them alone and not until they got home from the store in a few hours. I was not looking forward to dropping such a big bombshell on them.

I loved my parents, and I went out of my way not to do or say anything that would upset them. I'd only received a few whuppings a year when I was growing up. They used to brag to their friends about how "perfect" I was and to this day they still thought I was a virgin. They had told me more than a few times that I'd better not spread my legs for any man except the one I married. Mama had told me when I was twelve, on the first day of my first period, that being with a man "in the flesh" was not going to be a bed of roses for me, and that men would "pester" me to do it until the day I died. She also told me that the only acceptable excuse to have sex was to have children. I cringed when I thought about how my parents were going to react when I told them about my condition. I was scared to death.

When I stopped crying, Odell asked, "You want me to drive you home?"

"I can walk or take the bus. And—"

He cut me off and wagged his finger in my face. "Uh-uh! That's a long walk for a pregnant woman. I ain't about to let you do nothing that might hurt you or our baby. And one of the first things I want you to do is take a break from drinking."

"Drinking?"

"No alcohol. Not even elderberry wine."

I was happy that Odell was so concerned about me and our baby. "I didn't mean for this to happen," I said with fresh hot tears flowing down my face again like a waterfall. I hadn't shed so many tears since I was a baby. But I was not as "upset" as I appeared to be. Things were going just the way I'd hoped they would. I'd been trying to get pregnant for years so I wouldn't have to grow old alone. Now that I'd reached part of my goal, I no longer cared if I had a husband or not. I was prepared to be a single mother in case Odell took off.

I was so busy thinking about my future and what I was going to name my baby, I didn't hear Daddy, Mama, and Sadie approach us. "What's going on here?" Daddy boomed. I was glad Odell still had his arms around me. "Joyce, what you crying about?"

I immediately stopped crying. I never had a handkerchief when I needed one, so I wiped snot and tears off my face with the back of my hand. "Daddy, Mama, we all need to talk," I sniffled. I paused long enough to clear my throat, and when I spoke again, my tone was much stronger. "I have something to tell y'all, but it can wait until we get home."

"We ain't waiting for nothing! Whatever it is, you need to tell us *now*!" Daddy fired back.

After a stern look from Mama, Sadie skittered back out to her cash register.

"I don't think this is something we should discuss here," Odell said gently. He took his arms from around me and placed his hands on his hips. I was happy to see that he didn't look nervous or scared.

"You let us decide that. Now what's going on here? Joyce, you look sick!" Mama howled as she felt my forehead. "We ain't leaving this spot until one of y'all tell us."

"Joyce is fixing to have my baby and I want to marry her," Odell blurted out. For about five seconds, it seemed like the world had come to a standstill. Mama and Daddy stood rooted in place looking as grim-faced as undertakers. Odell still didn't look nervous or scared, but I was both.

After letting out a loud breath, Daddy looked at me and whimpered, "Gal, you . . . you done fooled around and got yourself *pregnant*? How did this happen?"

"We had sex," I confessed in a flat tone.

"Do you mean to tell me that you up and spread your legs—AFTER ALL YOU BEEN TAUGHT?" he roared with his nostrils flaring and his eyes bugged out.

"Great balls of fire, girl! Didn't we tell you to wait until you got married?" Mama threw in.

"I couldn't wait," I sniffled.

"I guess not! What about them other men?" Daddy's voice had dropped almost to a whisper. But from the scowl on his face, I knew he was still stunned and mad.

I gave him a curious look. "What other men?" I asked as I hunched my shoulders.

"Them ones you used to go out with!" he boomed. "You couldn't wait with them neither?"

Mama didn't give me time to respond. "Lord save us!" she yelped, and covered her mouth with her hand. There was a wild-eyed look on her face as she glared at Odell. I was glad Daddy's shotgun was not close by. "I . . . I wanted your first time to be special," she said, choking on a sob.

It was hard to imagine that my mother was naïve enough to believe that Odell was the first man I'd slept with. "My 'first time' was special, Mama, sixteen years ago." The look on her face was a combination of horror, disbelief, and disappointment. But I thought it was important for her and Daddy to know the *real* me and that when it came to sex, I was no different from other women my age.

The look on Daddy's face was the same as the one on Mama's. "If you couldn't keep your bloomers on with them other men, how do you know Odell is the one that got you in this mess?" he asked.

I was absolutely horrified to hear him ask such a question! He knew that I hadn't been out with another man since last year—something he couldn't stop broadcasting.

"Shame on you, Daddy. You ought to know better! Yes, I'm sure Odell is the one!" I hollered. My heart was beating so fast and my blood pressure had shot up so high, I was surprised I was still conscious. "And for your information, I am not in the 'mess' you say I'm in. I already love this baby and I can't wait to have it."

Odell put his arm around my shoulder. "I want to

marry Joyce as soon as possible. But if she don't want to be my wife, I'll understand," he mumbled.

I swallowed hard and looked around the room. Sadie and Buddy were busy waiting on customers, but I knew they had heard at least part of the conversation. I expected them to start running off at the mouth about me the first chance they got to everybody who would listen. But I didn't care. For the first time in my life, I felt like a real woman.

"Do you want to marry this man, baby?" Daddy asked. This was another question I couldn't believe he was asking. I knew that Odell was probably my last chance, so I was going to take him and run before he changed his mind.

I nodded.

"Y'all ain't even been together that long," Mama pointed out. "Do you really love this man? You know how we feel about marriage. It's a one-way street and once you get on it, it's for life on account of divorce ain't part of God's plan. When a couple get married, they is duty-bound to stay together until death claims one of them."

My heart skipped a beat. "We're not even married yet, so there is no reason for you to even be thinking about something like *divorce*!"

"Marriage ain't no fun and games, girl. It's a real big step," Daddy piped in, sounding tired now. He was running out of steam, so I knew that this hot discussion wouldn't go on too much longer.

"I don't care," I choked.

"Joyce is not going to deal with this on her own," Odell said. I was glad to hear him say more about this situation. "I'm just as responsible for this as she is, and I'm going to stand by her all the way." His words were like music to my ears. He'd just said exactly what I wanted him to say.

"What's the big deal about us getting married?" I wailed. "I don't want to raise a baby on my own."

"You ain't going to raise no baby by yourself as long as me and your daddy is alive," Mama said. "But if you don't *really* want to marry this man, you ain't got to."

I was disappointed to hear that Odell had suddenly become "this man" in her eyes. She and Daddy knew how I felt about him, and he'd just made it clear to them how he felt about me. A couple of weeks ago, when they realized how serious our relationship had become, they had mentioned the fact that Odell had dropped out of school in the eighth grade and hadn't done much with his life since then. And they never let me forget that he'd worked in a whorehouse. I had argued with them that all that was in his past and he deserved to be judged by what he was doing with his life now. I also reminded them that they'd had enough faith in him to give him a job, and they'd encouraged me to go out with him, so he must not have been too bad. I couldn't understand why they were reacting the way they were now especially when they'd previously been afraid that I'd never get married at all.

"I think we need to talk about this some more when we get home. We'll pray for guidance all night if we have to," Daddy decided. He looked from me to Odell, and then he added with a smirk, "Just the family."

"I'm having Odell's baby, so he's family now. And if we need to talk about this some more at home, he needs to be there," I insisted.

"That's all right, baby," Odell said, holding up his

hand. "I'm real sorry this had to happen before I got a chance to properly court Joyce and ask her to marry me."

Mama opened her eyes so wide, she reminded me of an owl. "You mean you was going to ask her to marry you anyhow?" she asked.

"Yes, ma'am. I made up my mind right after I met Joyce that I wanted to spend the rest of my life with her." Odell stopped talking and looked at me and smiled before he continued. "Matter of fact, I had planned to ask her to marry me anyway this coming weekend."

"Huh?" I mouthed. His last statement surprised me as much as it did my parents. "You mean you don't want to marry me just because I'm pregnant?"

Odell squeezed my shoulder and started talking in a slow, gentle tone. "I had a itching to propose a couple of weeks ago, but I didn't think it'd be a good idea if I rushed things. I needed to be sure you loved me."

"You know I do," I squealed.

"Humph!" Daddy shrugged and looked from Mama to me. "It sounds like y'all done already made up your minds, so it don't matter what me and Mother say, huh?" He suddenly stopped talking and started coughing so hard, he choked on some air and Mama had to slap him on his back.

"Daddy, I can see how hard this is on you and I'm sorry. That's why I wanted to wait until we got home to finish this discussion," I told him, trying to sound as apologetic as I could.

"Don't worry about me getting upset. You the one with a baby in your belly, so you need to be worrying about yourself. I just hope y'all making the right decision." Daddy's voice was getting weaker by the second. "A baby is supposed to be a blessing. . . ."

"Sure enough," Mama agreed with her voice cracking. "Oh well. What's done is done. Now we just need to move on." All of a sudden, her mood changed. Her eyes softened, and there was a hint of a smile on her face. "I . . . I never thought me and Mac would live long enough to enjoy a grandchild. It's been a dream for a long time, and it's finally going to happen."

Odell looked straight into Daddy's eyes first, then Mama's. "Y'all will live long enough to enjoy this baby and several more."

This was the moment when I knew for sure that Odell Watson was the man God had been saving for me.

Chapter 12
Odell

*F*ROM ALL THE STUFF I'D HEARD FROM BUDDY AND Sadie, and the things Joyce had told me out of her own mouth, I had been under the impression that her mama and daddy couldn't wait for her to get married. Now I wasn't so sure. They had not reacted the way I had expected. Instead of hugs and kisses, and congratulating me, they'd just stood there looking at me like I was crazy and talking all kinds of bullshit. What was the matter with these people? I didn't even want to think that they thought I wasn't good enough for their daughter. So what if I didn't have much education and nothing other than myself to offer? As long as they'd been waiting to see her get married, they couldn't be crazy enough to think that a better man would come along some day.

Even though Millie had eased up a little and started gushing about being a grandmother, I was still apprehensive. I decided not to go home with Joyce and her parents to continue the discussion. I knew she wanted to marry me, but I didn't know if she'd still want to by the time they got through with her. Right after I'd confessed that I'd been planning to propose to her anyway, the three of them left abruptly. The fact that they'd left in such a hurry was something else for me to worry about. It seemed like they couldn't get away from me fast enough. They didn't even say good-bye. If Joyce stood up to her folks and decided to marry me anyway, I wasn't so sure it was the right thing for us to do now. I kept thinking about all I had to gain if I went through with it. If I had not been in such a rush to make love to her, things might have turned out much better. Even though she'd been ready, willing, and able to hop into bed with me, I still should have held out.

Had I screwed myself out of a job by sleeping with the boss's daughter? If that happened, I had nowhere to go and only enough money to pay this month's rent. And I had too much pride but not enough nerve to go back to the same "friends" who had let me sleep on their couches during my downtime. I couldn't stoop low enough to beg Daddy and Ellamae to let me stay with them until I got back up on my feet. I'd rather live in a hole than live with them again.

The more I thought about the situation, the more worried I got about losing everything I had accomplished since my last job. I didn't have a damn thing to fall back on. I had to come up with a backup plan. And I didn't know where to start. I couldn't rob any of the banks still in business. That was too risky anyway. Everybody was still conversating about the stories in the newspaper and on the radio about what had happened to a young white couple over in Louisiana just a couple of months ago back in May.

Bonnie and Clyde had become such well-known outlaws, some of the news reports didn't even have to mention their last names no more. They had robbed banks, grocery stores, gas stations, and shot and killed folks for four years before the law shot them to pieces. If the cops could do something that extreme to white folks, there was just no telling what they would do to a colored man for committing the same crimes. With my luck, they'd lynch me and let me hang until the rope rotted. And then they would shoot me to pieces. I had to be smart and figure out a safe way to keep my ass out of the hole I had already got too close to.

When I finished my shift and got back to my dreary room, I stretched out in the same rollaway bed where Joyce and I had created a baby. And I was on pins and needles. For the first time in my life, I was really scared.

I got back up around midnight, slid back into my clothes, and decided to take a walk so I could get some fresh air and clear my head. Since I didn't have no key to the house, I had to prop open the front door with an empty Dr. Pepper bottle so I could get back in.

When I reached a little park two blocks from the boardinghouse, I sat on a bench for over a hour, trying to come up with a plan. I needed a drink, but I didn't have no alcohol in my room, and the few colored bars within walking distance had closed for the night. I went back home and got into the jalopy Mac had sold me. Without giving it much thought, I drove to the last place I ever expected to visit again: Aunt Mattie's whorehouse.

"What you doing here?" she barked when she opened

the door and saw me standing on her front porch. "Didn't I tell you not to bring your sorry ass back around here?"

"Yes, ma'am, you sure enough did. But I got a problem."

"You'll have a heap more problems if you don't get your black ass the hell away from here!"

"Please give me a break, Aunt Mattie. Can I come in and talk to you for a few minutes?"

"Naw! Whatever you got to say, say it here and you better say it quick. I got things to do."

Matilda Pennington, a well-known battle-ax that everybody called Aunt Mattie, was real unpredictable. It was no secret that she dabbled in hoodoo. When I was a little boy, me and my friends never knew if she was going to threaten to put a hex on us for raiding the two pecan trees in her front yard, or get drunk and chase us with a switch. She was a small woman with a heart-shaped face that was probably pretty at one time. Now she looked like a dried-up, droopy-eyed witch with wrinkles on every inch of skin you could see, and a head full of long, brittle white hair that always dangled around her shoulders like snakes. She had been chewing tobacco for so many years; the few teeth she had left had turned the same shade as her copper-toned skin. Nobody knew how old she was, but like a lot of other elderly people in town, she'd been born into slavery.

Aunt Mattie didn't have no relatives that I knew of, except a husband that nobody had seen in over ten years. She claimed he'd run off with another woman. But before she fired me, one of her girls got drunk one night and told me a gruesome story that chilled me to the bone. According to her, Aunt Mattie had hacked her cheating, violent, controlling husband to pieces with a hatchet, stuffed his body parts into gunnysacks, and buried them in her back-yard. I didn't ask that crazy old bitch about it because I didn't want her to know I'd heard the rumor. If she'd killed one man, what would stop her from killing one more? If I hadn't been so greedy and careless, she never would have caught me trying to empty the pockets of Mongo Petty, one of her regular customers. Aunt Mattie had cussed me out and had given me fifteen minutes to collect all of my belongings and get out of her sight, or I'd be "real sorry." I'd done it in ten minutes because I didn't want her back-yard to be my final resting place.

"Um, I never told you how sorry I was about what I done to Mongo. He worked too hard for his money for me to be trying to steal it," I said, trying to sound as hum-ble as I could.

"Well, you ought to be sorry on account of you didn't even get nothing from him. Mongo was lucky I walked up when I did. I wonder how many others you clipped that I didn't walk up on in time." Emptying an uncon-scious trick's pockets was nothing new in Aunt Mattie's house. Usually, when one passed out, she'd order me and Rufus to take his money and everything else of value. Then she'd make us haul him away from her house and dump him on a rival madam's porch two houses over. Since Mongo had already passed out, if I had waited a few minutes longer, she probably would have had me clip him anyway! I was so mad with myself for jumping the gun, I would have kicked my own ass if I could have.

"I swear to God, except for the ones you had me and Rufus do, Mongo was the only one. And I only did what I did because I'd been drunk myself that night and some-body had picked my pocket and stole my money. One of the girls claimed she'd seen Mongo going through my pockets, so I figured he was the one. I thought I'd just be getting back what belonged to me in the first place." I was so used to lying, it felt natural. I swallowed hard and tried to look as pathetic as I could, which wasn't hard for me to do.

"Well, do say. It don't matter now no more no how. What you come back here for? I heard you was working for them snooty MacPhersons now."

"That's true. But . . . uh . . . I might not be there too much longer."

"Why come? You can't even stock shelves right?" Aunt Mattie sneered.

"No, it ain't nothing like that."

"And another thing I heard was that you and that horsey gal of theirs done got real tight," she smirked. "Mosella told me at church last Sunday that you and Joyce been eating at her place quite a bit lately."

"I'm real fond of Joyce and I enjoy her company. We've had some good times."

"I bet! And there's no telling what some of them good times was. She ain't cute, but a gal with legs as long as she got could have done real good working for me. Poor thing. She is such an oddball. She got some nerve trying to talk all proper. I guess she think she too good to speak the way a normal colored woman is supposed to."

"Someday I hope to speak with more better grammar like Joyce do."

"Like I just said, she *tries* to talk proper, but she slips up now and then. She ain't as smart as you think. Matter of fact, for years a lot of folks thought she was retarded."

"Joyce ain't no more retarded than me or you. She finished high school and she's been working at a school for years and years, helping the teachers with the kids."

"That don't mean nothing. Look at all the things a dumb dog can be trained to do. A smart enough idiot can learn how to do just about anything. Roosevelt is one of the biggest idiots in the world and he was smart enough to make it to the White House." Aunt Mattie laughed. And then she got quiet and gave me a suspicious look. "Let me ask you again, what you doing back here?"

"I think I done got myself in a fix and I didn't have nobody else to turn to for help but you."

Aunt Mattie's eyes got big and her mouth flew open. "Me? Humph! If you think I'm the only one you can turn to for help, you in a bigger fix than you think! What in the world do you want me to do for you?"

"Give me another job."

"Pffft!" Aunt Mattie waved her hand at me like she was shooing a fly. "You done lost your mind or I ain't hearing right. I gave you a job and you fucked it up. What's wrong with the job you got now?"

"Things ain't working out for me there."

"Oh? What did you do? They fixing to fire you on account of they caught you trying to rob them too?"

"No, ma'am. It ain't nothing like that. It's just that . . . well, the job ain't what I expected, and I was thinking about leaving on my own. I need something to keep me from getting bored and me and Buddy and Sadie don't get along too good."

Aunt Mattie narrowed her eyes and glared at me. Her beady black eyes looked like ink spots. "Is that the only reason you dragged your tail back over here?"

I nodded. "Yes, ma'am." I hoped I sounded distressed enough for her to take pity on me. It had worked with Mac.

"Humph! I'll tell you one thing right now, I don't need

nobody working for me that I can't trust. I can't have no independent thief mingling with the men my girls service. If I did, it wouldn't take long for me to be out of business."

"I can understand that and I don't blame you. But I can do anything else you want me to do that'll keep me from coming in contact with your tricks. I know quite a bit about cars, so I can keep yours in good running condition and I play a mean piano. I can fill in when Rufus needs to take a break."

"Two of my girls play the piano just as good as Rufus do, and they always happy to take over when he ain't available. I already got a good mechanic and I got a feeling he robbing me blind, so I ain't about to take a chance on having *two* crooks shaking me down by claiming one thing or another need to be done on my car. For all I know, you might take off with my car."

I could see that I wasn't getting nowhere with this old bitch, and I was sorry I had come to her. "Aunt Mattie, thanks for listening to me. I'm sorry I disturbed you. If you change your mind, send one of the girls to get me. I got a room at that boardinghouse on Pike Street. Now you have a blessed—"

She cut me off with a weird question. "You squeamish?"

"No more than anybody else, I guess. Why?"

"Some folks is more squeamish than others. Anyway, Emmet had a stroke day before yesterday, so I need to find somebody to replace him."

I gulped. Emmet Williams was a retarded man in his sixties and had one of the worst jobs in the whorehouse industry. He emptied the spittoons that guests used to spit their tobacco and snuff into, dumped and cleaned out the piss and shit buckets people used when they couldn't make it to the toilet in time, and emptied trash cans that the whores filled up every night with cum-stained tissue. If all that wasn't nasty enough, Emmet also helped change the bedsheets after each fuck session. Working on a chain gang appealed more to me.

I glanced at my feet for a few seconds. My stomach felt like somebody had tied my insides into knots. I was going through all this aggravation because I hadn't been able to keep my pants zipped up. If I didn't watch my step, my stupidity and bad judgment would be my downfall. "I do declare, that's a pretty nasty job."

"Sure enough," Aunt Mattie grunted, sounding just like a hog. "But somebody got to do it. It's the best I can offer, and you ought to be glad I'm still nice enough to even let you do that. Rufus will be doing it until I can find somebody else or until Emmet recovers from his stroke." She tilted her head and gave me a thoughtful look. "When you want to start? I can only hold the job open for another day or two. You want it or not?"

"I'll let you know by tomorrow." I started backing off the porch and as soon as my feet hit the ground, I took off running. I didn't stop until I had made it back to my car where I had parked across the street in the next block. I got in and sat in the dark trying to picture myself emptying shit, piss, spit, snot, cum, and no telling what else. By now my stomach felt like something was crawling around in it. I didn't care what I had to do or say, I was going to keep my job at MacPherson's.

And I was going to marry Joyce. Just like I had planned.

Chapter 13

Joyce

I DIDN'T KNOW WHAT WAS GOING TO HAPPEN NEXT. I HAD no idea what Mama and Daddy wanted me to do if they didn't want me to marry Odell. I was too old to ship off to relatives so they could help hide my shame. Even if I had been a young girl, I wouldn't have agreed to that anyway. I didn't see anything shameful about an unmarried woman having a baby. I had been raised to believe that God didn't make no mistakes, and if he'd allowed me to get pregnant, I had to look at it as a blessing.

I was concerned about how upset Mama and Daddy were, but there was nothing I could do about it now. I knew them well enough to believe that they would eventually come around. They'd dote on a grandchild the same way they had done with me. Another thing I knew was that they'd help me raise my child, but for how long? They were two of the oldest people in town, so they were not going to be around too much longer. I predicted that both of them would become disabled within the next few years, and have to be cared for like babies. That responsibility would be on my shoulders. It was one of the disadvantages of being an only child. I didn't let my mind dwell on these disturbing thoughts too long. What was important now was my condition and my relationship with Odell. I prayed that my folks wouldn't make me choose between them and the man I loved. That was a decision I would never be able to make and be happy.

Mama and Daddy hadn't said one word during the ride to our house. As soon as we got inside, I went straight to my room and closed the door. But I could hear them in the living room mumbling nonstop. They were speaking in tones so low, I couldn't make out what they were saying. And I was glad I couldn't. I had a feeling they were saying a lot of things I didn't want to hear.

I had been lying across my bed crying off and on for at least an hour when Mama opened my door and stumbled into my room. I sat up and swung my legs to the side. I was already in my nightgown and I had no desire to eat supper, so the only time I planned to leave my room this evening was when I had to use the toilet. This was going to be a long night for me. I would be lucky if I got any sleep at all. I didn't want to think about what I'd have to face in the next day or so.

"Odell don't make enough money to take care of you," Mama said, sitting on the side of my bed, which was cluttered with some of the Gothic novels I hadn't read yet. If things didn't work out the way I hoped, I'd be right back to where I was before I met Odell. Then I'd have to order a bunch of new books so I'd have something to keep me occupied until I met another man. By then I'd probably be so old, I might not even want to get involved with another man. But at least I'd have my baby.

"I make enough money for us both," I pointed out. "And why are y'all making such a fuss? I wouldn't have even come to the store to meet him when I did if y'all hadn't raved about him so much."

"Yeah, we did do that. But we just wanted you to have somebody to go out with now and then. We didn't figure on you getting yourself pregnant and now wanting to marry a stock boy," Mama sneered.

"In case y'all forgot, before Odell came along, I hadn't been out with a man since last year. I was getting tired of sitting around the house twiddling my thumbs and reading about other women's romances. I thought y'all would be happy that I found somebody new," I grumbled.

"Yeah, but we don't want you to be supporting no man."

"If it doesn't bother me, it shouldn't matter. Don't y'all want me to be happy?"

"We do." Mama looked at the floor and shook her head. "But . . ." She stopped talking and just sat there staring at me.

"But what?"

"We thought that if you went out with Odell a few times, he'd pull you out of that shell you been hiding in all these months. He did, and I give him credit for that. Your disposition is a lot more sweet-natured on account of him."

"That's true. Odell brought me out of my shell and sweetened my disposition, so I don't see anything wrong with us wanting to get married. He's a good man and it'd be a shame if I let him get away. A lot of women would jump at the chance to marry him. Besides, we all need to think about what's best for the baby I'm carrying." I was close to tears again, but I refused to let Mama see me break down. If Odell changed his mind and ran, I'd break down in a way that I'd probably never recover from. And I wasn't going to let that happen without a fight.

Mama blew out a loud breath and gave me a weary look. I was surprised when she smiled and reached over and rubbed my knee. "Me and your daddy been wanting to retire for a real long time. We need somebody who can jump in and manage the store for us."

I racked my brain for a few seconds, but I couldn't figure out why she had suddenly taken such a drastic detour in the conversation. "Don't look at me. I told you and Daddy years ago that I didn't want to keep working in the store. I love my job at the school and I'm going to stay there as long as they let me."

"That ain't what I was getting at. I was thinking about what me and Mac could do to help Odell." Mama took another detour, but at least it was more related to me and Odell. She really had my attention now. I wasn't going to get too excited about it because I had no idea what direction this one was going in.

"Oh?"

"With a little help from me and Mac, he could be a real good catch."

"We're not talking about a fish, Mama," I said with my jaw twitching. "And I've already caught him."

Mama exhaled and blinked several times. "Even though he didn't get far in school, Odell is real smart and is better with numbers than me and your daddy put together. He wouldn't have no trouble keeping our books straight and doing all the other paperwork we been struggling to keep up with all these years. He can read real good and he know the acceptable way to talk to white folks. Every time one of our regular white customers come in the store now, they go right up to him and start chitchatting like magpies about everything from the price of cotton to the best brand of doughball to fish for catfish with. Besides all that going for him, he ain't shy about working hard, and ain't missed a day or been late since we hired him."

"Mama, I wish you would get to the point. I'm tired and I want to get some rest."

"Me and your daddy had a long talk before I came in here."

"About what? And what did you mean when you said you and Daddy could help Odell? Help him how?"

"If you really want to marry Odell, we know we can't stop you. But we can make sure he'd be able to take real good care of you and our grandbaby."

"What are you trying to tell me?" I knew the answer, but I wanted to hear it from Mama's mouth.

"Like I said a little while ago, me and your daddy been itching to retire. We know you ain't going to change your mind about managing the store. And Lord knows we can't put more responsibilities on Buddy and Sadie. They'd run the place into the ground because if they was in charge, they'd spend even more time gossiping with the customers than taking care of business. Me and Mac will talk to Odell tomorrow and see if he would be willing to take over for us. He so smart, it wouldn't take long to train him. I doubt if he'll need a backup manager to assist him. We'll let him decide if he do or don't. Now you get some rest; I'm fixing to do the same."

* * *

I wanted to get married right away, so we weren't going to have a big church wedding. But the main reason I wanted to do it so soon was because I didn't want to take a chance on Odell changing his mind.

We didn't bother to send out invitations. Most of the people we knew showed up at weddings whether they'd been invited or not. Mama and Daddy told everybody they knew that I was getting married. Buddy and Sadie took care of everybody else. We had the ceremony in my parents' living room a week after the conversation in my bedroom with Mama.

It turned out to be a big wedding anyway. There was standing room only. People I didn't know, or couldn't remember, showed up. Mama and a lady from our church had spent the day before cooking up all kinds of dishes for our guests to gobble up at the reception. But Mosella also brought several platters of food straight from her restaurant. "Since you one of my best customers, the food I brung here today is all on the house," she told me. Winking her lazy eye she added, "I closed down my restaurant today—for the first time since I opened thirty years ago—because I had to come in person to see this wedding with my own eyes to believe it." If I hadn't been so happy, Mosella's words would have hurt my feelings big-time. I knew most of the other guests had come for the same reason. But I didn't care.

My head was so high up in the clouds, I wasn't going to let anything faze me. Not even when I saw Aunt Mattie among the crowd with two of her sleazy prostitutes in tow.

Chapter 14
Odell

JOYCE LOOKED LIKE A PRINCESS IN THE OFF-WHITE, floor-length dress she had bought for the wedding. I wore the same secondhand suit I'd wore on our first date. It was the only one I owned, but now that I'd be making more money, I planned to upgrade my wardrobe. Everybody else was also dressed to the nines. Buddy was decked out in a lime-green pinstripe suit; one of the most popular items MacPherson's sold. He'd brought his current girlfriend. But he was flirting with a dozen other women, including Miss Kirksey, the attractive teacher Joyce worked with. Daddy had such a bad cold, he refused to get out of bed. Ellamae had to nurse him, so they couldn't make it to the wedding. Sadie was the only other person I knew who hadn't been able to make it because she had to attend her older brother's funeral.

Aunt Mattie showed up in an outlandish gold-trimmed maroon ballroom gown. The only reason I didn't go up to her and give her a piece of my mind for bringing her sorry ass to my wedding was because the preacher was still in the house. And besides that, this was a special day for Joyce and her parents, and me too for that matter, so I didn't want to cause a commotion.

I got sure enough disgusted when I noticed how Aunt Mattie and her whores was roaming from one side of the room to the other getting too friendly with some of the men. I didn't want these men's wives and girlfriends to act ugly, so I had to say something after all. But I had to wait almost thirty minutes before I was able to talk to Aunt Mattie in private. She went to the bathroom, and when she came out, I was standing by the door. "What you doing here?" I asked. It was the same thing she'd said to me when I'd tried to get her to give me another job last week.

"Pffft!" She waved her hands in the air and snickered. "You kidding? I came for the same reason everybody else came. Nobody wanted to miss this sideshow."

"You the last person in the world I expected to show up at *my* wedding."

"I can say the same thing about you," she sneered, talking out the side of her mouth. "I figured something was up when you didn't come back the next day for that job I offered you."

"Humph! That wasn't no job, it was a insult! And for your information, Mac and Millie promoted me to a much better job than the one I had. They retired a couple of days ago and now I'm in full charge," I said proudly.

"Full charge of what?"

"Everything! I'll be managing the other employees, doing the books, paying the bills and writing out the paychecks, and I'll oversee all the orders."

"Well, I do declare. I'm sure enough impressed! You a better trickster than I gave you credit for. Now I'm sorry you didn't come back to work for me. I could have groomed you to help me make some serious money."

"The only tricksters up in here is you and your girls," I said, getting madder by the second.

Aunt Mattie gave me a sympathetic look and shook her head.

"Why you looking at me like that, Miss Pimp?" I asked.

"Because I feel sorry for you and I'm going to pray for you because I think you'll need it somewhere down the road. You done got on too high of a horse too quick and when you fall off, you going to hit the ground real hard. Even after what you tried to do to Mongo, I still like you, Odell. Your daddy used to be one of my best customers, even before your mama died." This news almost made me lose my breath. I even stumbled back a few steps. "Don't act so surprised. Your daddy ain't no different than no other man."

"What my daddy done ain't had nothing to do with me," I shot back. "And I don't know why you telling me this shit—especially on my wedding day."

Aunt Mattie shrugged. "I just thought you might want to know. Some folks ain't what they appear to be, if you know what I mean."

"No, I don't know what you mean and I don't give a damn. Please don't bother to tell me nothing else unless it's something that'll benefit me in some way."

"I'm glad you said that. See, I'm a little on the psychic

side. Otherwise, I wouldn't be able to tell you what I'm fixing to tell you."

"Whatever it is, keep it to yourself."

"Uh-uh. I want you to know what I know. It'll benefit you."

"All right then. Go ahead and spit it out and get it over with," I growled.

Aunt Mattie pursed her lips and squinted. "Right after the preacher told you to kiss Joyce, I got a real bad feeling about y'all. A cold chill shot through me like a bullet. The same way it did a month before my mama died, and a few months before one of my used-to-be boyfriends got bit by a rattlesnake and died. It was a sign. Things might be hunky-dory for you and Joyce for a while, but don't count on it lasting. That sign I got was proof. When the shit hit the fan—and it'll be some real big turds—you come see me. I got a few tricks up my sleeve that'll straighten things out for y'all. I know you done probably heard about my hoodoo candles and all the folks' lives they done restored."

I laughed and waved my hand in her face. "Woman, you crazier than I thought! Don't worry about me and Joyce. We don't need no *witch doctor* to keep us happy. Save your prayers, hoodoo bullshit, and everything else for somebody that needs it!" I blasted. "Now if you don't mind, I'd like to go mingle with my other guests. And I advise you not to say nothing crazy to my wife. If you do, I'll have to ask you to leave."

Aunt Mattie's eyes got big, and she rolled her neck so hard, I was surprised it didn't break in two. "W-what? Well, I never! Look, black boy, you ain't got to ask me to do nothing. I'm already gone!"

I'd finally taken her down a few pegs, and it felt good.

* * *

Mac put up the money for me and Joyce to spend a few days in a motel near Mobile. We bought every one of our meals to go from one of the nearby restaurants and we made love for hours at a time. Between sessions, we talked about our future.

"I hope I get pregnant again right after I have this baby," Joyce told me as she lay in my arms. The mattress on the bed sagged and the springs creaked, but that didn't bother us. The cheap motel's walls was so thin we could hear the people snoring in the rooms on both sides of ours, so I knew they'd heard us making love. But we didn't care about that, either. I was feeling so good, you would have thought that we was lounging in the presidential suite at the most expensive *white folks only* hotel in the state.

"I'll do my best to make sure that happens," I told her, giggling as I squeezed one of her breasts.

"And I hope we stay this happy for the rest of our lives."

"We will," I said as I recalled that crazy shit Aunt Mattie had told to me about the "bad feeling" she'd had about me and Joyce. "I'm going to make sure of that." I meant what I said, and I hoped it was true. Even with her ordinary face, big feet, and long, strapping body—which now resembled a gigantic sausage because of her pregnancy—she actually looked beautiful to me.

As much as I cared about Joyce, I never thought I'd end up with a woman that looked like her. I had always been more attracted to petite, fair-skinned women with good hair. If it was long, that was a bonus. A redbone was the kind I had wanted to marry and raise children with. But every time I seen one I liked, some other man had got to her first. I didn't marry no beauty queen, but I was going to pretend like she was one. I frowned at the thought of that because there was nothing in the world that could change the facts. My thoughts was bouncing around in my head like rubber balls. I was glad when Joyce brung me back to her attention.

"Baby, are you all right?" She sat up and looked at me with a worried expression on her face. Even with her makeup smeared, she still looked good to me. I knew that if I told myself this often enough, I would forget all about the pint-sized redbones I used to fantasize about.

"I'm fine, sugar pie." I gave Joyce a quick peck on her forehead and tickled her chin.

"Then why is that strange look on your face all of a sudden?"

"I was just thinking about the wedding," I muttered. "We had a roomful of guests, but I can't get over the fact that we didn't get nary a gift."

Joyce laughed. "Since we didn't send out invitations and people just showed up, I'm not surprised. We did everything so fast, they probably didn't have time to go out and buy us something."

"Another thing I can't get over is that so many people came."

"That was probably because they couldn't believe a man like you was marrying a woman like me," she said with a heavy sigh.

"Baby, how many more times do I have to tell you that you are the only woman I want? I don't know why you are so hard on yourself."

I felt Joyce's body stiffen. "Odell, I know I'm ugly—"

"You hush up!" I cut her off so fast, she shuddered and geared up like she was going to jump off the bed and fly

out the window. "Don't you never let me hear you say
something like that about yourself again!"

"Well, maybe I'm not *that* ugly," she mumbled.

"Come with me!" I yelled. I grabbed Joyce by her arm
and pulled her up off the bed and ushered her into the
bathroom. I put my hands on her shoulders and held her
in place in front of the mirror. "Look at yourself. There
ain't nobody in the world that thinks your face is ugly except you. Did you stay stupid shit like that to your other
men friends?"

"Well . . ."

"Well nothing. If you did, no wonder they didn't hang
around with you for too long. The shit you say would
make most men begin to think the same thing if you keep
putting that idea in their heads. You been your own worst
enemy and that's why you been by yourself so long."

"Odell, I couldn't hold on to a man even when I didn't
put myself down in front of them!" Joyce griped. "I just
wasn't the woman they wanted to be with too long."

"Well, I'm going to be with you until the day I die and
I'm getting sick of trying to convince you of that. If you
was half as ugly and undesirable as you seem to think, I
wouldn't have asked you out in the first place. Now
promise me you will stop all that crazy talk about the way
you look. The last thing our child need to grow up listening to is his or her mama putting herself down so much."

"You don't have to be so mean about it. I feel bad
enough," Joyce pouted. "I can't help the way I feel about
myself. I've felt this way all my life."

"Your opinion of yourself is the only thing that's ugly
about you," I fired back. "Now, if you want to keep looking at yourself that way, you go right ahead. But do me a

favor and keep them ridiculous comments to yourself. I done told you over and over how beautiful you look to me. So it don't matter what you really look like to yourself or nobody else anyway. Shit."

Joyce giggled. "All right. You made your point. Now can we go back to bed?"

I lifted her up off the floor, carried her back to bed, and we made love some more.

Chapter 15
Joyce

I NEVER THOUGHT THAT IT WAS POSSIBLE FOR A WOMAN TO be as happy as I was. Each day was better than the last. Odell gave me so much attention and he was so affectionate, I didn't care if I looked like a baboon. He still made me feel beautiful, and that was all that mattered. My happiness must have been contagious, because people who used to look like they were constipated or disgusted when they were around me smiled and cracked jokes now. Even the birds that perched on my bedroom windowsill chirped louder and longer than before. My life was almost too good to be true. If I hadn't known any better, I would have sworn that somebody had paid a visit to one of the hoodoo women out by the swamps on my behalf. I knew that was unlikely. For one thing, I only knew a few people who dabbled in foolishness like that. Aunt Mattie was one of those people. During our wedding reception, I had noticed her in the hall outside the bathroom taking to Odell. When I'd asked him about it, he'd told me that she had been complaining because she didn't get any of the meatballs and deviled duck eggs that Mosella had brought. If they'd been discussing hoodoo, I didn't want to know. I scolded myself for even letting a thought like that enter my mind. Especially since Odell and I were too scientific to believe in any kind of black magic.

What I did believe in was that God had answered my prayers and with Him, I didn't need anybody else to help me. My life was moving so fast now, I could barely keep up with it. And I didn't want it to slow down.

I finally knew what it felt like to have some real self-esteem. At the rate mine was growing, by the time my baby arrived I'd be as confident as the most beautiful women in town. Now that I felt better about myself, I took more pride in the way I looked. But I'd gained twenty pounds since I got pregnant, and it didn't look good on me. My body was still slim and as straight up and down as a rod, but with a big bump in the middle. What I couldn't understand was why with all my height, most of the extra weight had settled mainly in three places. I had expected my stomach to swell, but not my neck and face, too. My legs and arms still looked like beanpoles, though. None of that bothered Odell. He still couldn't keep his hands off me. The only other thing on me that had gotten much bigger was my head. Odell had me thinking my shit didn't stink. There was nothing I wouldn't do for him.

Mama and Daddy had told us that we could stay with them as long as we wanted. Odell didn't care, but I did. I was anxious to move into my own house so I could fix it up the way I wanted, especially the nursery. When we got

back from our honeymoon the Tuesday after our wedding, we went to that tacky boardinghouse where he'd
been living and packed all his stuff. Odell didn't have
much, so we only had to make one trip.

Summer school was in session and I worked every day
even though we had only half as many students during
the summer months. And even less since the Depression
started. I planned to work as long as I could before I had
to take maternity leave. I loved my job even though the
Mahoney Street Elementary School building was shabby.
Everybody got nervous during tornado season because
we knew that a strong enough wind could blow the building down, like it had done to so many other places over
the years.

The only other elementary school for colored kids in
Branson was actually a church and didn't even have indoor plumbing. When somebody had to go, they used the
outhouse a few hundred feet behind the church, or
ducked behind the nearest bush. It was no wonder they
couldn't keep good teachers on the staff for more than a
year or two, and they'd never had a principal. I was lucky.
The same teachers and principal who had been employed
when Mahoney hired me more than ten years ago were
still on the payroll. Another thing I loved about my job
was the convenient location. It was close enough for me
to walk when I felt like it. But most of the time, especially on rainy days, I rode with Patsy Boykin in her five-
year-old DeSoto, or one of the other aides. Patsy and I
had graduated the same year, but she'd gotten married
right away and already had five kids. She was the closest
thing I'd ever had to a best friend. When she wasn't too
busy or tired, I'd badger her to pick me up so we could go

shopping or to a restaurant. I wouldn't have to do that now because I wanted to spend as much time as possible with Odell.

With my nest egg and Odell's new salary, we could afford a place in the same nice, quiet neighborhood where I had grown up. All of the homes were attractive and well tended, which was the reason my folks had never wanted to move. The problem was, the only house available was two blocks from Mama and Daddy. It sat on a corner next to another nice house. As much as I loved my parents, they had been smothering me all my life. I knew that if I lived close to them, they'd drop in on us whenever they felt like it, which would probably be every day of the week.

The first night Odell spent in my bedroom with me, Mama must have barged in every five minutes, even after we'd gone to bed and for the most mundane reasons. She wanted to know if we needed more pillows. She wanted to make sure we'd cracked open a window so the room wouldn't get too stuffy, and so on. I knew that if Mama visited me too often in my house, it'd drive me crazy. Another bad thing about the location of the vacant house was that some of the grumpiest elderly people in town lived on the same block. But after spending two weeks with my parents, we decided to move into that vacant house anyway. There were ways to get around my parents' interference: We wouldn't answer the door when we didn't want to be bothered. That's what Mama did when she didn't want to entertain company.

We didn't have to spend too much of our money on things for our house. We took all we could from the store: cookware, linen, dishes, food, and a few other necessary household items. We picked up a few nice pieces of new furniture from a discount store, but everything else came from a secondhand store.

After living with my parents most of my life, I knew that living close to any senior citizen would not be a cakewalk. I was prepared for all kinds of bullshit from Clarabelle Copeland and her husband, Henry, the eighty-something-year-old couple that lived right next door to the house we'd moved into. They didn't waste any time getting on our nerves. Two days after we moved in, Clarabelle cussed at me for spitting on the sidewalk in front of her house. The next day, Henry stuck his head out their living room window and cussed me out when Patsy dropped me off after work. The problem was, the loud muffler on her car had woken them up from their naps. Each time we did something they didn't like, we apologized and promised we wouldn't do it again. Other than that, everything else was perfect.

As far as I was concerned, nothing could go wrong for me and Odell. We couldn't have been happier if we'd died and gone to heaven.

Chapter 16
Odell

SOME DAYS I ACTUALLY PINCHED MYSELF TO MAKE sure I wasn't dreaming. Each day I loved Joyce a little bit more. I made love to her two or three times a day, three or four times a week. I joined the same church she and most of the other colored folks on our side of town belonged to, and I did everything else I thought she wanted me to do. We spent hours at a time with my in-laws drinking tea and discussing all kinds of mundane subjects. Things like that bored the hell out of me, but I went along with it because I didn't want to ruffle nobody's feathers. I had a damn good thing going and if I played my cards right, it would get even better.

I looked forward to going to work each day, especially now that I was the one in charge and my in-laws didn't come in too often. The fly in the ointment—or two flies I should say—was Buddy and Sadie. They was slow, unpleasant to some of our customers, and they complained all the time. What they enjoyed doing the most was running their mouths and blabbing other folks' business. I'd made it clear to them that I didn't like that kind of foolishness, so they didn't do it as much when I was around. But they were dependable and didn't mind doing other things around the store. We didn't have a cleaning person or a janitor, so Buddy and Sadie took care of things like dusting, sweeping, and mopping after hours—and only because Mac had promised they'd get paid time and a half when they worked past their shifts. Being as slow as they were and because they got paid by the hour, they made almost as much when they did a few hours overtime as they made doing regular time. Since part of my previous job had included some light "housekeeping" and other miscellaneous chores, I continued to do those things too. Not because I wanted to, but to show Buddy and Sadie—and the MacPhersons—that I was still eager to do some of the same unpleasant chores they had to do.

No matter how much grunt work I performed, I knew that Buddy and Sadie didn't like the fact that Mac and Millie had made me the new boss, and I could understand why. I'd only been an employee for a few weeks and they'd both been working at MacPherson's a lot longer, but were still in the same positions. That was bad enough. I could tell from their whispering, eyeball rolling, and the hostile looks I got when I told them to do something that they didn't like taking orders from a man young enough to be their son. As long as they continued to do their jobs, I didn't care what else they did. I tried to keep at least two stock boys on the payroll, but they came and went for a lot of different reasons. The teenage boy that me and Mac had hired to take over my old job had lasted only two days. Other than those minor things, everything was good.

On the first weekend in our new home, Joyce and I gave a cookout in our backyard that Saturday afternoon and invited two dozen of our friends, which included people from church, Joyce's school, and customers who shopped at the store. Everybody had a great time. When it ended, the Copelands came over and complained for ten minutes straight about all the noise we'd made and the smoke. Joyce and I promised them that we wouldn't give another cookout for a while and when we did, we'd be more considerate.

"Let's be patient. Them old fools can't live too much longer, and then we can do whatever we want on our own property," I told Joyce after the crotchety old couple left.

"Odell! That's a mean thing to say," she laughed. "But I hope you're right." We both laughed.

I loved spending time with Joyce. She was the most pleasant and kindhearted person I ever met. She tried to accommodate everybody. One Friday evening she was excited about a tent revival she had been looking forward to for weeks. She canceled just so she could babysit one of her coworkers' three kids. The oldest one was eight and the youngest was five, but they cussed like grown folks and acted like wild savages. That didn't bother Joyce at all. She still fawned over them like they was little angels. "There is no such thing as a bad child, just bad behavior." That was what she told me when I offered to break a switch off the pecan tree in our front yard for her to use on them little devils for sneaking into our elderberry wine. I knew she was going to be a good mother to our children, and that was one of the reasons I wanted us to have several.

Joyce had opened up a whole new world for me. She worked with some nice, intelligent people that I enjoyed socializing with because being around them made me want to be smarter. She and her friends read books and magazines and newspapers on a regular basis, so I started doing that too. I thought it would help me speak more proper. But English was such a complicated language, not only was it a struggle for me to understand most of what I was reading, it wasn't helping me improve my sorry grammar. I was going to keep trying, though, because I wanted my wife to be as proud of me as I was of her.

It was such a joy to wake up each morning with this wonderful woman in my arms. Some mornings I gazed at her as she slept. She looked so serene, and I was going to make sure she stayed that way. On top of all the other things I loved about my wife, she liked to party as much as I did. When we wanted to let our hair down, we picked up a bottle and sat on our front porch with a few of our friends. We wanted to avoid the rowdy jook joints. Especially after a man shot off a gun in one of the ones we used to go to.

Joyce even went fishing with me whenever I wanted to go. But she got tired of that real fast. She didn't like baiting hooks and waiting for hours at a time for the fish to bite. She didn't complain when I went by myself, which was what I liked to do on weekends and some weekday evenings after I closed the store at five p.m.

When we had our next backyard barbecue, a week after the last one, it was just me and Joyce. Ten minutes after I fired up the grill, the Copelands came hobbling out to their back porch, looking like they wanted to cuss out the world. "Oh shit!" I said through clenched teeth. Joyce bowed her head and snickered.

"I hope y'all don't be out here too long with all that damn smoke drifting over here," Mr. Copeland wheezed. The scowl on his face was so extreme, it looked like he'd been sucking on lemons all day.

"We got asthma," Mrs. Copeland added, looking just as bitter.

"We won't be long and I'm sorry about the smoke," I told them.

"Y'all want a couple of plates?" Joyce asked. "Me and Odell can't eat a whole slab of ribs by ourselves."

"Yup. I wish y'all had offered us a plate that last time, too," Mrs. Copeland snipped. "Just cut it up when it get done and bring it on over here."

As soon as they went back inside, I looked at Joyce and shook my head. "Baby, you must be a saint. I can't figure out any other way you can stand to be nice to them mean old fools. I wish I could figure out what I did to deserve you."

"Just keep being yourself, Odell. That was all you did, and that's all you'll ever have to do for me."

There was no end to my pleasure.

Even with all I had, every now and then I thought about what I *didn't* have. Like the petite, beautiful wife I'd been dreaming about all my life. I didn't let myself think about that woman too often because it was too late, and it didn't really matter that much now anyway. If anybody had asked, I would have told them that life had blessed me enough to keep me satisfied for the rest of my life.

But I was wrong.

If I had not decided to drive the fifty miles to Hartville that Sunday afternoon the first week in August, or if Joyce had rode shotgun with me, I never would have met the sweet young thing who would send me on a detour I never saw coming.

Chapter 17
Odell

I DIDN'T KNOW NOBODY IN HARTVILLE. I'D BEEN THERE only a few times when I was a kid. They had more sugar-cane fields than most of the other little towns, so when we would drive through it, Daddy would stop and me and him would sneak into a cane field and grab as many stalks as we could carry. We did the same thing during watermelon season.

Hartville was even smaller than Branson, but I'd heard that they had a lot of colored churches and just as many jook joints, bars, and beer gardens, so there was some-thing for everybody to do. They also had some good fish-ing holes that me and Daddy used to go to.

As much as I enjoyed Joyce's company, I needed a lit-tle space now and then. She felt the same way, so when-ever she wanted to go shopping or out to lunch by herself, I didn't make a fuss the way some husbands did. But whenever I was away from her, she was on my mind. That was why I never stayed away from her too long.

I had been roaming up and down one dirt road after another and it was getting late, and I was beginning to miss my sweetie. One reason I planned to head back to Branson soon was because the Ku Klux Klan was busier than ever terrorizing and lynching colored men and boys, especially the ones they caught alone on isolated country roads.

It would take me about an hour to get back home, and I didn't think I could wait that long to get something to eat. I hadn't had a bite since the oxtails I'd ordered at Mosella's for lunch. There was a long line of people in front of a place with a sign nailed on the wall outside next to the door that said PO' SISTER'S KITCHEN. I parked across the street and got in the line. When it didn't move for ten minutes, I changed my mind. I had spotted another restaurant nearby that didn't have folks lined up all the way outside, so I decided to go there instead. I turned around to leave and accidentally bumped into a young girl approaching the entrance.

"You must not be too hungry," she said.

I did a double-take and had to blink a few times because I couldn't believe my eyes. For the first time in my life, I couldn't speak. All I could do was stare at the most beautiful girl I'd ever seen in my life, a true redbone. She had smooth, high yellow skin, big brown eyes, full, juicy lips, and long straight black hair. Even in the baggy flowered dress she had on, I could tell that she had a firm, small-boned body with a butt that would have made Jesus throw in the towel!

"Cat got your tongue too?" she asked.

"Oh! I'm sorry . . . um . . . I didn't realize you was

talking to me," I fumbled. "Yeah, I am hungry but I don't want to stand here too much longer. I was going to try that place down the street. I think it's called Pigs, Hogs, and Sows."

"Yup, that's what it's called. They specialize in anything pork from pig snouts to pig tails. But I wouldn't go there if I was you."

"Excuse me? Why shouldn't I go there?"

The girl rolled her neck and eyes at the same time. "Only white folks can eat there. If you still want to go, you have to enter through the back door and you have to order your food to go. And, no matter how mean they treat you, you better not sass none of them crackers."

I let out a little chuckle. "Humph! That ain't nothing new to me. I been used to that mess all my life."

"And another thing: Even if they let you in and nobody ain't ahead of you, they'll take their good old time taking your order. If they do at all. And I don't care what you order, it's going to include something you didn't order."

"What do you mean?" I asked, giving the friendly girl a confused look.

"I guarantee you them crackers will hawk some spit into your food before they give it to you. If a real mean person fixes your order, they might include some rat shit, puke, and no telling what all else."

My mouth dropped open. I was dumbfounded, but from the look on this girl's face, she was serious. "Excuse me for asking, but how do you know all this?"

"One of the daughters of the family I clean house for told me. Her boyfriend is the day cook and he told her."

"And how come she told you?"

"Well, we got the same daddy. My mama used to clean

for this same family and when she had me, she had to take me to work with her. Me and that girl used to play together when we was little kids. She don't claim me as her half sister, but she still likes me and loves to run her mouth. That's something me and her got in common. I guess you can tell I love to talk, huh?"

I chuckled again. "I kind of figured something like that. Anyway, what you just told me about that other restaurant is hard to believe. I didn't know anybody, white or colored, could be that low-down and mean."

"Pffft!" The girl waved her hand and looked at me like I had just crawled out of a crow's nest. "Where you from? I know you ain't from up north on account of you don't sound like it. You talk like the folks in Mississippi. They speak real sharp."

I shook my head, which was now feeling kind of light and dizzy. Being close to so much beauty was making me feel something I'd never felt before, and it was scaring me. "I was born and raised in Alabama."

"Then you ought to know better. If you don't want to believe what I just told you, go on down to that other restaurant and let them racist motherfuckers poison you. In case you didn't know, if a person eats enough shit or other nasty scum, they could get sick and even die. You seem like a really nice man and I like you, so I'd hate to read about you in the newspaper in the death notice column."

We laughed at the same time. "Well, you must know what you talking about, so I'll take your word." I let out a loud breath and shook my head. "I guess I'll have to wait until I get back home to eat. But whatever they cooking up in this place, it sure smells good."

"Come on in with me. I'll get you fixed up real quick."

Before I could say anything else, she grabbed my hand and pulled me along with her and told me, "I'll take you straight up to the counter. You can get your food right away."

"Well . . . I hope it's all right. I don't want to make none of these folks in front of me mad." A bull-faced man directly in front of me turned around and gave me a dirty look. The rest of the folks ahead of me didn't look too friendly neither. "I really don't mind waiting like everybody else," I said loud enough for everybody in front of me to hear.

"Oh, you ain't got to worry about them. I know every last one of these knuckleheads and they know not to mess with me. Besides, my sister work here and I never wait in line."

I followed the young girl as she brushed past everybody in front of us. "Alline! I'm here!" she yelled when we got up to the counter.

A slightly older redbone, who was almost as pretty as the one holding on to my hand, came through a side door. "What you want, Betty Jean?" she barked, looking directly at me as she wiped her hands on a soiled apron.

"Can I get a double order today?"

"Yeah, I reckon so," the second woman drawled, still looking at me. She looked as unfriendly as the folks standing in line, but I smiled at her anyway. I was surprised when she smiled back. "Who is this handsome devil?" she asked, nodding toward me.

"My new friend," Betty Jean replied with a giggle. "Now hurry up and go get my stuff. We in a hurry." She whirled around and looked at me. "It won't be but a few minutes. Can you stay here that long, Mr. . . . uh, what's your name?"

"Odell Watson, but just call me Odell."

I was enjoying the unexpected attention, but I was getting uncomfortable. I couldn't wait to leave. But since my "new friend" had gone to the trouble to help me get something to eat, I decided that the least I could do was show my appreciation by staying with her. Even though I'd never see her again, I didn't want to hurt her feelings. "I guess I could stay a few more minutes," I mumbled.

"I'll be right back directly," the second woman said before she went back through the door.

Betty Jean gripped my hand even tighter. "I pick up my order at the same time every day," she told me.

"So your name is Betty Jean?"

"Yup. Betty Jean Bonner."

"That's a beautiful name. And it sure enough fits you."

She gave me a skeptical look. "Do you really think I'm beautiful?"

One thing I didn't like about pretty women, especially real young ones like the one with me now, was that even though they knew they looked good, they still needed to hear it from other folks. There was no way this Betty Jean didn't know how good she looked. "Your name fit you like a glove." I was already feeling like a clumsy fool and didn't want to sound like one too, so I stopped talking while I was still ahead.

"It was my grandmama's name." Betty Jean narrowed her eyes and stared at me for several seconds without blinking. "I been living in Hartville all my life. This is a real small town and I know most of the colored people. I ain't never seen you around here before. And I don't know no Watsons, period."

"I was born and raised in Branson. I ain't been over

here since I was a young boy. Me and my daddy used to fish in that lake out by the highway."

"What you doing way over here today?"

"Nothing in particular. My father-in-law sold me his car and I'm still getting used to it. I work long hours five days a week, so I don't get much free time to drive. I thought I'd cruise around so I could see what it feels like to drive more than a few miles at a time."

"So you got a wife, huh?"

I nodded. "Joyce."

"When you get home, tell Joyce I said she is a lucky woman. And she better not let you get loose on account of there's a heap of women laying in wait to snatch up a man like you. . . ."

Chapter 18
Odell

JUST AS I WAS ABOUT TO ASK BETTY JEAN WHERE SHE lived and if she had a man, her sister came back out the same door holding a big brown paper bag with grease seeping out on every side. "We didn't have no more hot sauce," Alline said, handing the bag to Betty Jean.

"It don't matter. We got plenty at home. I'll see you when you get off," Betty Jean told her sister. Then she motioned with her head for me to follow her back out.

I had no idea why it had even crossed my mind to ask this strange young girl more about herself. There was no reason for me to know where she lived or if she had a man, because I would never see her again unless we bumped into each other by accident. I shook my head to get rid of the thought. "How much do I owe you?" I asked when we made it back outside. The line still hadn't moved and now there was half a dozen more people in it.

"Don't worry about it, Odell. It's on me," she said, grinning. Everything on this girl was perfect. Her teeth looked like pearls. I couldn't stop myself from wondering if her lips tasted as sweet as they looked. I sure should have shook this thought out of my head too, but I didn't. She licked her lips and that made them look even juicier. "The next one'll be on you." I could hear Betty Jean talking, but my mind was still on her lips. I just stared at her. "You all right?"

"Oh! Yeah, I'm fine."

"Did you hear what I just said?"

"Yeah, I heard. You said the next meal's on me." I swallowed hard and blew out a loud breath. "The thing is, I don't know when I'll be coming back this way."

"We won't worry about that for now. But if and when you do come back this way, you owe me."

"Okay. By the way, what did you order for me?"

"Deep-fried catfish. They soak it in buttermilk first for about twenty minutes. And then they sprinkle it with a little bit of cayenne pepper before they coat it with meal and deep-fry it in lard. It's the best fish in town. Even the mayor says so. He sends his colored handyman over here at least once a week to pick up his order. Last week that greedy peckerwood had the nerve to come over here hisself to complain about them being stingy with his orders. They gave him another order for free. That's just how good the food is here."

"Buttermilk-soaked, deep-fried catfish sure sounds real tasty and I can't wait to see for myself, Betty Jean." I looked toward my car. "I guess I'd better be on my way. I got a long drive ahead of me."

"Well, since I treated you, you can treat me to a ride home. You can eat your order there while it's still hot. If you wait until you get back to Branson, it'll be cold and soggy. Come on. I live with my sister just down the road apiece and around the corner to the right. It'll be the first house you get to."

"All right," I mumbled.

We didn't talk during the short ride to the shabby, tin-roofed house near some railroad tracks. I was glad it was only about half a mile away. I didn't want to spend too much time alone with this beautiful girl. I was going to gobble up my fish order as fast as I could and be on my way. Before I could even turn off the motor, Betty Jean swung open the door on her side and jumped out. I parked and followed her as she trotted toward the porch, even though I knew that what I should have been doing was running my ass in the opposite direction. But I couldn't. Either she had already put a spell on me, or I was weaker than I thought.

Once we got inside, she waved me to a plaid couch in the middle of the living room/dining room floor. I eased down and looked around the sorry place. The odor of stale turnip greens was so thick, it seemed like it was seeping through the walls. Every piece of furniture looked like it belonged in the city dump, especially a chair with no legs facing the couch. But everything looked clean and was neatly organized. Several run-over shoes sat in a crooked row on the floor by the front door. If Betty Jean hadn't been so cheerful, I would have felt sorry for her.

She dropped the bag on top of an empty crate used for a coffee table and then she disappeared behind a flowered curtain in the back of the room. She came back a couple of minutes later with a bottle of hot sauce and two different-size glasses filled with some kind of juice. She plopped down next to me and immediately started telling me about her family. Her daddy had died before she was born and her mama had died three years ago. She had three siblings and a bunch of other relatives scattered all over the state. While we ate our food, which was pretty good, I let her do most of the talking. She hadn't asked me much about myself yet. And if she did, I hoped she didn't ask about Joyce. "You look nervous. You ain't got to be nervous around me. I don't bite." She laughed.

"I ain't nervous," I declared, with my hand shaking.

Betty Jean took my hand and kissed it. "Like I said, your wife is a real lucky woman."

"I hope she thinks so too," I said dryly. I had lost my appetite, but I managed to continue eating. Having to pick bones out of the fish slowed me down, so it was taking longer to finish than I wanted it to. I was walking on some thin ice and it was getting thinner by the minute. When I swallowed my last bite and hawked up a fishbone, I wiped grease off my lips with the back of my hand and then I got nosy. "Where is your man at?"

"What makes you think I got a man?"

"You look old enough and you sure got what every man wants. . . ."

"I do? Well, if you don't mind, can you tell me what I got that every man wants?"

My laugh was so nervous, I almost choked on it. "Slow down now. You old enough to know what I mean, so ain't no need for me to say it. And another thing, you moving kind of fast for a man my age. I'm surprised I'm able to keep up with you."

"You ain't that old. My ex turned forty on his last birthday."

"Oh well." I coughed because my words kept getting stuck in my mouth so it was getting harder and harder for me to spit them out. "Not that it'll make no difference, but I'm thirty-one. What about you?"

"Old enough to marry but too young to bury," she giggled. "My grandmama used to say that. She had five husbands. But if you really want to know, I turned eighteen last month."

She looked more like fourteen, so I was glad to hear that she was grown. If I ever went to jail, I didn't want it to be for getting involved with a minor.

"I'm old enough and you young enough." She winked and slid her tongue across her bottom lip. Sweet Jesus! Why did she have to do that? I knew the wink was a flirt, but there was no telling what the lip-licking deal meant. I crossed my legs, hoping she wouldn't see the bulge between my thighs. But if she got any closer to me, she'd feel it.

"I don't believe that a girl like you ain't got a new man yet. Shoot. I just hope he don't come up in here and cold-cock me for being alone with you."

"You ain't got to worry about nothing like that happening. I ain't found me no new man yet." Up until now, her tone had been real cheerful. Now it was dry and humdrum.

"The men around here must be blind or crazy."

A sad look crossed Betty Jean's face. "The one I lost was real good to me. I miss him on account of I sure hate being by myself."

"Maybe you should get back with him."

She shook her head and sniffed. I thought she was going to bust out crying. "He got a wife and four kids. He said I was taking up too much of his time so he decided to cut me loose." She stared at the wall for a couple of seconds. When she looked back at me, the sadness was still in her eyes. "I want me some kids so bad. How many you and your wife got?"

"One on the way, but we plan to have a bunch."

"I want a bunch of kids myself someday. What kind of work do you do?"

"I manage a full-service convenience store. Our slogan is: 'We sell everything from aprons to mens' pinstripe suits.' We even have a meat counter and a produce section. It ain't no real big store, but we usually have enough of anything we need at any given time."

"Is business good these days? Half of the restaurants and stores we used to have, and all but one bank, done gone under. We have to go all the way to Scottsboro to shop for most things."

"Business couldn't be better for us. All the colored people in Branson, and quite a few white folks, come in at least once or twice a week."

"That's good for y'all. Things recently started to pick up again in Hartville. I just hope that when we get out of this depression, we won't have to deal with another one no time soon."

"I don't think we will. Roosevelt and his wife keep coming on the radio saying things is slowly getting back to normal." I didn't like the way Betty Jean was looking at me. There was another smile on her face and a twinkle in her eye that made my heart pick up speed. I knew I was a handsome man, but I was almost old enough to be Betty Jean's daddy. A few fast teenage hussies who shopped in the store flirted with me from time to time. That didn't mean nothing, though. They flirted with Buddy, too. Some women was so hot to trot, they'd pull down their bloomers and spread their legs for any man that asked them to. I didn't think Betty Jean was like that, but I could tell she liked me. She was looking at me the same way Joyce had the first time I met her. Just thinking about Joyce brung me back to my senses. "Um . . . I think I'd better get going—"

Betty Jean cut me off real quick. She rubbed my arm and scooted closer to me. It was a good thing I had on long sleeves so she couldn't see the goose bumps on my skin. "Odell, don't go yet. I was hoping I could get to know you better."

I gulped and my chest tightened. "Better than what?"

"Better than I knew you when I first laid eyes on you."

"W-why?"

"Because I really like you. Do you believe in love at first sight?"

I had used the same line on Joyce, and it had worked. "Uh, it's possible, I guess."

"Well, I do too," she purred. "As soon as I laid eyes on you, I wanted you to be my man. Don't ask me why because all I can tell you is that there is just something about you. . . ."

The shit I'd walked into was rising so fast, I'd have to swim my way out if I didn't get going soon. But I couldn't move. My butt felt like it had melted into the couch. I stared into Betty Jean's eyes. "You must be the prettiest girl I ever seen and I do believe in love at first sight. And if I was still single, I'd be . . . well—like I told you, I'm married."

"So what? Like I told you, the man I was with for two years got a wife and it didn't stop him, so why should it stop you?"

"It's . . . it's complicated."

"You can't fool me, Odell."

"Who said I was trying to fool you?"

"I know you like me so I don't know why you trying to come up with enough reasons to scare me off."

"No, it ain't that." I exhaled and gave Betty Jean a hangdog look. "I'm sorry to hear you feel that way. But I work forty hours a week and me and my wife do a lot of things together. Even if I wanted to be with you, I don't have a lot of time to spare. And since I live fifty miles from you, I'd have to allow time to drive over here and back. Then I'd have even less time. You'd be in the same situation with me that you was in with your other man."

Betty Jean leaned over and kissed me. If somebody had shot me with a crossbow, I couldn't have felt more shocked. "Odell, if you really wanted to see me, you'd make time."

"Please don't do—"

She cut me off by kissing me again, this time poking my tongue with hers. When she pulled away she whispered, "If you don't like me and don't want to get to know me, just tell me."

I looked dead in her eyes and told her, "I . . . I . . . do like you, Betty Jean." My voice was so hoarse, I could barely talk.

"I'll make you feel so good, you'll find time for me. And I *promise* you won't regret it."

I didn't know if I was crazy, stupid, or both. The last thing I wanted to do was cheat on Joyce, so why was I even telling Betty Jean I didn't have time to spare for her? Why had I left that restaurant with her in the first place? Why was I sitting here alone with her? My head was telling me to let this girl go on about her business and for me to get in my car and get my horny ass back to Branson.

Running into some members of the Ku Klux Klan was

not the only death threat I had to be concerned about. Betty Jean could cause me to get killed too, because if Joyce ever found out, she'd skin me alive. And if she didn't, her daddy or mama sure would.

Even with all the outrageous thoughts swimming around in my head and my common sense, my dick was telling me that if I didn't get a piece of this beautiful girl now, I never would.

Chapter 19

Joyce

WHEN I WALKED INTO THE LIVING ROOM THIS EVEning, I didn't even know Mama and Daddy had stopped by on their way home from church. They had kicked off their shoes and made themselves comfortable on the couch. Daddy had even unloosened his tie and unfastened the two top buttons on his shirt.

"It's high time you dragged your tail in here," Mama complained as she adjusted the hat she had on, which looked like a doughnut without a hole. "We been sitting out here for twenty minutes."

"I was in the bedroom folding clothes and didn't hear y'all come in," I explained. "Y'all want some lemonade or a bottle of Dr. Pepper?"

"Naw. We ain't going to stay but a few more minutes. We just wanted to drop in to say hello. We came by last night but y'all wasn't home," Daddy said in a gruff tone. "Where was y'all?"

"We went to Mosella's for dinner," I said, clearing my throat.

"Again?" Mama said. She and Daddy looked at each other at the same time, then back at me. "Where is Odell now?"

"He left this afternoon to go run the car. It's taking longer for him to get used to it than we thought it would."

"No wonder y'all didn't make it to church today or last Sunday," Daddy said harshly. "That's a black mark against your name in the sin book." Every time I missed church, he reminded me how important it was to go. But as far back as I could remember, he would always doze off within minutes after Reverend Jessup started his sermon. He would sleep until Mama woke him up when it was time to leave. "I just hope you don't backslide too far." When Daddy was in a grumpy mood, his eyes darkened and his jaw twitched. He was in a real grumpy mood today. "Now that you done finally got a husband, I hope you'll start behaving more like a married woman."

"I thought I already was," I snapped.

Daddy reared back in his seat, gave me a critical look, and started talking in a loud voice. "Humph! I can't tell. For one thing, you don't need to let Odell go off by his-self too often. Last Sunday he went to 'run the car' and was gone for hours. The next time he go run the car, you need to go with him so you can start learning how to drive yourself."

"I don't know why you don't do that already," Mama slipped in with her eyes narrowed. "Besides that, it ain't fitting to let a man have too much freedom. It's a recipe for trouble. Especially after all that ruckus you put us through so we'd let you marry him."

I didn't think it was smart for me to remind my mother that I was a grown woman and didn't need permission from her or Daddy to "let" me do anything. That would have led to another argument and we would have been going back and forth for hours. It was a good thing Odell was not in the house. He would have said something in my defense, and I knew it would have upset Mama and Daddy even more.

"Odell gives me just as much freedom as I give him," I said hotly. "And he did ask me if I wanted to go with him today. If he was going to get in some kind of trouble, it would happen whether I was with him or not. Things couldn't be better between us. But they won't stay this way if I start badgering him, or tagging along with him every time he leaves the house."

The "few more minutes" that Mama and Daddy said they'd stay was two hours. By the time they left, my head was aching on both sides. They had complained about everything from the weather to the wrinkled-up dress I had on.

It was almost time for me to put supper on the table and Odell still hadn't come home. I figured he was still just driving around, or had changed his mind at the spur of the moment and gone fishing. Then again, the car could have broken down and he was stranded somewhere waiting for help to come along. That really worried me. One of the worst things that could happen to a colored man was for him to be stranded by himself on a country

road without a weapon. I'd told Odell that after we had
the baby, we were going to save up enough money to buy
a better car and a shotgun.

Right after I took the cornbread out of the oven, I
heard a commotion in the living room. I ran from the
kitchen with the pot holder and the pan of bread still in
my hand. I made it to the living room just in time to see
Odell moaning and stumbling across the floor, looking
like he'd seen a ghost. "What in the world happened to
you?" I asked. I set the pot holder and pan on the coffee
table and ran up to him and wrapped my arms around him
because the way he was hobbling, it looked like he was
about to collapse. "Where all did you go?"

"Joyce, I'm so glad you home!" he hollered, swaying
against me like a man with one leg.

"I was getting real worried. Did the car break down or
did you get lost?"

"Baby, you won't believe what all I been through!" He
was almost out of breath as I guided him by the hand to
the couch, where he dropped down like a sack of rocks.
The way he was huffing and puffing, you would have
thought a dog had chased him in the house.

"What happened? You left here almost five hours
ago." I could tell from the bug-eyed look on his face that
he was already in enough distress, so I kept my voice soft
and low. I sat in his lap and draped my arm around his
shoulder. He started wincing like he was in pain. "And
why do you have bruises on your neck? Looks like you
ran into a nest of yellow jackets."

"That's exactly what happened. Let me tell you the
whole story first." Odell stopped talking long enough to
let out a few deep breaths and rub his neck.

"As I was creeping along that dirt road that leads to Carson Lake, I made too sharp a turn and ended up in a sand trap. I tried to spin out, but the more I mashed on the gas pedal, the deeper the tires sunk down. I had passed a few houses a couple of miles back, so I decided to walk back to one and see if I could get some help. Well, would you believe that the old white man who lived in that first house came to the door with his shotgun? He told me that if I didn't get my black behind off his property, he'd fill it full of buckshots."

"My Lord in heaven! What did you do?" I checked out Odell's neck again. When I looked back at his face, I noticed a bruise on his cheek, too.

"I got back on the road and started walking until I got to the next house. There was a pickup truck in the front yard, but nobody came to the door when I knocked. I tried the back door but nobody answered that one neither. Since I wasn't having no luck, and was taking a chance on getting myself shot or worse, I went back to the car. I decided to get me some tree limbs and slide a few up under the tires hoping that would help me jiggle the car out of that sand. The first tree I went up to had a yellow jacket nest and it was a big one! Right after I had plucked off a few limbs, the nest fell and them damn things got on me like white on rice."

My mouth dropped open and I shivered. I'd been stung by yellow jackets before, so I knew the kind of damage they could do to a human being. I'd had the same kind of bruises Odell had on his neck. I had been lucky that day because I'd been able to duck before they got to my neck and face, so they had only stung me on my hands and arms. But ten years ago, one of my teenage cousins stepped on a nest that had fallen from a tree. So many yellow jackets stung him, he died later that night. I didn't know what would be worse, my husband getting shot to death by a mean old cracker, or stung to death by a swarm of yellow jackets.

"Odell, I waited too long to get you. If something ever happens to you, they'll have to bury me with you. . . ."

Chapter 20
Odell

"*I* WISH YOU WOULDN'T SAY THINGS LIKE THAT. IT'S bad luck," I told Joyce. I rubbed one of the spots where Betty Jean had sucked on my neck. I couldn't believe Joyce was naïve enough to swallow my story about the yellow jackets. And I couldn't believe that I'd been so caught up in Betty Jean I hadn't even noticed how hard she was nibbling on my flesh until it was too late. She had done the same thing on other parts of my body too. But as long as I kept my drawers and undershirt on and got naked in the dark like I usually did, Joyce wouldn't see the rest of the damage.

Words couldn't describe how good Betty Jean had made me feel. She had made me see sex from a whole different angle. I was still in a trance, which I'd been in from the minute I'd scrambled out of her bed. As much as I had enjoyed her amazing body, Joyce was still the most important woman in my life. I knew that the sooner I returned to reality and focused on her, the better off I'd be.

"Let me put it this way, Odell. If I ever lose you, I wouldn't want any other man in my life."

"Now you talking even crazier. If something was to happen to me, I'd want you to find somebody else. We both know what it feels like to be alone and I didn't like it no more than you did."

"If I died, you'd get married again?" Joyce wiggled in my lap and that got me excited all over again, but not for her. I slapped the side of her hip and pulled her closer to me.

"Hell yes."

"Oh." She sounded disappointed, so I had to soften the blow.

"But it would be hard for me to find another woman as wonderful as you, and I probably wouldn't. Because when God made you, he broke the mold."

That compliment seemed to cheer her up. She smiled and squeezed my knee. "Do you think you could ever love another woman as much as you love me?"

"I don't know about that." I coughed and scratched the side of my face. Not only was this conversation making me uncomfortable, holding Joyce too long on my lap was no picnic. She weighed almost as much as I did now, which was over two hundred pounds. "Look, I don't like to talk about things like this, and the only reason I'm doing it now is because you brung it up."

"I just want to know what I'd have to face in case something did happen to you," she pouted.

"If something happens to me and you don't want to get married again, that's your business. Whatever you decide to do, I hope you'll be happy."

"Thanks, baby. I feel better now. In the meantime, I'm going to enjoy every minute we have together and worry about the rest when and if it happens."

"Good. Let's talk about something else."

Joyce let out a loud breath and glanced at the side of my neck again. She tapped it. I winced and let out a soft groan. "I'm sorry, baby." She moved her hand and placed it on my shoulder. "So how did you get out of that sand trap?"

"Well, with them yellow jackets after my blood, I couldn't take the time to use them tree branches. Right after I'd been stung a few times, I jumped back in the car and sat there until this young boy drove up in a pickup truck. He pushed me out. Come to find out, he was the son of the man that had chased me off with his shotgun."

"Well, at least you got out of that mess all right. Did you have a good drive?"

"Uh-huh."

"I'm glad to hear that. Pretty soon you'll be so familiar with that old car, you'll be able to drive it with your eyes closed. But I'm telling you now, you'll be driving up and down the roads without me. If I had been with you today, I would have had a heart attack as soon as I saw those yellow jackets. Where all did you go?"

"Um, I drove through Scottsboro—"

Joyce wasted no time cutting me off with a gasp and a slap upside my head. "*Scottsboro*? Odell Watson! Have you lost your mind? You know how dangerous it is for colored men in that town! What's the matter with you?" Three years ago, nine colored teenage boys had been accused of raping two white girls on a train in the hick town of Paint Rock near Scottsboro. They had all hopped on that train illegally so they could travel around to look for work. The Depression was responsible for a lot of colored men and boys doing some foolish things, but raping white girls wasn't one of them. Even with no evidence, no witnesses, and one of the girls claiming later that she and her friend had lied about being raped, eight of the boys had been found guilty by an all-white jury and sentenced to death. The other boy got life in prison because he was only thirteen at the time of the bogus rapes. Newspapers all over the world covered the story. Some of the colored people who had lived in Scottsboro during the trial moved away. Things had cooled off over there, but it was still a dangerous place. I had enough sense to keep my distance, but the lie about driving through that town had rolled off my lips before I could stop it.

I rubbed the side of Joyce's arm. "Calm down, sugar. I'd never rape nobody."

"You don't have to! Those boys didn't either. But if a white woman says you did, that's all the law needs to hear and your life wouldn't be worth a fake nickel."

"Joyce, I was born and raised in Alabama, just like you. You ain't telling me nothing I don't already know about the Jim Crow laws. One town is just as segregated and dangerous for a colored person as the next. We can't keep living in fear of white folks and be happy. Until I have a problem with some peckerwood, I'm going to keep going wherever I want to go. And every white person ain't crazy, or racist. I know a bunch of good crackers. They spend a lot of money in the store and treat us real nice."

"I know all that. But that's not enough to keep me from worrying about you. Just promise me, you'll always be careful."

"I promise you, I'll always be careful."

Joyce swallowed hard and looked pleased. But a split second later, her body got as stiff as cardboard and she started sniffing my neck. "Y-you smell like fish."

"I ain't surprised. I had my fishing rod with me so I tried my luck in Carson Lake before my run-in with them yellow jackets."

"What did you do with the fish? I hope you didn't leave them in the car to stink it up."

"I caught a few blue gills but they was so small, I threw them back in the water."

Joyce sniffed some more, frowning the whole time. When she leaned back and rubbed her nose, there was a puzzled look on her face. "You don't smell like raw fish. You smell like *fried* fish," she pointed out.

I was a good liar, even better than I was before I married Joyce. I could make up a believable fib at the drop of a hat. "I stopped off at this hole-in-the-wall restaurant along the way and picked up a few fried catfish fillets to nibble on during the drive back home."

"Well, I hope you didn't nibble too much. I'm going to put supper on the table in a couple of minutes." I was so happy Joyce stood up because my lap had become numb. Betty Jean had also sat in my lap, but compared to Joyce, she was as light as a chicken feather. "You sit here and I'm going to go get some salve to put on the spots where you got stung. You can't go to work tomorrow with your neck and jaw looking like a beaver's been gnawing on you."

While I waited for Joyce to come back, I stretched out on the couch and thought about what had happened between me and Betty Jean. I could still smell her sweet scent. And her firm young body had felt so damn good! I didn't know what to think about her being so eager to make love with me a few hours after we'd met. I didn't give that detail too much thought, because Joyce had done the same thing.

As much as I had enjoyed Betty Jean, she was just another piece of tail to me. But she had a different opinion about me. She hadn't asked if I'd ever visit her again, she'd told me, *"I'll make you feel even better the next time you come over."* I hadn't said I would visit her again, and I hadn't said I wouldn't. All I had done was blink and then I'd stumbled out the door and trotted all the way back to my car with my pants still unzipped.

The only thing I was concerned about was me and Betty Jean accidentally crossing paths again. I wasn't going to worry about that because it was not liable to happen. She had no reason to come to Branson, and I had no reason to go back over to Hartville.

But the following Sunday, I did. And I ended up in her bed again. The same thing happened the Sunday after that. By the time I realized what I was doing, it was too late. Betty Jean Bonner had become part of my regular routine and I couldn't stay away from her.

Chapter 21
Joyce

*T*HE MORE TIME I SPENT WITH THE CHILDREN AT WORK, the more anxious I was to give birth. To me, nothing was more important and precious than motherhood. I couldn't understand why every woman didn't feel the same way. Some of the mothers of the children in my school couldn't have cared less if their kids got an education or not. A lot of the kids felt the same way. I realized that certain people grew up to be fools because that was all they ever wanted to be in the first place. But I couldn't put too much blame on them. Our school system didn't encourage colored kids to do much to prepare themselves for the future. It made me angry and more determined than ever to make a difference. I complained about it to Daddy and Mama. They supported me, but they didn't see things the way I did.

The subject had been on my mind a lot lately. I

brought it up again yesterday when Daddy came by the house to drop off the laundry Mama had done for me earlier in the day. "Joyce, you can't save the world. My mama and daddy was slaves, so they never got no education, period. Just be glad that some of the colored kids do want to go to school."

"I'm just tired of our people settling for just enough to get by on. I might even start tutoring a few of the slower kids in the evenings and on weekends," I said.

"Don't be no fool."

"What's that supposed to mean? I thought you cared about helping folks."

"I do. But I always took care of me and mine first. You want to tutor somebody, tutor yourself."

"Daddy, what in the world are you getting at?"

"Stay on top of your marriage, that's what. Keep your mind on Odell and what *he* needs. You need to be more concerned about him than improving the lives of other folks' kids. And another thing; I don't care what he do to you, you better stay with him."

Odell laughed when I told him what Daddy had said. "Honey, I don't need for you to babysit me. I'm glad you want to do so much for other people, especially the children. You spend as much time as you want working overtime, tutoring after hours and anything else. I'm proud of you and I'm sure the folks you work with is too."

Knowing I had Odell's support made me enjoy my job even more. I loved going to work almost as much as I loved being at home with Odell.

Branson had four public elementary schools, one private school, and two high schools for the white kids. The colored kids had two elementary schools and one high school, period. Each one was so crowded the students didn't get half of the individual attention they needed, which was the reason some of them attended summer school every year. Our elementary schools went from the first grade up to the eighth. Most of the students that made it that far didn't even bother to go on to high school because they had to go to work. With a lot of the girls, they couldn't continue their education because they usually got married and started having babies. Mama had only completed elementary school and Daddy had dropped out halfway into the fifth grade. But they could read and write well enough to get by.

Even though I'd never really liked school, I'd promised myself and my parents that I would finish high school. I studied just enough to get by, so I'd graduated by the skin of my teeth. I could read and write as well as some of the people I knew who had attended college. My grammar was not perfect, and I made a lot of effort not to speak like a country bumpkin, especially around more educated people. But I had better things on my mind than speaking perfect English. My marriage was the most important thing in my life now.

As anxious as I was to give birth to my first child, being pregnant was no picnic for me. I couldn't eat some of the things I'd been eating all my life. The sight and smell of collard greens—one of my favorite dishes— turned my stomach and sent me running to the toilet to throw up. Mornings were the worst. Bacon and grits made me cringe, and I would rather eat a spider than a scrambled egg. I couldn't even drink and keep down the ginger tea Mama claimed would stop the morning sickness.

By the middle of my fourth month, my ankles and legs looked like tree stumps. I tried not to stir around too much because I got tired real quick. Other than work and church, I didn't go too many places. If I got home before Odell, Mama came over and waited on me hand and foot. She cooked for us two or three times a week, and washed our clothes and cleaned the house. Odell did those chores when she couldn't. He never complained, but I had a feeling he didn't like rearranging his schedule and doing extra work around the house on my account. I didn't want him to feel smothered, and I didn't want to feel that way myself. As much as I loved him, I still enjoyed having a little free time to myself once in a while. It allowed me to relax and catch up on my reading. He loved to fish and visit his daddy after work and on weekends, so I encouraged him to keep doing that. Besides, I didn't want him to see how miserable and clumsy my pregnancy was making me.

My condition was causing other discomforts too. Sex was painful, even when Odell was gentle. When I noticed some bleeding tonight after we'd made love, I decided to put sex on hold. "Honey, we can't risk hurting the baby, so we need to take a break until I deliver."

"No problem," he said, sounding too nonchalant. His reaction surprised me.

"You . . . you mean you don't care?" I asked, holding my breath.

"Hell yeah I care. But I care more about our baby. We got a long time ahead of us to make love, so a few dry months won't kill me." He laughed. Then he said something that made me blush. "In the meantime, I can think of a couple of other things we can do to have fun."

I gave him a disgusted look and jabbed his side with my elbow. "Hush up, you nasty dog you!"

"What?"

"I know what you got on your mind. I told you from the get-go that I don't do nothing with my mouth but eat, talk, and kiss. I ain't never put my head nowhere near a man's privates and I don't want to start doing it now."

"Aw, shuck it! Giving up a little head now and then ain't never hurt nobody," he griped. And then he started grinning like a fool and tracing my lips with his finger.

"Not this 'head.' That's why they have women like the ones that work for Aunt Mattie. They do all kinds of unnatural things."

"Baby, don't be like that. You ain't got to go that far. But I understand. I don't want you to do nothing for me that you think is 'unnatural.'"

"You ought to be ashamed of yourself, Odell. I hope you never bring up this nasty subject again."

"Don't worry. I won't."

It pleased me to know that it didn't bother Odell too much that we couldn't make love for a while. He didn't pester me, even when it looked like his pecker was hard enough to bust out of his pants. But I gave him as much attention as I could. One night in bed when I felt how aroused he was against my backside, I did something I thought I'd never do. I stroked and massaged his crotch until he was satisfied, and since that did the trick and calmed him down, I planned to volunteer to do it every time he got frisky.

If I had known that a simple hand job could keep him from feeling neglected, I would have started doing it a lot sooner.

Chapter 22
Odell

I WAS DISAPPOINTED THAT JOYCE HAD DECIDED WE NEEDED to stop having intercourse for a while. I was just as concerned about her health as well as our baby's. But I was still a man. I couldn't help myself. Instead of me controlling sex, it was controlling me. Some men fucked to live and others lived to fuck. I did both. To me, sex was like food and water, so I needed some to keep going.

There was only one thing I could do to keep from going crazy until Joyce gave birth: keep seeing Betty Jean.

Every time I paid her a visit, I told myself that it would be the last time. That was easy to say, but hard to do. I felt like I was sinking deeper and deeper into a bowl of quicksand and I cussed the day I'd gotten myself into this mess. That pretty young girl in Hartville really had a hold on me, but I had to break loose eventually. And I would as soon as Joyce was back in commission.

I knew what I was doing was wrong. But I didn't feel too guilty about it. I justified my actions by putting some of the blame on Joyce. For one thing, when a woman puts a hold on sex—no matter what the reason—a man has to do something to ease the pain. I didn't have no problem jacking off, but that only took me so far. Without having a woman's body to hold on to, it didn't please me no more than if I'd been humping a wall.

As "perfect" as Joyce was, I realized she had a few flaws after all. I had been so blinded by love, I hadn't been able to see them until now. One thorn in my side was the way she reminded me how "lucky" I was because of her. She took credit for me landing the high position I had at the store. But the subject only came up if she was having a bad day. And today was one of them days. She came home from work almost in tears because of an incident with one of the students. He was a rowdy little scalawag. He'd cussed Joyce out and bit her on the leg because she'd whacked his palms with a ruler to punish him for dropping a baby scorpion down the blouse of the girl who sat in front of him. I thought it was funny, but Joyce didn't. When I laughed, she almost bit my head off.

"You better watch your step, Mr. Man. I'm the last person in the world you need to piss off. If it hadn't been for my folks hiring you, you'd be back in the cotton and sugarcane fields, or working in another whorehouse," she blasted. Since Joyce was usually so easygoing, I didn't let what she said bother me. I kept my mouth shut and slunk out of the room. If I'd had a tail, it would have been between my legs. She was fine and very apologetic when I came back to the living room ten minutes ago with a fresh cup of tea I'd made for her.

I eventually noticed flaws in another area too: my in-laws. Even though they had put me in charge of the business and told me on a regular basis what a good job I was doing, they never let me forget that I was still just an employee. They also let me know that when they passed, Joyce would be the only one authorized to handle their estate. And I'd only be in charge if she died or went crazy. I didn't think that was fair to me, but I didn't make a fuss. Shit. My mama didn't raise no fool. I was not about to bite the hands that was feeding me. Besides, I knew that when Joyce had to take over and control her parents' affairs, I'd be in an even stronger position because I was controlling Joyce. The only thing I had to do was keep her happy and that was as easy as licking a lollipop. All of that was good for me, but there was times when it made me feel less of a man, and it had a lot to do with me getting even more seriously involved with Betty Jean. That was what I kept telling myself so I wouldn't feel even guiltier. But the bottom line was, Betty Jean was not the kind of girl a healthy man could ignore. Not only was she too beautiful for words, which would have been enough to make any man act like a fool, but she was also a stone freak in the bedroom. Nothing was too nasty for Betty Jean. I had known a lot of women, but only a couple had enjoyed doing things other than straight sex as much as she did.

"At least I can't get pregnant by sucking you off," she told me on my last visit.

"Pregnant? Lord Jesus, girl! Don't even let that cross your mind." Just the thought of her getting pregnant sent a chill up my spine. But I knew that if we kept wallowing around in her bed, making a baby was a strong possibility. I *had* to break off the relationship and I had to do it soon. Matter of fact, I had decided that the next time I visited her, I'd tell her I couldn't see her no more.

I had never thought too much about Betty Jean getting pregnant. From day one, we'd been careful and I'd pulled out in the nick of time. I'd been too late a couple of times, but so far we'd been lucky.

Until today, the last Sunday in September.

I came straight home from church a few minutes past noon to change out of my new black suit into some jeans and a plain shirt. The house was empty, so I had time to sit down and have a glass of wine and go over in my head what I was going to say to Betty Jean. I wanted to wrap things up as fast as I could so I could put her behind me, and forget I ever met her.

Joyce and her parents had gone to visit some relative in Mobile. They'd invited me to tag along, but I'd told them I needed to go check up on Daddy. He was the best excuse I could use when I needed to get out of something I didn't want to do. In addition to his other ailments, which included diabetes and arthritis, now he had the grippe. What my wife and in-laws didn't know was that none of Daddy's problems was as bad as I made them out to be, so I actually only visited him once or twice a week. All the extra "visits" to him in the last couple of weeks had been to Betty Jean's house. My "fishing" trips didn't actually happen as often as I claimed either. I kept my reel, a net, and bait cans in the trunk of my car, so a lot of the times when I wanted to be with Betty Jean for only a couple of hours, I'd pick up fresh fish from one of the markets on my way home and told Joyce I'd caught them. She put up a mild fuss about cleaning the fish, so I eventually took over that chore. But she enjoyed cooking and eating them so much that she even encouraged me to go fishing more often. And, I did. . . .

The drive to Hartville seemed longer this Sunday. I figured it was because I had made up my mind that this would be the last time I'd be making this trip. I was concerned about how Betty Jean was going to react when I told her I was ending our relationship, because I knew she loved me. And, I loved her, so it was going to be just as hard on me as it was her. By quitting while I was still ahead, it would be easier for me to forget how I'd ignored my wedding vows.

When I pulled into her front yard, she was standing on her front porch. Since this last visit was not going to end on a happy note, I was going to get frisky as soon as she'd let me. Before I lowered the boom, I wanted to make love to her one last time, or at least get a nice farewell blow job. I was convinced that that would hold me over until Joyce got back on track.

I knew Betty Jean would be hurt when I told her I couldn't see her anymore, but I'd be hurt too. She was a feisty little woman, so I expected her to at least cuss me out and maybe even bounce a skillet off my head. Before I even parked, I could tell that something was bothering her. There was a tight look on her face, and she was wringing her hands and shifting her weight from one foot to the other.

I piled out of the car so fast I didn't even shut the door. I was gasping for air as I ran up to her. "Baby, what's the matter?" Instead of answering me right away, she folded her arms and took a long deep breath. "Did you get some bad news?" I asked. My heart felt like somebody with big hands was beating on it like a bongo drum.

"That depends," she said real quick, and then she pressed her lips together, narrowed her eyes, and poked my chest with her finger.

"Well, tell me what it is. Is it something I can help you with?"

"You sure will help me with it. I'm pregnant," she told me in one breath.

The sun was as bright as it could be, but everything suddenly went dark. I froze like a icicle. When I tried to speak, my lips and tongue moved, but nothing came out of my mouth but gibberish.

"What do we do now?" Betty Jean wanted to know. "I can't take care of no baby and work, too."

"I swear to God, you won't have to," I assured her. My head felt like it was about to explode. I couldn't believe I'd let myself get into such a mess! I had cooked my own goose. Coming out of this in one piece was going to be the biggest challenge I'd ever faced. I didn't want Betty Jean to know how stupefied her news had made me. So I smiled and wrapped my arms around her. "Sugar, don't you fret none. Everything is going to be all right," I assured her. And I was determined to make sure it was.

Chapter 23
Odell

I WAS MADLY IN LOVE WITH TWO WOMEN AND IT WAS THE best feeling in the world. I'd been in love a few times before, but it had never felt this good. I kept a smile on my face and I felt so cocky you would have thought I was the only rooster in a barnyard with nothing but hens.

Having a pregnant wife *and* a pregnant woman on the side was probably enough to drive any other man over the edge. But in my case, it was a double blessing.

I had started walking around with my chest puffed out back in July when Joyce told me she was having my baby. I couldn't wait to be a daddy. I had been with a lot of women, so it was possible that I had children already out there somewhere. None of my exes that still lived in Branson had come up to me and told me that I was a daddy, so as far as I was concerned, my baby with Joyce would be my first.

Now I had *two* babies on the way. I was happy and scared at the same time. If Joyce ever found out about Betty Jean, my life would be over. I'd lose her, my job, and my good reputation in the community. And there was just no telling what her daddy would do to me. He still had that shotgun. My mother-in-law would probably do something crazy to me too. Millie was a mild-mannered woman. But one time I seen her beat a would-be shop lifter over the head with a whisk broom, so I knew she wouldn't hesitate to do the same thing or something worse to me. I was leading a double life now, and a dangerous one. One wrong move and somebody could even end up dead. . . .

Sneaking to see Betty Jean a couple of times during the week wasn't enough. It only made me want to see her even more. The store was closed on weekends, so I started visiting her on Saturdays and Sundays, too. Each time I told Joyce I was going fishing or to check up on Daddy. And each time she told me, "Drive carefully, baby, and stay as long as you need to." She was so determined to keep pleasing me, she never got nosy or suspicious. The more I "fished" and "visited Daddy," the easier it got for me to pull the wool over her eyes. I pitied the men who had passed up marrying this wonderful woman. The women in the Bible couldn't have been more devoted to their husbands.

A week after Betty Jean had dropped her bombshell on me, Joyce dropped one the first Saturday in October. Just as I was about to go "fishing," she came stumbling out of the bathroom crying up a storm and holding her stomach. "Odell, something's wrong with the baby!"

She had a miscarriage and for the next three days she stayed in bed. I only left her side when I had to use the bathroom or to get us something to eat or drink. I didn't even go to work the following Monday.

"Son, why don't you go on back to the store? Joyce will be fine and there's nothing more you can do for her," Millie told me the next day. "You look awful, so you need to do something for yourself before you get sick and we'll have to nurse you, too."

"Mama's right, Odell. Go fishing or take a long drive," Joyce suggested, still sounding as weak as a kitten. She was in bed with her head propped up on three pillows.

"Yeah," I mumbled, giving her a thoughtful look. "Maybe I'll do just that. I guess I should go check on Daddy." Then I turned to my mother-in-law. "Millie, do you mind staying here for a few hours? Um . . . I ain't been out to visit Daddy since last week, so I might even spend the night."

"Boy, you know I don't mind staying with my baby girl. Now you go on. You been cooped up in this house long enough." Millie snapped her fingers and waved me to the door.

I didn't feel good about leaving Joyce when I thought she needed me. But Betty Jean needed me too. I knew she was wondering why I hadn't come to her house last Saturday like I had promised her I would. She didn't have a telephone, but when I got on the road a few minutes later, it dawned on me that I could have called her sister at her job and gave her a message to give Betty Jean. I made a mental note to do that the next time something interfered with my plans. I prayed all the way to Hartville that she was all right and that she wouldn't be too upset about me not showing up when I was supposed to.

She was mad as hell when she met me at her front door. "Oh, so you finally decided to come back, huh?" she hollered, rolling her neck and giving me one of the meanest looks I'd ever seen on a woman's face. Her sister Alline came stomping into the living room. She looked just as pissed off as Betty Jean. I stood close to the door in case I had to make a run for it. They stood side by side in the middle of the floor, looking at me like I'd stole their last dollar.

I held my breath for a couple of seconds. "Alline, can I talk to your sister alone, please?" As far as I knew, Betty Jean's big sister didn't know I was married.

"Ain't nothing you can say to her that you can't say in front of me," Alline snarled.

"Girl, please go on to work. You know more than enough of my business already," Betty Jean said in a gentle tone. Alline huffed out a loud breath, grabbed her purse off the coffee table, and stomped out the front door.

"How much do she know about me?" I asked, moving closer to Betty Jean. I wanted to lean over and kiss her. But from the way her lips was poked out, she probably would have bit mine in two.

"You ain't got to worry. She don't know you got a wife. Even if she did, it wouldn't be no big deal. Her last boyfriend had a wife and nine kids."

"Well, let's keep that part of your business from her as long as we can. If she find out I'm married, she might blab to the wrong people. And sooner or later, they'll talk to somebody who might know people in Branson that know the MacPhersons and will tell them about us. And my butt would be theirs."

"I ain't going to tell my sister nothing about you that she don't already know. Now why didn't you show up last Saturday? I had baked some turkey wings and made cornbread dressing just like you asked me to."

"Let me explain." I held my hand up to her face. "I had a real emergency." I was glad Betty Jean stayed quiet long enough for me to tell her about Joyce's miscarriage.

"I'm sorry about your wife losing your baby, and I'm glad it wasn't nothing more serious than that." We sat down on the couch at the same time. Betty Jean gave me a sympathetic look and started rubbing my knee.

"What could be more serious than my wife losing my baby?"

"A bunch of things. I thought maybe you'd been in a car wreck, or had a run-in with some crazy peckerwood along the way," she told me, giving me a hopeless look. "And, I thought maybe Joyce had found out about us."

"Betty Jean, I don't want you to worry about Joyce finding out about us. That ain't going to happen. As long as I tell her everything she want to hear and keep treating her like a queen, she ain't got no reason to think I'm involved with another woman."

"Can I ask you something?" She stopped rubbing my knee.

"You can ask me anything you want."

"Am I the only other woman?"

"Huh?"

"You been with anybody else since you married Joyce?"

"Goodness gracious no! Why? And what difference would it make? I love you and you the only other woman in my life except my wife."

"And you really love us both?"

"Damn right I do."

"Men who *really* love their wives don't cheat on them."

"Look, you can think whatever you want. But I really do love my wife and I really do love you. I'm going to be with both of y'all until the day I die. Happy?"

"Yeah, I guess."

Chapter 24
Joyce

I HAD LOST MY BABY TWO WEEKS AGO, BUT I WAS STILL happier than I ever thought I'd be. And, I was confident that I'd get pregnant again real soon. Right after Dr. Rogers gave me the okay to have sex again last Monday, I practically jumped Odell that first night. After riding and slurping on his sweet dick for three days straight, I'd slowed down and it was only because he'd started complaining about me wearing him out. I laughed long and hard because that was the last thing I ever expected to hear from a man who loved sex as much as he did.

I waited a couple of days before I started up on him again. He enjoyed all the attention and the sex. But three more months went by and I hadn't gotten pregnant again. I was getting worried that we'd never have a child. "Maybe it wasn't meant to be," Odell said, trying to make me feel better. "Maybe God got other plans for me and you."

"Like what? What other plans would God have for us, especially when He knows how desperate we are to have a baby?" I cried.

"Joyce, we ain't that old. We got a lot of good years left and I'm sure my jism and your eggs won't expire no time soon."

"Well, I don't want to be forty-eight-years old like Mama was when she had me. Even if we have children within the next three or four years, by the time they get old enough to go to school, Mama and Daddy will be too old to enjoy doing things with them."

Mama was so anxious to be a grandmother she had already knitted several pairs of booties and blankets and was about to do a few more. Daddy was even more anxious. He couldn't stop talking about how much fun he was going to have teaching his grandchildren how to fish. It got to where I hated when the subject of babies came up.

"I wish you would stop all that unnecessary worrying. I know we'll have a baby way before you get as old as your mama was when she had you, sugar."

"I just don't want you to be disappointed in me." It was hard for me to speak and hold back my tears.

"You ain't disappointing me by not giving me a baby. But you do disappoint me when you keep harping on it. That ain't helping the situation at all, and it's just making you feel even worse. Now let me tell you again, I'm very happy with you and I'm always going to be happy with you, whether we have children or not."

I was so glad Odell had such a positive attitude. If any man deserved to have children, it was him. Somehow I *knew* he was going to get what he wanted and I knew it wouldn't be too much longer. That was one of the things that kept me going. Another one was all the attention he gave me.

Some days I couldn't walk past him without him lunging at me. If we were in the living room, he'd wrestle me to the floor or the couch and we'd make love. Then we'd move to the bedroom and start all over. The last time that happened, he told me, "I'm just getting started on you." Those words made me tingle all over. I couldn't imagine how much more he could show his love for me. I didn't know what I had done to deserve a man who practically worshipped the ground I walked on.

Even without makeup and my hair fixed, Odell had me believing that I still looked good to him. We made love every way possible two human beings could. I'd even started doing things I never thought I'd do. Once I got used to oral sex and French kissing, I enjoyed it as much as he did. On the nights that he didn't jump on me, I jumped on him. I liked to hem him up in the bathroom and make love leaned up against the wall. Another favorite location for me was the kitchen. I looked forward to the times when we'd get buck naked and do our business on top of the same table where we ate most of our meals. One time we got so carried away, we rolled to the floor and Odell's foot hit the stove and knocked off a boiling pot of collard greens. It missed our naked asses by a few inches. We never made love in the kitchen again.

People noticed how much I had changed since Odell had come into my life. "I'm so pleased to see how much you've blossomed," Miss Kirksey, the teacher I worked with, told me one morning a few minutes before our students arrived. "I guess love is the cure-all some folks claim it is."

"Sure enough," I agreed, grinning from ear to ear.

I still enjoyed working with young kids and I felt that the practice was going to come in handy for when I had my own. However, there was one little girl named Minnie that I didn't care for. She lived with three divorced women: her mama, her grandmama, and an aunt. One was just as bitter and miserable as the next, so I was not surprised that Minnie had such a bleak outlook on life. She was a pretty little thing, but she was a bully and had no friends. It seemed like every time she opened her mouth, she let out something offensive, mean, or just plain nasty. "Mrs. Watson, how did *you* get such a handsome husband?" She had asked this rude question in front of the whole class last Thursday when Odell came by the school to bring me some flowers for no reason.

"What do you mean by that, Minnie?" The minute I asked that question, I regretted it.

"Did you hoodoo him? My mama said you must have." She had a serious look on her round face, but the other kids snickered.

I was so shocked and annoyed, I wanted to slap that nosy little heifer. "No, I don't believe in all that hocus-pocus and you and your mama shouldn't either." I was so glad Miss Kirksey returned to the classroom before Minnie could say anything else. And the next time she got a little too personal with me, I ignored her. That was the end of that. But every now and then something else happened or was said to me that ruffled my feathers. Last night while Odell was visiting his Daddy, my daddy paid a random visit to our house and made a remark that really bothered me. "I hope Odell ain't too disappointed about you not having no babies yet."

"You don't have to worry about Odell. He already told me that even if we never have children, he'll still love me just the same," I replied.

"I hope he meant it," Daddy added. "Nothing completes a marriage like children. Odell ain't no different from other men, so I know he's pining away for some children of his own."

"Daddy, you worry too much," I teased.

"And you don't worry enough, girl."

"Except for not having a baby yet, I don't have anything to worry about," I insisted.

"Yeah, you do! And so do everybody else. It just take some folks longer to realize what it is."

I didn't give much thought to Daddy's comment, and by the time he left, I had forgotten all about it.

I refused to worry or let anything else bring me down. My life was so good. I was going to do everything I could to keep it that way or die trying. . . .

Chapter 25
Odell

June 1938

JOYCE TRUSTED MY JUDGMENT JUST AS MUCH AS HER parents and had decided right after we got married that I should be the one to handle all our finances. She got paid every other Friday, kept only what she needed out of her paycheck, and gave the rest to me. I was one of the few people who still had faith in the banks, so I maintained a savings and checking account. Joyce's name was on both accounts, but since I paid all the bills and took out money when we needed it, she never checked on the balance or anything else.

Even though my wife was a very humble woman and always agreeable, I didn't take that for granted. One thing

I had learned over the years was that life was unpredictable. Joyce was still human, so I knew that no matter how meek she was, she could still do something out of character, if pushed far enough. Other than her finding out about me and Betty Jean, I couldn't think of nothing else I could do that would make her snap. I couldn't afford to take no chances and end up unemployed, back at that boardinghouse, or worse. That was why I'd opened a secret bank account so I'd have something to fall back on in case things fell apart. It was a necessary move on my part because I had a lot more responsibilities now. I finally had the "several" children I'd always wanted.

But not with Joyce.

Betty Jean had given birth to our third son last year, three days after Labor Day. I supported her in every way, especially financially. She still lived with her sister, but she had stopped working after the birth of our second son. I was happy about that because I wanted her to spend as much time as possible with the boys. Our oldest, three-year-old Daniel, resembled me so much we could almost pass for twins. Two-year-old Jesse and nine-month-old Leon looked more like Betty Jean.

"Y'all have any more babies, we'll have to move into a bigger house," Alline told us five minutes after I walked into the house this particular Sunday morning. I liked Alline and couldn't understand why a beautiful woman like her, with men coming on to her every day, was still unmarried. If and when she decided she didn't want Betty Jean and the children to continue living with her, I'd have to make some drastic changes. Even though Betty Jean and the boys had to share the same bed (me and her slept on a pallet when I visited), Alline had assured me that her baby sister and children could live with her as long as they wanted to. That was fine with me because I didn't want to start paying out any more money than I already was.

When Alline broke the news this morning that she was going to marry some joker she'd been seeing for a couple of years and move him into the house, Betty Jean told me that she couldn't stand the man and that I needed to find a place for her and our children. I had saved quite a bit over the years, so it was not going to be too much of a hardship on me. But she was so persistent, I went out and found a place for her three hours after Alline had announced that she was going to get married.

Betty Jean wasn't too happy about my choice, though. For one thing, the house was near a swamp, so she'd have to deal with snakes and other creatures. It had only two bedrooms, the toilet was outside, and she would have to get all her water from a nearby spring.

"For ten dollars a month rent, you could have found a much better place," she whined.

"Baby, it was the best I could do on such short notice," I explained. "I'll keep looking until I find something better. In the meantime, it'll have to do for now."

Betty Jean and the children stayed in the first house only six months. In December, I found one in a much nicer neighborhood with three bedrooms and indoor plumbing. It was close to the two elementary schools for colored kids in Hartville, so when our boys got old enough to attend, they could walk. This was a blessing. There wasn't no school buses for colored kids and some lived four and five miles away, and had to walk. It was no wonder so many of us dropped out so early.

With all the good things about the new house, I assumed this would be the last move for Betty Jean until the kids got grown and moved out on their own. It was well worth fifteen dollars rent a month, especially since she was so happy with it. The only thing she didn't like was that all of her friends and family lived on the other side of town and none of them had transportation. The city bus situation in Hartville was just as bleak as it was in Branson, bad or no service in the colored neighborhoods. "You'll have to come over more often to drive us around," she told me. It was ten p.m., the first Saturday night in the new place. We had put the kids to bed and plopped down on the new couch I had recently purchased.

"Baby, I'm already pushing my luck by spending every Sunday, and two or three Fridays and Saturdays a month with you—not to mention a few weekday evenings, too. Joyce ain't stupid. Sooner or later, she'll get suspicious about all the time I spend fishing and visiting my daddy," I said, draping my arm around Betty Jean's shoulder. All I had on was my drawers, which I planned to slide off in a few minutes because she was looking too sexy in that flannel nightgown she had on. I couldn't wait to hoist her up and tote her to our bedroom so we could make love again. "And to tell you the truth, I don't like lying to my wife."

Betty Jean's mouth flew open so wide, I could see the base of her tongue. "What did you just say?" she screamed, pushing my arm from around her.

"Woman, you heard me."

"I heard you! I can't believe you had the nerve to say what you just said! So you don't 'like lying' to your wife, huh? Hah! You got a funny way of showing it!" Betty Jean was mad, but she laughed long and loud. "If you feel that way, why don't you just be a man and tell her the truth. Tell her about me and our sons and how much you love us. I'll even go with you when you tell her if you want me to. From what you done told me about her, she sounds like a mild-mannered, forgiving Christian lady."

I looked at Betty Jean like she was crazy. And if she wasn't, she wasn't too far from it. I had never hit a woman before in my life, but I wanted to slap some sense into her head. "Joyce wouldn't be no mild-mannered, forgiving Christian lady if she knew about you and me and the boys!" I hollered. "I ain't *never* going to let that happen! How could you even fix your lips to say something like that?"

"Pffft! You know I'm just playing," she laughed again. "Can't you take a joke?"

"Well, don't play with me about something so serious."

"Then maybe you should find me a house in Branson so you won't have to drive so far to see us," she said next, which was almost as ridiculous as what she'd said a few moments ago.

The thought of my two women living in the same city sent a shiver up my spine. "Woman, you must be out of your mind! Branson is a small town and almost everybody there knows me. And what about the boys? If they lived there, they could be the ones to let the cat out of the bag to one of their new little friends."

"Like I said, I'm just playing. I know I can't live too close to you. I promised you from the get-go that I wasn't going to cause you no trouble with your wife and I still mean that. It's just that, well, I'd like you to spend at least one more day during the week with us. Your wife sounds like she's always on the go anyway, so I don't think she'd make a fuss if you spent just a few more hours away from her a week."

"Betty Jean, I got enough on my plate for now."

"Like what? Don't tell me there's *another* woman in the mix," Betty Jean teased, which I didn't appreciate. "Forget I said that. I'm just playing with you."

I wagged my finger in her face and gave her a harsh look. "Well, don't play with me because I don't like it. You know I ain't involved with no other woman except my wife. Now you just be a little more patient and things will work out."

The first month's rent for the new house and some new furniture for Betty Jean and the kids put a big dent in my savings account. But I was still in pretty good shape financially. Mac had given me quite a few hefty raises over the years. And when Betty Jean or the kids needed clothes, food, or anything that we carried in the store, I had no problem packing up a few boxes and hauling them to Hartville.

The first Sunday evening in June when I got home from my latest trip to Hartville, Joyce met me at the door with a huge smile on her face. "Baby, guess what?!" she boomed, almost out of breath as she ran up to me. I could smell fresh tea cakes baking in the kitchen and she only cooked them for special occasions or when she was slaphappy about something. I could think of only one thing that would make Joyce happier than she already was.

"Good God!" I hollered. I put my hand on Joyce's shoulder and guided her to the couch. We sat down at the same time. "You finally got pregnant again?" Our fifth wedding anniversary was coming up next month and I wanted to do something special for her. If she was pregnant, I'd do something even more special. She was a good wife, and I was determined to continue showing how much I loved and appreciated her.

Joyce's voice dropped to almost a whisper. "I wish," she said with a sniff.

"Well, whatever it is, it must be something real good. I never see you this excited unless it's in the bedroom," I said, poking her crotch.

She looked exasperated as she slapped my hand. "Later on for that. Anyway, a nice couple moved in the house next door this morning and they're just a few years younger than us. I already went over and introduced myself, and they seem like the kind of people that like to have fun."

The Copelands, the grumpy elderly couple who had lived in the house next door, had moved out two weeks ago. They had been a major pain in our butts since the day we moved to the neighborhood. I was glad that they'd moved to Miami to be closer to their son. I was surprised to hear that new neighbors had moved in already. "Oh. That's nice."

"I can't wait to get acquainted with them. It'll be nice to have some young people one house over for me to visit while you're off fishing or out there fussing with your daddy and his crazy-ass wife," Joyce said, grinning. I didn't think us getting new neighbors close to our age was anything to get that excited about. But it didn't take much to excite Joyce. She sounded like a little kid on Christmas morning.

"I can't wait for us to get acquainted with them too. Where did they move here from?"

"They've lived right here in Branson all their lives. But on the lower south side." Joyce dropped her voice to almost a whisper, like she was afraid our new neighbors could hear what she was fixing to say about them. "Uh, the only thing is, they're bootleggers."

"They sell illegal alcohol? Hmmm." I exhaled and scratched the side of my head. "That's a mighty risky business."

"Tell me about it. But they don't seem to care who knows it. The wife didn't waste any time telling me."

"Hmmm. Most of the bootleggers I ever knew was well up in age and couldn't find no other way to make money. Oh well," I said, hunching my shoulders and shaking my head. "Whatever our new neighbors do, it's their business."

"I feel the same way. They seem like nice enough people and I still can't wait to get to know them. But I don't know just how close we should get to bootleggers. Most of the ones I know are real shady and rowdy."

"Well, let's give them the benefit of the doubt. Unless they do or say something to offend us or make us feel unsafe, we'll do all we can to make them feel welcome. What's their names?"

"Yvonne and Milton Hamilton. She's *real* cute. Looks like a little colored Kewpie doll and knows it. I could tell by the way she kept slinging that long hair of hers."

"So what? If a woman is cute, she'd be pretty dumb if she didn't know it. What about the husband?"

Joyce shook her head and gave me a pitiful look. "Dogmeat. He's short and tubby, beady-eyed, moon-faced, and real countrified. His hair looks like a black sheep's ass. I wonder what in the world a woman as good-looking as Yvonne sees in Milton. But wait until you see the way they look at each other. I can tell they are very much in love. They've been married for a few years, but they act like they are still in the honeymoon stage."

"Just like us, huh?" I poked Joyce's crotch again. She didn't slap my hand this time.

"Just like us," she agreed. And then she led me to the bedroom.

Chapter 26
Joyce

*A*FTER ODELL AND I MADE LOVE, WE GOT BACK UP AND ate the lima beans and gizzards I had cooked for dinner. He was anxious to meet our new neighbors, so we decided to visit them this evening before it got too late.

"Shouldn't we take them something else other than them tea cakes you baked?" he wanted to know, standing next to me while I wrapped the plate with the tea cakes in wax paper.

"Like what?"

"Well, like a bottle of wine? That's what my folks used to take over to new neighbors when I was growing up."

"Wine?" I laughed. "The Hamiltons are bootleggers. If they are in the business of selling alcohol, I'm sure they already have enough of it on hand already. If they don't, they won't be in business too long." I laughed again.

During Prohibition, which had ended five years ago,

people had to make their own alcohol or get it from bootleggers. Even though we had a lot of bars in Branson now, all of the nice ones were for white folks only. The few owned by colored people often ran out of alcohol too soon, or had to close for a few days for one reason or another. Usually when the people got too rowdy. The people I knew preferred to continue dealing with the bootleggers anyway. I could understand why. They didn't care how rowdy somebody got in their houses, as long as they didn't kill anybody. Most of them stayed open all hours of the day and night, seven days a week. Also, sitting in a nice house drinking with friends made people feel a lot more comfortable. And, the majority of the bootleggers had shady backgrounds, so they couldn't get liquor licenses. They bought their alcohol from the local moonshiners and sold it a lot cheaper than the bars and stores.

Yvonne opened her front door and greeted us with a huge smile. "Girl, I was just talking about you. Y'all come on in," she squealed, waving us into her living room. "You must be Odell." She grabbed his hand and started shaking it so hard, I was surprised it didn't fall off. "That's Willie Frank, our best friend," she introduced, nodding toward a slender, barefoot white man sitting on the beige couch with a Mason jar in his hand. He had on a dingy white shirt and brown pants rolled halfway up his legs.

"Howdy do," Willie Frank said, grinning. He stretched out his hand as we approached the couch. He shook Odell's and kissed mine. He was only in his early or middle thirties, but three of his front teeth were missing and the ones he had left had chewing tobacco stains. He was still fairly good-looking with his baby blue eyes and thick blond hair.

"Nice to meet you," I chirped as I sat down next to him. His clothes were neat and clean, but he smelled like stale tobacco.

"How you doing?" Odell said cheerfully. There was plenty of room on the couch, but he plopped down at the opposite end.

"Milton, get out here! Our new neighbors is here!" Yvonne yelled over her shoulder. Almost immediately, her chubby, plain-featured husband shuffled into the room. He was holding a jar even bigger than the one in Willie Frank's hand.

"How y'all doing? Odell, it's good you could make it," Milton said, stumbling across the floor. Odell stood up and shook his hand. "Joyce, it's good to see you again." Milton sat down on a footstool facing the couch and Yvonne stood in the middle of the floor.

"Um, I brought y'all some tea cakes," I said, handing the plate to her. Her long, thick hair was in a ponytail. She was so pretty, she didn't need make-up, but she had on some blood-red lipstick and enough rouge for two other women. The blue sundress she had on was so thin I could almost see through it. Milton had on a pair of dusty over-alls and a plaid flannel shirt with the sleeves rolled halfway up his arms. He was also barefoot and so was Yvonne. After we'd made love before we left our house, Odell put on a fresh pair of black pants and a white shirt, and I put on a lime green dress and pumps I usually wore to church, so we looked out of place. Based on the shabby beige couch, lamps on the end tables with no shades, and a huge, cheap, framed picture of Moses parting the Red Sea on the wall right next to one of two knights fighting with swords, I could already tell that these people were not very sophisticated. After living next door to the stuffy old Copelands and having to walk on eggshells every time I got close to this house, I couldn't wait to see what kind of relationship we'd have with a bold, fun-loving couple like Yvonne and Milton.

"Thank you. I love me some tea cakes. It's been a while since we had some. I can cook a mean pot of greens and any kind of meat, but when it come to baking, I still need a lot of practice," Yvonne said, rolling her eyes. "Well, Joyce, like I promised you this evening, let me get you and Odell a drink—on the house."

Yvonne skittered over to a shabby wooden crate on the floor in a corner and took out a large, long-necked bottle and two jars. "We still got a little unpacking to do," she explained, as she set the jars on the coffee table in front of us and poured a bluish white liquid into each one.

Odell drank first. After a mild belch, he cleared his throat and rubbed his nose. "Ooh wee! That's real good," he swooned, smiling. It was the best homemade whiskey I'd ever tasted, and the most potent. I got an instant buzz. Odell took another sip and continued. "So, Milton, since you and Yvonne don't work real jobs, bootlegging must be paying off, huh?"

Willie Frank snickered. Milton gasped and hollered, "Bootlegging is cool, but we work real jobs too." He took a long pull from his jar and then let out a belch that made Odell's sound like a sigh.

"Oh? What else do y'all do?" I asked.

"Well, like most colored folks, me and Yvonne been working 'real jobs' since we was youngbloods. Farm labor mostly. We work at Cunningham's Grill these days. Yvonne wait on tables and I'm a fry cook," Milton said proudly, puffing out his chest. "It ain't no fancy place, but the food is good so we do good business anyway."

"Well do say. A waitress and a cook . . . uh . . . in that little place over by the city dump? Hmmm. I don't know about the food or the service because I've never eaten there and never will," I declared. "A woman that goes to my church said she got food poisoning when she ate there. Me and Odell usually go to Mosella's when we eat out."

"I ain't never heard about nobody getting food poisoning at Cunningham's Grill, but my cousin said she seen a fly in her peach cobbler the last time she ate at Mosella's," Milton shot back.

"Oh well. I guess no restaurant is perfect," I quipped.

"Cunningham's sure ain't perfect, but we like it," Yvonne threw in. "What school you work for, Joyce? And ain't school out until September?"

"I work at Mahoney Street Elementary, fourth grade. I love what I do so much, I don't mind being there for summer school, too. I do it every year."

"Woo wee. At least you in the nicest school in town for colored kids. Me and Yvonne had to attend classes at that old church out by the cemetery that they used for a school on weekdays."

"You a teacher, Joyce?" Willie Frank asked.

"A teacher? Goodness gracious no. I'm just a teacher's aide," I chuckled.

"What is a teacher's aide job?" Willie Frank and Milton said at the same time.

I told them the same thing I had told Odell when he'd asked me the same question on our first date. "My job is real easy and the pay is pretty decent. I wouldn't work anyplace else."

"Joyce, it's all the same to me. I ain't never been inside

no schoolhouse nohow," Willie Frank grunted. "But I can read and write just as good as anybody."

"Oh? Where did you learn?"

"In prison. A few years ago, the husband of my used-to-be girlfriend jumped me. I pulled out my knife and he landed on it. Self-defense I said. But the law didn't see it that way so I was their guest for a few years."

"Oh," I said again. "I never would have guessed that. You don't look like a criminal."

Willie Frank tee-heed. "Lady, let me tell you something. Criminals don't look like criminals until they get arrested and convicted. I took my punishment like a man, and I swear on my granddaddy's grave"—he paused and raised his hand—"I ain't been in a lick of trouble since the state turned me loose."

Knowing I was in the same room with an ex-convict made me a little nervous, but I managed not to show it. I was glad Yvonne spoke next.

"We don't make much at the restaurant. But we like it and the boss man lets us take home some of the leftover food at the end of each day. We just started bootlegging about a year ago. Us both working two jobs was the only way we could scrape up the money to move here."

I was overjoyed when the conversation took a slight detour. Willie Frank talked about how much he enjoyed operating a still and selling alcohol to Milton and Yvonne, and a few other bootleggers. Odell jumped in and bragged about his job managing MacPherson's and how much he enjoyed it. "I don't have to work half as hard as I did when I worked on farms and in Aunt Mattie's whorehouse. I could do the job I got now in my sleep if I had to."

"I wish somebody had gave me a good break so I could be doing a real job," Willie Frank whined.

"Let me tell you something, my friend: Good breaks is what some people get when they happen to be in the right place at the right time. With me, it wasn't that. It was hard work and perseverance. I didn't even make it to high school but I am living proof that *anybody*—even a colored man—can succeed and land a dream job like mine if they really try." Odell puffed out his chest and there was a smug look on his face. I was proud of him and how far he had come. What I didn't like was how he never mentioned my role in him getting such a "dream job."

Milton shifted in his seat, and Yvonne started coughing and scratching the side of her neck. From the corner of my eye I saw Willie Frank roll his eyes.

"The bottom line is, it don't really matter what nobody had to do to be successful," Milton offered. "Getting there is all that matters."

"That's a good point, I guess," Odell said with a sigh. "But what made y'all want to get off into bootlegging, of all things?"

"There's good tax-free money in running a speakeasy," Milton said quickly. "But it's a fickle business. We can make a lot of money one night, and hardly nothing the next night."

"I'm sure it's risky, too. Y'all have to worry about the law getting involved or hoodlums causing trouble," I commented.

"Pffft!" Yvonne gave me a dismissive wave. "We ain't never had no problems like that. Some of the bootleggers in Branson been in business for twenty, thirty years and the law ain't never bothered them, so that's one thing we ain't worried about. As far as hoodlums causing a ruckus, we only let in folks we know and we don't know nobody crazy enough to thug us. At the end of the day, all we want to do is get together with people we like and make some money. Let me get y'all another drink."

Odell and I had two more drinks—on the house—and we discussed a few more subjects. But when everybody started yawning and slurring their words, I told Odell it was time for us to leave.

Chapter 27
Odell

"*I* HAD TO FORCE MYSELF TO KEEP FROM LAUGHING when Milton called his business a 'speakeasy.'" Joyce snickered as we made our way back to our place. It was a few minutes after nine p.m.

"Tell me about it," I said as I clicked on the living room light. "And what about all that tacky furniture in the living room? I've seen better-looking stuff at the city dump."

We sat down on the couch at the same time. "What do you expect tacky people to have, Odell? I almost fainted when they gave us drinks in jelly jars! And what about that musty hillbilly?" Joyce howled with laughter.

I groaned and shook my head. And then I howled even louder and longer than Joyce. "White trash to the bone! He probably done slept with every female relative in his family, including his mama. Low-level white folks like them is the only kind you can expect to associate with colored people like Yvonne and Milton."

"That's the truth. There was enough dirt under his fingernails to plant turnip seeds." Joyce screwed up her face and shuddered.

"And what about that shelf paper they got in the toilet to wipe your butt off with? That's almost as bad as them corn cobs I had to use when I was growing up in the boondocks. Milton and Yvonne couldn't be more countrified if they tried."

"They remind me of puppies nobody wants. Oh well. They are still God's children and I like them anyway. One thing I admire about them is the way they show their love to each other. The whole time we were over there, Yvonne looked at Milton like he was something good to eat. I could tell that he is hopelessly in love with her, too."

"You already told me something like that. But what man wouldn't be in love with a pretty woman like Yvonne?" I didn't put my foot in my mouth too often and when I did, I took it out as soon as I could. I knew how self-conscious Joyce still was about her looks, so the comment I'd just made was equal to both my feet.

"You noticed her looks, huh?" Joyce's words was so stiff, you would have thought she'd dipped them in starch.

"Well, kind of. She was so loud, how could I not notice her?"

"That's not what I meant. Milton and Willie Frank were loud, too, and so were we for that matter." A hurt look crossed Joyce's face and I felt like a piece of shit. "I guess you also noticed how much prettier she is than me. I can understand why colored men act a fool when it comes to redbone women. It's as close as they will ever get to having a white woman. . . ."

"Now you putting words in my mouth," I accused.

"I don't have to. You brought up Yvonne's good looks."

"Yeah, but so what? She ain't got nothing on you! You the cream of the crop."

"You really think so?"

"I don't *think* it, I *know* it. Women that look like her is shallow and self-centered and that ain't enough to keep a man like me happy. I wouldn't take five Yvonnes for one of you." That compliment must have really impressed Joyce. She sucked in some air and smiled. But the smile stayed on her face only a few seconds. The next thing I knew, she had tears in her eyes.

"I don't care how much I got going for me, I would give anything in the world to know what it's like to look like Yvonne." She looked at her hands, which was even larger than mine. Her feet was too. "Every morning I have to coat my face with face powder and rouge, just to look decent. Women like Yvonne don't have to do all that. They can roll out of bed looking as glamorous as the models in the Sears and Roebuck catalogs."

"It don't matter. I done told you and I hope I don't have to keep telling you: You still got more going for you than Yvonne!"

Joyce's jaw dropped. "Oh yeah? Like what?"

"You a lot smarter and got way more class. You come from a real good family. Just from the few things she mentioned about her folks, I suspect they are just as trifling as mine. Yvonne Hamilton ain't got a damn thing for you to be jealous about. Shoot! She just a pooh-butt waitress in a pooh-butt restaurant. You work for the nicest colored school in town. You give me everything I want from a woman."

"Not everything . . ."

"What do you mean?" I asked, holding my breath. This was one question I already knew the answer to.

"I don't care what you keep telling me, I know you won't be satisfied until we have some children, and neither will I. Only then will our family be complete."

"Um . . . it'll happen, baby. Just give it a little more time," was all I could say.

A little more time was what I needed so I could make extra trips to see Betty Jean and my boys. I just needed to find a way to justify some additional absences. That turned out to be easier than I thought it would be.

The day after our first visit together to the Hamiltons' house next door, I came up with a plan that would allow me to spend at least one more night a week with Betty Jean. "Daddy ain't doing too well. He wants me to start spending at least one more night a week with him," I told Joyce a few minutes after I got home from work at five-thirty Tuesday evening.

"What's the matter with him now? He's not getting any better, huh?" she asked as she helped me take off my jacket. Joyce hadn't been with me to visit my daddy in weeks, and I didn't blame her. If Ellamae wasn't in the picture, Joyce would have been as close to my daddy as she was to hers. Daddy liked her and he asked about her every time I saw him. But he understood why she didn't like to come to his house. I didn't want Joyce to change

the way she felt and want to see Daddy more often because it would mean that I really would have to visit him
more often and Betty Jean less.

"The same old things, just worse. He done convinced
hisself that death is right around the corner. But according to him, it's been that close for the past twenty-five
years." I chuckled. "Oh well. He have his good days and
his bad days. I just wish he lived closer. The drive to get
out to his place ain't that long, but I don't like them dirt
roads and all them creatures jumping out the bushes in
front of my car. Last time I drove out there, I ran over
three different squirrels and almost hit a deer."

"I'd go with you every time you went if Lonnie would
get rid of Ellamae. The way he mean-mouths her to us, I
can't for the life of me understand why he keeps her
around. They haven't slept in the same bed in ten years.
She talks to him like he's a dog, and he's caught her
cheating on him! He should want her out of his life."

"Getting rid of her wouldn't solve the problem. After
my mama died, every woman he got involved with was a
she-devil. The next one might be even meaner than Ellamae. The thing is, he don't like to live alone."

"Then if the only reason he keeps her around is because he doesn't want to live alone, he can move in with
us," Joyce said. "Let him know that if he only wants to
take a short break from her, he's welcome to stay with us
for a few days or weeks."

"I'm sure he'll be pleased to hear that, honey," I
replied. "But Daddy would never let that woman stay in
the house he paid for by herself for a few days, let alone a
few weeks. Knowing Ellamae, she'd probably have another man up in there in no time."

"Or burn down the house." Joyce heaved out a sigh. "Yvonne said she'd show me how to make a quilt, so I'm going to get started on that later this week. After that, she's going to show me how to press and curl hair. It'll be nice to have a girlfriend this close to do things with when you have to go away."

"Yup. I'm glad you won't be by yourself the extra nights I have to spend with Daddy."

Chapter 28
Joyce

By THE END OF THE FIRST WEEK, ODELL AND I HAD SPENT three evenings in a row since Sunday in the house next door drinking with Yvonne and Milton and a few of their other "guests." Mama and Daddy, and even Reverend Jessup had advised us not to get too close to bootleggers, especially since we didn't know enough about them. We had told Yvonne and Milton almost all of our business, even the fact that I'd had a miscarriage and we'd been trying to have another child for five years. They told us that their parents were deceased and they had other relatives "here and there" that they were not close to, so they only communicated with them "now and then." They were vague when it came to more details. Each time we brought up the subject, they changed it, so we let it alone. Odell and I really liked them and didn't want to scare them off by being too nosy. "If and when Yvonne and Milton want us to know more about them, they'll let us know," I told Odell. I had told my parents and Reverend Jessup the same thing.

"One thing I do know about them is that they ain't too shy about asking for money," Odell volunteered on Friday morning before we left for work. We had just finished eating breakfast.

"What do you mean?"

"Milton came into the store Wednesday afternoon and asked me to lend him five dollars."

"So what? You can afford to help a friend out every now and then. We've been lending money to some of our other friends for years."

"True. And them same friends keep coming back again and again. And don't none of them never pay us back when they said they would."

"Did you give Milton the five dollars?"

"Yeah. And he came to the store again yesterday and paid me back. Just like he said he would."

"Then I wouldn't worry about it, Odell. Besides, they've been letting us drink on the house all week and I noticed that they always asked other guests to pay."

"Let's enjoy the freebies while we can. I guess they really want to impress us."

"Well, it's no wonder. They probably think that if they get close enough to us, some of our class will rub off on them. Lord knows they need all the grooming they can get," I snickered.

"That's fine with me. I'm a people person. As long as somebody treats me good, I'll treat them good."

"I feel the same way, baby. And another thing, until

they ask us to pay, we'll keep drinking on the house." We both laughed. "I wouldn't mind having some more of that homebrew the next time we visit them."

"Um, me too, but it won't be this evening. I'm going to pay Daddy a visit. Matter of fact, I was thinking about going straight to his house right after I close up the store and take the profits to your daddy. If that's all right with you . . ."

"Baby, you go right ahead." I gave Odell a dismissive wave as we walked toward the door, holding hands as usual. "I'm glad you decided to visit Lonnie more often. Don't worry about me. I'll find something to keep myself occupied."

I didn't want to spend the evening alone, so I decided to visit Mama and Daddy when I got off work. I had stayed at the school a little later than usual, so I didn't get a ride with Patsy. But since it was June and the weather was so nice, I took the bus back to my street and walked the two blocks to my parents' house.

They were sitting on the squeaky front porch glider when I got there, looking so anxious to see me you would have thought they hadn't seen me in years. If it hadn't been for the fact that they had on different clothes, I would have thought that they hadn't moved from the porch since my last visit three days ago.

"Where is Odell this evening?" Mama asked when I stumbled up on the porch. She stood up and gave me a big hug.

"His daddy is getting worse. He went to spend the night with him," I answered.

The two walking sticks that Daddy had recently started using lay across his lap. He didn't stand up to greet me. He just smiled and patted the spot next to him. Mama sat back down on the other end and started picking her teeth with a straw from one of her whisk brooms. "You mean to tell me Lonnie's got a wife—and a used-to-be nurse at that—but he still need his son to come out to them sticks to help him out?" Daddy asked with a frown.

"Odell doesn't mind going out there. He loves his daddy as much as I love you. And I sure wouldn't mind coming to help you or Mama out if you needed it."

Mama stopped picking her teeth and gave me a dry look. "How come you didn't go with him?" she wanted to know.

"How many times do I have to tell you I don't like his daddy's wife? That woman is so spiteful, she makes a rattlesnake look as tame as a butterfly. She must have ice water in her veins. I don't want to be around her any more than I have to. I haven't been out there in quite a while." I sniffed and looked toward the street. "I can't stay here long. I told my new neighbor I'd come visit her this evening."

"Them *bootleggers* that moved one house over from y'all?" Daddy asked in a harsh tone.

"Uh-huh."

"You better be careful with folks in that line of business, not to mention the kind of heathens they ply with drinks and no telling what all else! They can pull a whole bale of wool over your eyes!" he warned, wagging one of his canes in my face. "We ain't supposed to bury you, you supposed to bury us."

"You don't need to go overboard," I said, giving him an annoyed look. "I'm always careful. Nobody has pulled the wool over my eyes yet, so don't worry about me."

I stayed about fifteen minutes and would have stayed a little longer if I hadn't seen Yvonne, dragging her feet up the street toward her house. I didn't know her too well yet, but it was obvious to me that she was distressed about something. And it was no wonder. If I worked in a dingy grill like Cunningham's, had lost my parents, and was married to a pug-ugly like Milton, I'd be distressed every day.

I didn't like being nosy, but I wanted to know what, if anything, was going on for her to be looking so sad. When I got to my house, I decided to give her enough time to catch her breath and relax for a few minutes before I joined her.

Since Odell wasn't coming home for supper, I didn't have to worry about cooking, so I finished off what was left of the pig feet and turnip greens we'd had the night before. By the time I finally decided to go next door, an hour had passed. I was surprised to see at least a dozen people with drinks in their hands already in the house when I got there. "Oh, hi, Joyce. I'm glad you decided to come over," Yvonne greeted with a big smile and a one-armed hug. I was glad to see that she didn't look the least bit distressed now.

"Are you all right now? I saw you earlier this evening and you seemed upset."

At first Yvonne gave me a blank stare. Then she slapped her forehead and rolled her eyes. "Oh that? Pffft! A man I waited on this afternoon snuck out before I brought him his check so Mr. Cunningham docked my pay. Milton and Willie Frank went to that no-paying customer's house with a baseball bat a little while ago. They straightened him out and I got my money back and then some. I'm feeling fine now, but thanks for asking."

"I hope they didn't hurt that man. . . ."

"Oh, he's fine. They didn't even have to use that bat.

Now come on in here and make yourself comfortable." Yvonne waved me to the couch.

"Yvonne, go get Joyce a drink," Milton ordered, walking into the room. "And while you at it, bring me another one too."

I plopped down on the couch next to their snaggletooth white friend, Willie Frank. He had on shoes this time, but he smelled like sawdust. The bibbed cap on his head had so many stains I couldn't tell what color it was. His long straight blond hair flopped down over his forehead. "Joyce, Willie Frank left the last time before you got to know much about him. As you can see, he ain't colored, but he been my ace boon coon for a long time! Ain't that right, white boy?" Milton yelled. Willie Frank smiled and bobbed his head up and down like a rooster. "Anyway, him and his brothers and daddy make some damn good liquor. Their homebrewed beer is for beginners, sissies, and folks that can't hold much alcohol. But if you really want to get sure enough loose, you need some of their white lightning. It's the highest-proof moonshine in the county."

Willie Frank tipped his cap. "It's good to see you again, Joyce. I enjoyed your company the last time I seen you," he said, grinning with his eyes twinkling.

"It's good to see you again too," I said.

Willie Frank blinked and looked toward the door. "Is your husband coming later?"

"Uh-uh. He wanted to, but he had to go check on his sickly daddy," I replied.

"Well, tell him that the next time I come this way, I'm going to bring him a mess of that fishing bait doughball from the batch I'm going to make in a few days. Maybe he'll start catching more fish instead of spending all that time on the bank and coming home emptyhanded most of the time."

Before I could say anything else, Yvonne handed me a jar filled to the brim with a drink that had such a harsh smell it irritated the insides of my nostrils. I got a sharp buzz within seconds after I took the first sip. "This is white lightning. We didn't have none them other times y'all was here. Don't drink it too fast or you'll be sorry," she warned. "I ain't had but a few swallows and my head is spinning like a whirlpool." She threw her head back and laughed long and loud.

"Too late," I giggled. Not only was my head already spinning, my whole body was tingling, all the way down to my toes. And I liked it.

Willie Frank tipped his cap again before he stood up and staggered to the other side of the room where Milton was. They hugged and clapped each other on the back, and then their lips started moving real fast. Somebody was blowing on a harmonica and everybody else was talking at the same time. There was so much noise, I couldn't hear what people were saying. Not that I wanted to know. I had a feeling that some of the guests had more disturbing pasts than Willie Frank. Less than two minutes after he had left the couch, an elderly woman in a paisley dress and a hat that looked like the lid off a lard bucket flopped down next to me. She wore the same rose-scented sachet my mama was so fond of. It took a few moments for me to realize who she was: Aunt Mattie, the madam who operated the whorehouse where Odell used to work. Some folks claimed she was the richest colored person in town. Odell never liked to talk about his experience with her and that was just fine with me. As far as I was concerned, his past was his business. But I didn't like the fact that he had even associated with a hoodlum like Aunt Mattie. Especially after I'd heard the rumor that she'd chopped up her husband and buried him in her backyard. "Hello, Aunt Mattie," I greeted. "How are you doing these days?"

"I got one foot and a big toe in the grave. The rest of me is still kicking," she told me, wheezing like a sick mule. "I ain't seen you in public but a few times since you got married. How come Odell ain't with you? He done run off already?"

Chapter 29
Joyce

"*O*DELL DIDN'T RUN OFF. HE WOULD NEVER LEAVE me!" I was talking so fast, I almost bit my lip. I couldn't believe the nerve of this old woman. "Why would he and why are you asking me something like that?"

Aunt Mattie looked at me with contempt—like I was the one who'd insulted her—and hunched her shoulders. "Well, you here and he ain't. And, he is a man."

"So? He's also my husband. He told me he married me for life."

"Pffft!" Aunt Mattie waved her hairy, gnarled hand, which could have passed for a monkey's paw. "Gal, let me tell you something, and I hope you believe every word I'm fixing to say. So what if Odell is your husband and claims he'll be with you for life. Ha! You wouldn't believe how many times I done heard them famous last words from other women. If that's what you believe, you got a lot to learn. It'll take more than him being married to you for him to stay! People do fall out of love and split up. I see it all the time in my business."

It took a great deal of effort and a silent prayer for me not to get too mad. But I still wanted to slap the smug look off Aunt Mattie's face. I had never hit another person in my life and wasn't about to start now. Besides, I had to consider her age because another thing I'd never done was sass an elder. I would give her the benefit of the doubt, because I had heard from a lot of folks that she was just naturally rude. I had also heard that she had a good heart and was always willing to help people in need—as long as you didn't disrespect her or make her mad. "I'm sorry. I didn't mean to holler at you and get you upset," I apologized.

"Honey child, it'd take more than you hollering to get me upset. I done been through things most people ain't even had to deal with in their worst nightmares. Getting hollered at don't even faze me." Aunt Mattie gave me a thoughtful look and kept talking. "Being nosy and meddlesome is part of being old."

"Well, I can tell you myself that Odell is crazy about Joyce, and he ain't going no place. He treats her like a queen," Yvonne piped in, sitting down on the other side of me. "I wish I could train Milton to be more like Odell."

"Be careful what you wish for, Yvonne," Aunt Mattie advised. Then she got a glazed look in her eyes. "Sometimes you better off with what you already have. I got everything I ever wished for and look where I'm at."

"You got a good business and you still kicking. For somebody that used to be a slave, you lucky," Yvonne said, crossing her legs. "I bet most of the use-to-be slaves done already died."

Slavery was another painful subject to me. My parents had experienced it and every time they brought it up, I left the room. I didn't want to keep hearing about how the white folks had mistreated our people back in the old days. It was hard enough to listen to how they were mistreating us now. As much as it bothered me, I decided to encourage a conversation on this subject so I wouldn't have to listen to more of Aunt Mattie's comments about my marriage. "Daddy was eleven and Mama was seven when Lincoln freed the slaves. She can't remember anything about being a slave, but he remembers it all like it happened yesterday," I reported in a sad tone. "Aunt Mattie, can you still remember what it was like?" I knew this was an unnecessary question because she was several years older than my daddy and if he could remember slavery, she could.

"I hope I never forget. It was my hell on earth. I was a teenager when it ended," Aunt Mattie said with her voice cracking. Two women I hadn't been introduced to yet stood nearby. They stopped talking and moved closer so they could hear what Aunt Mattie had to say. "Um . . . I ain't talked about what I went through in more than sixty years. But for some reason, I got a few things I'd like to get off my chest and share with somebody tonight." Aunt Mattie sat up straighter and cleared her throat. There was an extremely sad look on her face. It was hard to believe that a few minutes ago she'd been laughing and whooping and hollering like a wild woman. "When I was eleven, they took me out of the fields and put me to work in the main house. I slept on a pallet in the room Master Buffington shared with his wife. I had to get up two or three times a night and go all the way out to the end of the backyard to empty the slop jar them two boogers used.

They had the nerve to call it a "night glass" but it was just as much a shit pot as the ones in the slave quarters. And every other night one of them peckerwoods had the runs. I hated being around Master Buffington. When that horny motherfucker didn't feel like pestering his wife—with his nub of a dick—he got down on that pallet and crawled on top of me. By the time I was fifteen, I'd had four baby girls by him and he sold them all before I could even wean them."

"Did you ever see them again?" I asked, feeling sorry for a woman I barely knew.

Aunt Mattie shook her head. "Naw. To this day, I don't know where they at. But a few years after the war, a woman on the next plantation over told me that he had sold them to other men who had sons so they'd have somebody to pester when they got old enough. By now I must have grandkids, great-grandkids, and great-great-grandkids all over the place that I'll never meet."

The mood around me got dark. It didn't seem like I was still in the same room with the rest of the rowdy guests. They were just a few feet away whooping and hollering, dancing, drinking, and talking all kinds of bull-shit, and I wished I was doing the same thing. I didn't want to be rude and get up and move, so I decided to stay put until Aunt Mattie finished telling her story.

"Did you have any other babies?" Yvonne asked.

Aunt Mattie shook her head again. "Just one. Ten years after we got our freedom, I got pregnant by a man I'd been in love with for years. He got kicked in the head by a mule and died a week before my son was born. I named him Aaron, after his daddy. He was a smart little rascal, but colored folks and smarts didn't go together back then, not that they do much now either. When he got old enough, he spoke up about the way we was being treated and how we needed to get some education. He even taught hisself how to read and write and had just started teaching other colored kids to do the same thing. Well, the white folks told him to behave and act like a nigger. They beat him up a few times, but even that didn't stop him. One night he didn't come home after visiting the girl he was planning to marry. The next day, we cut his body down from the tree where somebody had lynched him."

"Did they ever find out who done it?" Yvonne asked.

"Pffft! What's wrong with you, girl? Everybody knowed who done it! It was them same peckerwoods that was so pissed off about losing the war and was taking it out on used-to-be slaves. They put the entire blame for the war between the North and the South on us!"

Yvonne blinked hard and sniffed a few times. I blinked and sniffed even harder. Aunt Mattie wiped a few tears off her face. The other two women who had been listening stayed quiet. I didn't know what was going through their minds, but I had never felt so sad in my life. I motioned for Milton to replenish my drink, which he did immediately. Aunt Mattie sniffled a few times, but she perked up again right away. "Enough of that!" she said, clapping her hands. "So Joyce, where is Odell tonight? Do you know?"

"He's gone out to check on his daddy," I replied. "Lonnie's been having all kinds of problems with his health lately."

"Well, if Ellamae ain't taking care of him, he ought to get rid of her," Aunt Mattie snarled.

"She takes care of him, but she needs a break now and then. Taking care of that old man is a big responsibility.

Ellamae depends on Odell to come out and help a few times a week. And when he needs a break, he goes fishing."

"Hmmm. Fishing for what?"

"For fish!" I snapped harder than I meant to. Aunt Mattie flinched, but she stayed on the same subject anyway.

"That's nice. You ought to go with him."

"I don't like to fish."

"So what? I didn't like to fish when my man was still with me. But every time he went, I was right behind him. Sometimes it pays off for a woman to stay close to her husband."

"Well, I don't think that. Odell doesn't smother me, and I'm not going to smother him. Especially as close as we already are. Sometimes he knows what I'm thinking before I say it and I'm the same way with him. Now, if he likes to go fishing a few times a week by himself, I want him to do just that. But I don't need to go."

Aunt Mattie sucked on her teeth and gave me a dry look. "Maybe you should. For all you know, he could be doing something he don't want you to see. . . ."

Yvonne and the other two women stayed as quiet as mutes. I was exasperated, but I had to keep standing my ground. I was not about to let this *signifying monkey* get under my skin without speaking up for myself. "He used to ask me to go fishing with him every time he went and I went a few times. I never enjoyed it so I stopped going. I told Odell that if he's happy standing on a creek bank for hours at a time and don't catch but one or two fish, if any, more power to him. I think he'd rather go by himself anyway. He works hard taking care of my folks' business, so he needs to be alone when he wants to." The way Aunt

Mattie pressed her thin liver-colored lips together, I thought she'd decided to shut up. I was wrong.

"Humph. He sure is a busy man. And a right handsome one, too, you know. If he was my man, I wouldn't let him out of my sight as much as you do. I don't like to get too personal, but I'm just being nosy on account of I really like you and Odell, and I'd hate to see something bad happen between y'all."

I took a deep breath and swallowed hard. "If you mean him latching on to another woman, that's the least of my worries," I shot back. "Yvonne, can I use your toilet and if you don't mind, could you pour me a stronger drink?" I stood up and started walking toward the back of the room as fast as I could.

Chapter 30
Odell

"*D*ADDY, HOW COME YOU DON'T LIVE WITH US ALL the time?" my son Daniel wanted to know. I loved all my children, but he was the most special. He'd been born in the month of May in '35 at home in the same bed where me and Betty Jean had created him during one of the worst tornadoes we'd had since I was a little boy. In nearby Midland City, the wind had picked up and hurled a family of three a hundred and fifty yards from their farmhouse, killing the five-year-old son and seriously injuring the husband and wife. Some of the people who lived on the same block as Betty Jean had lost everything. Because of that storm, I'd had to spend a few extra hours in Hartville and so I'd been in the house for Daniel's birth. I'd also been present for the births of our other two, but things had gone a lot smoother. As big a fool as I was for women, I'd choose my children over them in a heartbeat. There was something about having another person in my life that I had helped create. Love was the strongest connection between a man and a woman. But with his children, it was love and blood. I would rather die than not be able to spend time with my precious sons. I had to blink hard to hold back the tear that threatened to roll out of my eye.

"Boy, you know your daddy got to travel for his work," Betty Jean answered before I could. We sat on the front porch steps of the house that I paid the rent for every month. My two younger boys was visiting with their aunt Alline.

Daniel gave me a curious look and hunched his shoulders. "How come you can't work around here, Daddy?"

"I wish I could. But we still going through the Depression and finding jobs is hard, so I need to hold on to the one I got."

The country was still in a slump. Millions of people was still out of work and scrambling like crazy just to put food on the table and keep a roof over their heads. I don't know what I would have done if Aunt Mattie hadn't let me work for her for almost five years and then for Mac and Millie to hire me. Without the job I had now, I couldn't take care of my family, and I couldn't imagine what my life would be like if I lost them. With things being so easy for me, at least for now, I didn't spend much time worrying about losing either one. Instead of wasting time dwelling on situations that sent shock waves throughout my body, I spent my time counting my blessings every day.

"Did that answer your question?" I asked, tapping the side of my son's head. The older he got, the more he resembled me.

He nodded. "I got another one."

"Oh? And what is it?"

"Do we have a grandmother and a grandfather? And what about aunts and uncles and cousins and stuff?"

A lump got stuck in my throat. I was relieved when Betty Jean jumped and answered that question for me, too.

"You know my mama and daddy both dead. But you got plenty of other kinfolks on my side. Your auntie Alline and her husband, and our cousin Roy and his wife and your three cousins come see us all the time." Betty Jean paused and gave me a sympathetic look. "Your poor daddy. He lost his whole family years ago. He ain't got nobody except us."

"Oh. Well, can we have a puppy, too?" Daniel asked.

Betty Jean and I laughed at the same time, but I felt really sad. Daddy loved children and he missed not having relationships with my siblings and their families. That made me feel worse than I already felt. I hadn't communicated with my sister and brother since before I got with Joyce, so they'd never met her. I had toyed around with the notion that one day I would load up Betty Jean and the kids and drive to Birmingham so they could get acquainted with my siblings and their families. But if I ever did, I could never let my siblings know about Joyce. It would be just my luck that one of them might decide to visit Daddy someday and he'd tell them about her. And if he didn't, Ellamae sure enough would. That was one pickle barrel I didn't want to be in, so I had to leave things just the way they were.

Everything else was going fine. I had nothing to complain about. My finances were still in pretty good shape. Other than our rent and the household expenses, me and Joyce didn't have a lot of money going out. We was generous with our friends who needed loans now and then, but we had recently started cutting back on that. And it wasn't because we had suddenly turned stingy, or had lost our compassion for people that had less than us. The problem was, every time we approached people about paying us back, half of them had a sad story about how the country's ongoing depression had set them back, and the other half didn't give no excuse or even attempt to repay the loans. It was Joyce's idea for us to stop lending out money. "Odell, we can't keep fattening frogs for snakes. The same friends we've been helping out for years ain't in no better shape than they were before. Besides that, I still see some of the same ones in Mosella's and other restaurants eating like hogs at a trough and spending money on other things like they didn't have a care in the world. If we keep paying for everybody else's good times, we'll be in the same boat with them," she said.

I agreed with her, but it cost us a few friends. After we stopped giving, they stopped coming around and started rolling their eyes at us in public and calling us "uppity Uncle Toms" behind our backs. It hurt when Buddy and Sadie told me some of the things people was saying about us, but it didn't change nothing. The only friends that didn't ask us for frequent handouts was Yvonne and Milton. I had a feeling that would eventually change because the first night we drank with them, they dropped a few hints about how some of the guests they'd entertained in their previous residence had been slow about paying up their drinking tabs. The subject had come up after me and Joyce had gulped down three drinks apiece that we'd been told was "on the house," so we didn't think to offer no tip or nothing else. But I couldn't decide if they was lumping us in with that deadbeat bunch, and I didn't ask. Me and Joyce had discussed the issue and like always, she went right along with whatever I said. We decided that until they straight up asked us to pay for our drinks, we'd continue to enjoy every freebie we could get from them. She'd joked about us having a "callous" attitude. But she changed her tune when I reminded her how free-handed we'd been to other people such as us loaning money, giving free rides, and whatnot. She agreed real fast that it was time for us to reap some benefits for our generosity.

Right after my other two boys had come home from Alline's house, I helped Betty Jean give them their baths and tuck them in for the night. After that, we went back out to the porch and relaxed with a pitcher of lemonade. The streetlight in front of the house had been out of order for weeks. But there was a lot of light coming from the coal oil lamp we had set on a brick near the front door in the living room. Mosquitoes, moths, and lightning bugs buzzed around our heads. I got so tired of swatting them with my hand, I gave up. Them creatures annoyed the hell out of me, but it could have been a lot worse. I re-called the lie I'd told Joyce about a swarm of yellow jack-ets attacking me the night I'd come home with sucker bites up and down my neck after my first date with Betty Jean. We had come such a long way since then. And I'd never felt better in my life. I walked around with my chest puffed out every day.

I had told Betty Jean about my new plan to visit and spend the night a little more often.

"Is your daddy really sick enough for you to get away with using him for a excuse for a few more times every week?" she asked with a worried look.

"Yup. Daddy is sick enough for me to use him as one of my most frequent alibis until the day he dies. I just wish I had thought of using him sooner so I could have been spending more time with you and the boys. One day real soon when I can spend the night, we'll drive over to Mobile and eat at one of them fancy restaurants. We might even go fishing and shopping and anything else you want to do."

"Baby, I'd love to do all that. I'd also like to take the boys to that duck pond they love so much, pick some blackberries if we come across a patch that ain't already been plucked clean, and we can have a picnic before the weather get too cold."

"Whatever you say, sugar."

"Odell, you so good to me. You sure know what to do to keep a woman happy." Betty Jean stopped talking long enough to clear her throat, which usually meant she had something to say I didn't want to hear. I was right. "By the way, how is your wife doing these days?" Her question caught me completely off guard. In all the years we'd been together, I could count on one hand all the times Betty Jean had asked me about Joyce. She hadn't even seen a picture of her, and I'd never even told her what she looked like.

"Who?"

"Your *wife*? Joyce is her name, right?"

"Yup, that's her name. Well . . . um . . . she's doing real good. Loves her job, is always busy, and don't give me no trouble at all. On top of helping out during summer school, now she is thinking about tutoring some of the slow students in the evenings. Joyce is a good wife."

"But not good enough . . ."

I had to take a deep breath before I could respond to Betty Jean's comment. "Not good enough for what?" My heart was ticking like a time bomb.

"Not good enough for you to be faithful to." I didn't like her tone. I couldn't tell if she was complaining, whining, joking, or just talking off the top of her head.

"What's that supposed to mean?"

Her next question made my chest tighten. "Is she fat, pitch black, and ugly?"

"No. Um . . . compared to some women, she is a good-looking woman . . . in her own way."

Betty Jean held up her hand. "Hush up. You don't need to say nothing else. What you just said told me everything: Joyce is as ugly as homemade sin," she snickered.

I sucked in some air and reached into my pocket and fished out my wallet. I snorted when I pulled out one of the pictures Joyce's mama had taken of us on our wedding day and held it up to Betty Jean's face. "She is a lot better-looking in person," I claimed. I put the picture back in my wallet.

Betty Jean gave me a sympathetic look and shook her head. And then she looked me straight in the eye and asked, "How much longer do you plan on staying with a *moose* like that?"

My jaw dropped. I was shocked and disappointed to hear her low-rate another woman, especially one she knew I was in love with. There was nothing Joyce could do about her looks. But she was better-looking than some of the women I knew. And in other areas, she had more going for her than any of them—especially Betty Jean. "What's wrong with you, girl? I told you from the get-go that I was *never* going to leave my wife. How long do you think her daddy and mama would let me work the store if I left her?" I reared back and gave her the most disgusted look I could come up with. "And what's the point of bringing this up after all this time?"

Betty Jean stared ahead for a few seconds and hunched her shoulders. When she returned her attention to me, the expression on her face was so sad, I thought she was going to cry. "I'm sorry. I'm just jealous."

"You ain't got to be jealous of Joyce. She ain't taking nothing away from you."

"She ain't got to take nothing away from me; she already got it: *your last name.*"

"There ain't nothing I can do about that now. Shoot! I think I'm man enough for both of y'all, so what's the problem?"

"The problem is, every woman would like to get married someday. When I was a little girl, I used to fantasize about the big church wedding I was going to have when I grew up. I never thought I'd spend my whole life being just a outside woman," she mumbled. "And, I don't know if I'm going to. . . ."

"Well, you can't have it both ways. If I leave Joyce and move in with you, we'll have to go on relief and let the government support us until I find a new job. And, you know I'll never find another one making the kind of money I make now. On top of all that, the scandal would kill Joyce and shame you and the children. You want to deal with all that?"

"Naw, I guess I don't." Betty Jean put her arm around my shoulder and then she hauled off and kissed my jaw. "Them little devils must be asleep by now. Let's go to bed."

Tonight was the first time I felt really guilty about what I was doing to Joyce. But it was way too late for me to do anything about it now. I was swimming in shit up to my neck and I had to do everything I could to keep from drowning.

Chapter 31
Joyce

*I*T WAS ALMOST MIDNIGHT AND I WAS STILL SITTING ON the couch next to Yvonne. Aunt Mattie and most of the other guests had left. I had had two large drinks in the last hour and Yvonne had just poured me another one. I wasn't worried about getting too drunk and having a hangover the next morning and I didn't care if I did. I had plenty of ginger tea in the house and it was the best cure for a hangover. I didn't feel like going home yet, because I didn't want to be alone with my thoughts. I had heard some disturbing things tonight. Willie Frank was an ex-con, but he seemed like a nice enough person anyway. I just wasn't sure that I wanted to be around him too often. But he was entertaining. He told funny jokes and when he got real drunk, he got his guitar out of his truck and sang and danced in his bare feet. I couldn't remember the last time I'd come across a man who behaved like he didn't have a care in the world. I was so pleased that I had finally reached that point myself. Except for me not being a mother yet, I didn't have a care in the world. I couldn't remember the last time I'd been depressed, but Aunt Mattie's story had put a damper on my peace of mind and pushed me closer to the doldrums than I wanted to be.

"I feel so sorry for Aunt Mattie," I commented to Yvonne. "I had no idea she'd had such a miserable life. That was one hell of a story she told us tonight." I shook my head and took a long drink. "I wouldn't trade places with her for all the money in the world."

"Me neither. I feel sorry for her too. But I got one hell of a story to tell myself. And it ain't pretty."

I widened my eyes and stared at Yvonne. I was surprised to see such an unhappy look on her face. Most of the pretty women I knew complained about breaking a fingernail, pimples, or gaining a few ounces. Some even had the nerve to complain about all the attention they got from men. I hadn't met one yet that had anything serious to complain about. "Oh? I never would have guessed that you'd ever had more than a few bad times in your life."

"Oh, I'm happy now. But I done dragged myself through a lot of gloomy days in my life."

After Aunt Mattie's depressing story, I didn't want to ask Yvonne to share hers. I'd heard enough dreary stuff for one night. But since she'd already started in the direction, I decided to be still and listen to her. "Like what?" I asked.

"My mama and daddy died in a tractor accident when I was six," she started, twirling a lock of her hair as she spoke in a low voice. "It was the most godawful time in my life. Me and my two older sisters had to go live with relatives. That was rough too. I dropped out of school, worked miserable jobs, got involved with the wrong men, and ended up losing my children."

I gasped. "I had no idea you were a mother!"

"I got three. My baby girl will be thirteen on her birthday this year, and it's coming up real soon. My boys is only ten months apart so they both eleven. They all got different daddies." Yvonne blew out a loud breath and sniffled. "I never really wanted kids, but I do love mine. Some of the folks I used to work for didn't mind me bringing them to work with me, but some did. When that happened, I had to leave my babies alone all day with peanut butter sandwiches and water. Everybody else I knew worked too so I couldn't ask them to babysit for me."

"You couldn't get any help from the daddies?"

"Pffft!" Yvonne waved her hand, did a serious neck roll, and looked at me like I was speaking gibberish. "Don't make me laugh. Neither one of them fools hung around when they found out I was pregnant."

"Where do your kids live?"

"With one of my mama's sisters and her husband. They're real good people. They don't drink or smoke and they read the Bible every night. They live in Mobile and I don't get to see my babies that much on account of my auntie and my uncle don't want them to be around folks that drink and get loose the way we do."

"That must be rough on you. If you don't mind me asking, how come you don't have your kids with you?"

"Well, like I just mentioned, I never wanted any. Since I lost my mama and daddy, I been real disappointed in the way things happen in life. The accident they died in happened just about half a mile from a hospital. They didn't admit colored folks so them white motherfuckers let my mama and daddy lay there on the ground and die. Because of that, it took me quite a while to look at another white person without wanting to break their neck. For a long time, I hated being colored. I didn't want to bring no babies into a world that had people so mean and hateful that they'd let human beings die just because they was the wrong color."

"All white people ain't bad," I defended. "Me and Odell do a little socializing with some real nice ones from time to time."

Yvonne nodded. "I know some nice ones myself. Willie Frank is one of our best friends—and it ain't because we buy his liquor. The rest of his family is pretty cool too. But that still don't make me feel better about what happened to my parents. Sometimes I wish I had been on that tractor with them."

"Girl, don't say stuff like that!" I scolded. "Life is precious." I caressed her cheek and gave her a hug. "You have too much to live for now."

"I know and thank you for reminding me of that." Yvonne sat up straighter. "Well, I don't know about you, but I can hardly keep my eyes open."

I didn't wait for her to ask me to leave. I should have done that on my own hours ago. With Odell gone until tomorrow and because Aunt Mattie's story had made me feel so glum, I had decided to stay around people as long as I could tonight. But now I wished that I had left earlier. Yvonne's story had made me feel even worse.

I went to bed as soon as I got home, but it took me a while to get to sleep. I had barely dozed off when I heard Odell come in just as the sun was rising. I got up and trotted to the living room.

"I'm so glad you're back!" I gushed. I ran up to him and wrapped my arms around his waist.

"Joyce, you acting like you stressed out. Is everything all right?" He leaned away from me, looked around the room, and then back at me with his eyes blinking hard and fast. "Did something happen to your mama and daddy?"

"They're doing just fine." I guided him to the couch and we sat down. "What about your daddy?"

"He's fine!" He glanced away again for a moment and then back at me with a pleading look in his eyes. "It's a good thing I decided to start spending more nights with him. That heifer he married spent the whole evening running around with some of her friends and was just coming home as I was leaving."

I gave Odell a puzzled look. "I thought you told me Ellamae didn't have any friends."

"She got a few and they all just as nutty and mean-spirited as she is." He let out a loud sigh and rubbed his head. "Poor daddy. That lazy bitch hadn't bathed him in two days."

"Honey, I don't like to keep saying it, but I will: When and if you want to bring your daddy to live with us, that's fine with me."

"Thank you, baby. I'll keep that in mind." Odell cleared his throat and glanced toward the door. "Uh, did you visit Yvonne and Milton last night?"

"Yes, I did and I almost wish I had stayed home." I told Odell everything that Aunt Mattie and Yvonne had shared about their lives. He was as shocked as I was to hear that Yvonne had three children. "I felt so bad for her and Aunt Mattie, I couldn't wait to get back home. Believe it or not, I was the last guest to leave. I knew that once I got home, and didn't have anybody to talk to, I'd think about everything they'd said."

"Well, baby, some of us got a bigger cross to bear than others. We just lucky."

"I hope we stay lucky. Poor Yvonne. I really pity her. Last night I saw a side of her I never expected to see. She didn't come out and say it, but something tells me that one of her regular guests is depression. It was bad enough she had to drop out of school and do odd jobs to make ends meet, she had to give up her babies, too. After all that, she ends up working in a dingy restaurant. Oh well. At least she's still got her looks, good health, and a husband. The poor little thing."

"Sweetie, don't feel sorry for her. Pity ain't never helped nobody feel better. Just be a good friend to her and I'm sure she'll appreciate it. Why don't you take her shopping with you next time you go? Or treat her to supper at Mosella's or any other restaurant she want to go to. Maybe you should introduce her to some of your friends from the school."

"Uh . . . I don't know about that. I mean, I really like to keep my work and my personal life separate. I don't think any of the folks I work with would be interested in socializing with bootleggers. I would die of shame if the police cracked down on Yvonne and Milton while we were on the premises and hauled us to jail."

Odell laughed. "I wouldn't worry about that happening. Them laws don't give two hoots about what colored people do out here as long as we ain't raping no white women."

"You're probably right. I'll be friends with Yvonne. But I think I should feed her with a long-handled spoon, just in case. . . ."

"Just in case what?"

"We don't know them that well yet, so we don't know what kind of people they really are. Most of the boot-leggers have shady backgrounds. Some have even been in prison. Remember that Jones man that used to run a house out by the cemetery? He's in prison now for shoot-ing a man to death one night during a card game in his house."

"I doubt if Yvonne or Milton got enough gumption to kill somebody." Odell laughed again. "They both stupid as hell and ain't got a lick of class, but they ain't got a murderous bone in their bodies."

Chapter 32
Odell

*T*HINGS MOVED REAL FAST BETWEEN ME AND JOYCE and our new neighbors. Yvonne and Milton didn't waste no time squeezing themselves into our lives. They were already acting like they were our best friends. We had told them on the first night we visited them that we'd like to have them over for a meal one evening soon. Before we could tell them what day, they showed up at our door unannounced the following Monday evening around six. "I hope we ain't too late for supper!" Milton whooped, looking over my shoulder with his eyes bugged out.

"Whatever Joyce is cooking sure do smell good. I could smell it all the way outside!" Yvonne squealed as I waved them in. They both had on the plain gray uniforms they wore to work, and house shoes so shabby they'd have been better off barefoot. Joyce was in the kitchen getting supper ready.

"Um, we didn't know y'all was coming." I smiled even though I was annoyed. I thought it was real rude of them to just show up for dinner without an invitation.

"We didn't feel like entertaining a bunch of drunks tonight, so we thought we'd come hang out with y'all for a few hours," Yvonne chirped.

A few hours? "A few hours," I gulped.

"Well, just one or two. We don't want to wear out our welcome too soon," Milton responded, clapping me on my back.

I felt a knot swelling in my stomach. I was not in the mood to entertain company tonight. It had been a very hectic day for me and I had spent a lot of energy on Betty Jean yesterday, so I was tired, too.

I had planned on a quiet evening at home with my wife listening to the radio. It was on the tip of my tongue to tell them to come back some other night, but I couldn't fix my lips to say that. Especially since they'd already shown us so much hospitality. "Joyce, we got company! You need to set two more plates!"

"All right, Odell. Is that Mama and Daddy?" she yelled back.

"No, it ain't them, baby. Um . . . it's Yvonne and Milton." Within seconds, Joyce trotted into the living room, wiping her hands on her apron. There was a puzzled expression on her face. I gave her a weary look and shrugged.

"I was going to ask y'all to eat with us this coming Thursday after I go to the market to pick up a few things. We're having leftover pigtails and turnip greens this evening," Joyce said. And being the gracious woman she was, she spoke with the most apologetic look I ever seen on her face.

"Pigtails and turnip greens is my favorite meal. Oooh wee," Yvonne yipped, sniffing and grinning.

They didn't wait for us to ask them to sit down. They casually strolled over to the couch and made themselves comfortable, and immediately started looking around the room. "Y'all sure got a nice place," Milton noticed. "We been itching to see the inside of this house."

"Sure enough," Yvonne agreed. "We would have come over before now, but we been so busy getting settled and folks been coming and going like crazy."

"Well, I'm glad y'all finally made it over here," I said, clearing my throat.

"I ain't never been in no colored folks' house that was this neat and coordinated. If I didn't know no better, I'd swear white folks lived up in here," Yvonne hooted. "Y'all got it made in the shade. Joyce, where you get them curtains from and how much did they cost?"

"They were free. My mother made them for us," Joyce announced proudly. "She and Daddy bought some our furniture, too."

"Humph. Y'all doing better than I thought," Milton commented. "If things go the way I hope they do for me and Yvonne, we'll be living like kings; just like y'all."

"Well, I don't think we living like 'kings' yet," I tossed in, forcing myself to chuckle. "We can't afford to spend money the way some folks do. We keep ourselves on a strict budget." I didn't like the way Milton was staring at me with his eyes narrowed. It was the same way he had looked at me last week when he'd asked me to lend him five dollars. Even though he was brazen enough to already be begging for loans, I still wanted to get to know him and Yvonne. I liked the fact that I didn't have to go too far now when I wanted to socialize and have a few drinks. But one of the main reasons I wanted to have a good relationship with them was because they'd be a good distraction for Joyce. They'd keep her busy so I could spend even more time with Betty Jean and the boys.

"Joyce, you need some help in the kitchen?" Yvonne asked, already rising.

"I need to set the table and if you don't mind, you can come in and fix up the Kool-Aid."

Yvonne and Joyce hadn't been gone two seconds before Milton stood up. He shuffled over to me and got so close up to my face, I could smell the cheap lye soap he bathed with. "Um, listen." He stopped talking and peered toward the kitchen. "I was wondering if you could lend me another dollar?"

"Again?" The only reason I had mentioned the fact that Joyce and I were on a budget a few moments ago was to encourage him not to get used to asking me for loans. Now here this clown was asking me for more money anyway!

"This'll be the last time for a while," he told me, giving me a serious look.

"I sure hope so, Milton." I took a deep breath and pulled out my wallet.

I was glad when we all sat down at the table. And I was pleased to see that Yvonne and Milton had good table manners. I was also pleased that they liked to eat and run. As soon as Yvonne scarfed down the last of the pigtails, she was ready to leave. "We'd stay a little longer, but I think Willie Frank is coming by the house tonight," she explained, wiping her mouth with the back of her hand, which was tacky since Joyce had put a cloth napkin right next to her plate.

"Y'all welcome to come over anytime you want," Joyce

said, and I was sure she meant it. Me, I was having some serious second thoughts about our new neighbors. We walked them to the door and as soon as I locked it, I peeped out the window to make sure they had left. Then I turned to Joyce with my hands on my hips. "Baby, would you believe Milton had the nerve to ask me for another loan already?"

"How much this time?"

"Just a dollar," I said in a tired tone. I rubbed the back of my neck and shook my head. "Now I'm a dollar short. . . ."

"Pffft!" Joyce waved her hand and gave me a dry look. "I wish you would stop making such a big deal out of Milton asking you for money. I'm sure he wouldn't have asked for it if he didn't really need it." Joyce paused and gave me a thoughtful look. "But if he's asked to borrow money twice in less than two weeks, and they both have jobs and a bootlegging business, maybe they are not doing as well as they want us to think. Or, maybe they are just downright greedy and like to use people. Next thing you know, they'll be asking us to ride them here and there."

It was a busy week for Yvonne and Milton. Each day there was so many cars and trucks parked bumper to bumper on our street, you would have thought a funeral procession had arrived. Thursday evening Joyce ran to the window and peeped out every time she heard a vehicle pull up. "They must really be jamming next door. That's the sixth car to drive up in the last fifteen minutes," she gushed. I walked up behind her and peeped out the window myself. "I wouldn't mind having a drink or two this evening. And, some of their guests are so entertaining."

"I'm sure Milton and Yvonne would be glad to see us again. You want to go over there?"

Joyce closed the curtain and put her arm around my waist. We moved over to the couch and plopped down. "Yeah, I'd like to go but one drink will be my limit tonight."

"One drink?" I said with my eyebrow raised. "What's the matter?"

"I don't want to get too carried away. Last Monday when we went over there, I had a hard time staying awake at work the next morning," Joyce sighed, and then her eyes lit up real quick. "Aw, shuck it! Let's go anyway. I don't want Milton and Yvonne to think we're trying to avoid them."

We spent only a hour next door and we had a good time. I was overjoyed that Milton was too busy talking to his other guests to bother me much. I figured he'd be up in my face again soon enough.

And I was right.

Friday afternoon around three thirty p.m., him and Yvonne showed up at the store. I didn't like people coming into my office, so when I heard them outside asking Buddy and Sadie where I was, I jumped up and went out to see what they wanted.

"Speak of the devil," Yvonne smirked as I approached them.

"What's going on?" I asked.

"We need a favor!" Milton sputtered. My chest tightened and I groaned. Even if the favor involved only a dollar, I decided I'd tell him I was flat broke.

I motioned for them to follow me to the back of the store. "How come y'all ain't at work?"

"Jacob Petty, one of our dishwashers, passed on Tuesday. His family just let us know this morning and Mr. Cunningham closed the grill early so all the staff could attend the funeral today. That's where we just came from," Milton choked. "Me and him was real close." He blinked hard and wiped a tear from the corner of his eye.

"It's all right, baby. Jacob is in a better place," Yvonne said, rubbing Milton's shoulder. She let out a loud sigh and blinked hard to hold back her own tears. "Jacob had a heart attack."

"Oh, I'm sorry to hear that. Me and Jacob used to work in the same cane field a few years ago. He was a good man." I cleared my throat and tried to look as sympathetic as I could. "We got some real nice sympathy cards in aisle eight and I would offer y'all some flowers half price, but the florist man didn't show up today like he was supposed to so—"

"We already got a card and we don't want to spend good money on flowers so they can die too," Yvonne said.

It was a shame to see such a sad look on her pretty face. Milton looked even worse. His eyes were red and swollen. I held up both hands, as if somebody had just pulled a gun on me. "Well, if it's money y'all want, I can't spare none this time."

"We didn't come to ask for no money," Yvonne said in a pitiful voice.

Before I could speak again, Milton sniffled and said in a gruff tone, "We need a ride home. We missed the last bus and it'll be a whole two hours for the next one."

I glanced at the clock on the wall and shook my head. "It'll be a while before I close up and y'all can't hang around up in here unless y'all going to buy something. Mac told me to stop folks from loitering so much. We been having a lot of trouble with shoplifters." As soon as that last word slid out of my mouth, I wished I could suck it back in. Yvonne's jaw dropped and Milton looked like he was going to start crying some more.

"You ain't got to worry about us because we don't steal," Milton said sharply.

"I'm sure y'all don't. But I still can't have y'all just hanging around here for the next hour or so."

"We can go over to Mosella's and wait until you close up," Yvonne suggested.

I shook my head real fast. "No, that won't work neither. See, I need to get out of here right at five so I can go out to my daddy's house. Driving y'all home would be too far out my way." I swallowed hard and folded my arms. "Anything else?"

"Naw. I guess we'll be seeing you when we see you," Milton muttered. "Have a blessed day, Odell."

"Y'all too," I said with a tight smile.

Chapter 33
Odell

I WAS SORRY I'D BEEN KIND OF HARSH AND ABRUPT WITH Yvonne and Milton, but they had come at a real bad time. I'd been thinking about Betty Jean all day and how she'd been badgering me lately to spend more time with her and the boys, and it really started to bug me. But I was glad I'd taken out my frustrations on Yvonne and Milton, not Joyce. In all the years that we'd been married, she'd never seen me upset. And she never would if I could help it.

I was feeling somewhat better now and I regretted not letting them hang around so I could give them a ride home. I made a mental note to be extra nice to them the next few days. Twenty minutes after they'd left, I gave Joyce a call. The only telephone in the school was in the principal's office, and she worked on the opposite side of the building. Whenever I called her at work, I had to wait anywhere from ten to fifteen minutes for her to come to the telephone. She must have been close by today because she came on the line five minutes later.

"Hello, baby doll."

She gasped and I could picture the look of ecstasy on her face before she spoke. "Oh, Odell! It's so nice to hear your voice, sweetie!"

I was amazed that after all these years, Joyce still swooned when she heard my voice. I had a feeling she'd never get used to me calling her cute names. It wasn't even necessary anymore because she was already putty in my hands.

"I hope I didn't pull you away from nothing too important."

"You didn't. I was just about to clean the blackboard, but it can wait. I'd much rather be talking to you. You still going to visit your daddy this evening?"

"Yup. I was just calling to tell you I probably won't be back home tomorrow until around noon or later."

"Oh?"

"Last time I was with Daddy, I told him I'd take him fishing for a couple of hours next time I came to visit. I figured we'd get up tomorrow morning, and go to Carson Lake. I hear them bluegills over there been biting up a storm lately."

"Hmmm. You know, I've been thinking."

"Thinking what?"

"It's been a while since I saw your daddy, and enough time has passed so I'm not as mad as I was about the way Ellamae talked to me the last time I went out there with you. What time did you plan to get on the road today?"

I gulped. "Huh?" There was no way I could let Joyce tag along with me. I wasn't going to visit Daddy. I had promised Betty Jean and the boys that I'd take them out to eat this evening and we'd take a long drive along the countryside. "Uh, baby, why don't you come with me the next time? I was going to leave as soon as I get off the phone so I can't wait until you get off."

"Don't worry about that. The school day is almost over anyway, so I don't think Miss Kirksey would care if I leave now. I just need to call and let Mama and Daddy know where I'm going to be tonight. Let me get off this phone so I can let everybody know I'm leaving early."

"You sure you want to go with me?" I held my breath, praying she'd say no.

She took her time replying. "Odell, what's going on? Is there some reason you don't want me to go?" These questions seemed out of character for Joyce. She had never cross-examined me like this before.

"Oh no, baby doll. It ain't nothing like that," I said real quick. "You know I would never try to keep something from you. I love you from the bottom of my heart, so I would never do or say nothing that you wouldn't like. It's just that . . . well, I know you don't like to go to Daddy's house on account of Ellamae. And even if she wasn't there, Daddy ain't no fun to spend time with." I stopped talking long enough to squeeze in a chuckle. "I know you only want to go to please me, but you don't need to do that."

"I know I don't. But I don't mind doing it when I do. And to be honest with you, I should offer to go with you more often. But if Ellamae is real nasty today, there's no telling when I'll feel like going out there again. This could even be the *last* time." Joyce laughed.

"Okay, sweetie. I'll see you in about twenty minutes." I had to think fast, so I said the first thing that came to my mind next. "Um . . . looka here, before we head out, I'd like to drop in on Milton and Yvonne and check on them. They was both down in the dumps when they stopped by here a little while ago."

"Oh Lord. I hope none of their guests got drunk over there last night and did something crazy!"

"Don't worry, sugar. It wasn't nothing like that."

"Then why were they down in the dumps? And how do you know?"

"They was on the way home from the funeral of one of their coworkers. They must have been real close to him, because they took his passing real hard. They both had red, swollen eyes from crying so much. I was busy and in a lousy mood myself so I wasn't as gracious as I should have been. I think I was probably a little too abrupt with them. So now I'd like to go over there and make up for it. I'll take them a few snacks because I know they'll have plenty company tonight."

"That coworker must not have been too close of a friend if they still want to party and drink with a house full of folks after attending his funeral today."

"Don't be like that, sugar. That's how some people deal with grief. They need sympathy more than they need you criticizing them."

"Yeah, you're right, I guess. I don't know what's wrong with me for saying something like that. Well, I wouldn't mind spending a little time with them before we go out to your daddy's house. I'll be ready when you get here, so just park out front and toot the horn."

"All right. I'll be there after I collect this week's profits from the registers and take them to your daddy." Joyce mumbled something under her breath I couldn't make out. "What did you say?"

"I said I get nervous every time I know you driving around with a paper bag full of money. That's the only thing I hate about Fridays."

"Baby, I agree with you. But this is the way your folks want to do it. I don't think they'll ever trust banks again."

"Well, you just be careful. There are some desperate crooks out there willing to do whatever they have to do to get some easy money."

"Tell me about it," I sniffed. I was one of them "desperate crooks" and I would probably be one for the rest of my life. Or, for as long as I had to take care of my boys and Betty Jean. One thing I planned to do soon was make arrangements to have a telephone installed for her. Since I couldn't call to let her know I had to postpone my visit, when I got off the phone with Joyce, I called Betty Jean's sister at her work and told her to relay the message.

"Why ain't you coming?" Alline wanted to know.

"Something serious came up," I explained.

"I bet," she said, which I didn't appreciate.

"It's something I can't get out of," I went on.

"Uh-huh. It's a shame it's more 'serious' than your children, Odell. They was really looking forward to spending time with you this evening and tomorrow. They'll be sure enough disappointed. . . ." This heifer was getting on my nerves with her suspicious-sounding comments, but she was too important for me to piss off. I didn't know what I'd do if she was to quit helping Betty Jean with the boys. Alline was usually nice to me, but lately she'd been acting standoffish and I didn't know why. I had always treated her with respect, but there'd been times when I wanted to cuss her out. I would never do that because at the end of the day, I needed to stay on her good side in case something happened to Betty Jean. Life was so unpredictable and unfair, I had to think about things like that. If Betty Jean up and died or decided to run off with another man, or by herself, I didn't want Alline to take my babies and relocate to Ohio where they had other relatives. She had told me more than once that the only reason she hadn't already moved north was on account of she wanted to stay close to her baby sister and her nephews.

"Nothing is more serious to me than my boys, Alline. You of all people should know how much I love them!" I snapped.

"I know you love them little devils. It's just a damn shame they don't get to see you more often."

"Well, I'm working on that. But for now, I'm doing the best I can do so cut me some slack."

"Odell, I'm kind of busy, so I have to go. I'll tell Betty Jean you called and I'll tell her everything you just told me."

I had never discussed my marital status with Alline, but she was no fool. She had to know that I was married. But one good thing about her relationship with Betty Jean was that they stayed out of each other's business. And, to stay on Alline's good side, every time I delivered a bunch of goodies from the store to Betty Jean, I always included a few items for Alline. It was because of my generosity that she had a huge supply of hair grease, makeup, and all kinds of other she-products that women had to have. And, at least two or three times a month, she borrowed money from me.

"Let her know that I'll see her either sometime tomorrow or Sunday afternoon. And tell the boys I'm real sorry, and I'll make it up to them."

I was sweating when I hung up. Daddy didn't know I

was coming, so he'd be surprised when me and Joyce showed up. That was one thing. The other thing I was worried about was him letting the cat out of the bag that I hadn't been visiting him as regularly as Joyce thought I had. Shit! This was the first time I was glad Daddy was having memory lapses. No matter what he said in front of Joyce, or how he acted when we got there today, I'd blame it on his mental condition. Ellamae never had much to say to Joyce and she usually left the house a few minutes after we got there, so I wasn't worried about her blowing the whistle on me.

In addition to having to pay Daddy an unplanned visit today, now I had to visit Yvonne and Milton, too! Well, I had to do what I had to do to keep everybody happy.

Chapter 34
Joyce

WHEN ODELL GOT TO MY JOB, HE APPEARED TO BE DIStressed. His eyes were watery, his lips were dry, and his hands were shaking. I thought he was coming down with something. "Baby, are you all right?" I asked as soon as I slid into the car. I glanced over my shoulder and was pleased to see that the snacks for Yvonne and Milton on the back seat included their favorites: crackers, hog head cheese, baloney, and two huge jars of pickled pigs' feet. "You don't look too good. Maybe you're coming down with something."

"Now that you mentioned it, I do feel a little under the weather. I think I'm coming down with a cold." He eased the car out onto the street and drove slowly toward our neighborhood, keeping his eyes on the road.

I put my hand on his shoulder and massaged it. Next I touched his chest. His body felt so tense, he was probably sicker than he thought. "A summer cold is nothing to play with. Our principal's niece caught one last July and died. Do you think it's a good idea for you to go around your daddy with him already being so sickly?"

"I hadn't thought about it. Since you brung it up, maybe I shouldn't go out there today. If he gets any sicker, he'll have another reason to badger me to come see him even more often." Odell's voice was so high-pitched, he almost sounded like a woman.

"Then you should stay home and take care of yourself first," I insisted. "You don't need to go next door with your germs and infect Yvonne and Milton and their guests. I'll go over there for a few minutes and drop off the snacks and tell them how sorry we are about their friend's passing. But before I do that, I'll fix you some soup and make a pot of ginger tea. I'm sure your daddy, and Yvonne and Milton, will understand if they don't see you today."

When Odell spoke again, he sounded normal, and that made me feel better. "That's fine, Joyce. You are so good to me."

"And you are so good *for* me."

We didn't talk during the ride home, but all kinds of thoughts were bouncing around in my head. Odell didn't put his arm around my shoulder or even look at me the way he usually did when we were in the car. You would have thought he was alone. I was concerned about his odd behavior. When we got home, I looked him in the eye and said, "Odell, is there something going on you don't want me to know about?"

He suddenly seemed so frightened, I thought he was going to jump out of his skin. "What do you mean?" he asked in a voice I almost didn't recognize. "Somebody been putting bugs in your ear?"

"No. I know you like a book, so there is nothing anybody can tell me about you that I don't already know."

"It's just that today was real busy and I had a run-in with some teenagers that was trying to steal a few items. Them same punks I had to chastise last week."

I blew out a sigh of relief and gave Odell an incredulous look. "Is that all? Shoot!"

"Baby, it could be a problem if I don't nip it in the bud in time. The last thing I want your folks to think is that I can't keep things under control."

"Some unruly young crooks snatching a few cheap items ain't worth you getting so bent out of shape over. Come on." I grabbed Odell's hand and led him to the couch. With a groan, he dropped down on it like a lead balloon. "Now, you stay here and I'll make you some soup. After I do that, I'll take the snacks next door." I blinked and rubbed my chest, which had been aching from worry a few moments ago. "I wish I had told you to pick up some flowers for me to take over there too."

I boiled some chicken necks and backs and made a small pan of soup for Odell. After I got him situated, I put all the snacks in a metal dishpan and went next door. "Odell couldn't make it, so he asked me to bring y'all some goodies," I told Yvonne when she let me in.

She gave me a puzzled look before she said anything. "It's nice to see you again, Joyce. But I didn't know you was coming over tonight." She turned around and stared at Milton hovering a few feet behind her.

"I'd love to stay for a drink, but I'm going to meet up with some friends from work in a little while," I lied as I glanced around the room. I was surprised and disappointed to see that the only other guest so far was that mealy-mouthed Aunt Mattie. She was kicked back on the couch with a jar of homebrew in her hand. Her beady black eyes were glassy and her makeup was so smeared it looked like she'd put it on with a whisk broom. Though she was even older than my parents, and drank like a big fish, she was still healthy and spry. She didn't even need a cane to walk with like Daddy did. I didn't want to hear any more of her sad stories or listen to her make more comments about me and Odell, so I didn't plan on staying long. "It's good to see you again, Aunt Mattie."

"Sit down and chew the fat for a while, *Mrs. Watson*," she slurred, patting the seat next to her.

"I wish I could. But like I just told Yvonne, I'm going to go out for drinks in a little while with a couple of ladies from work." I returned my attention to Yvonne. "Odell told me about your coworker passing, so I wanted to come by here first and offer my condolences and bring y'all a few snacks," I said, handing her the dishpan. I had no plans to go out with my coworkers, but it was the best ruse I could come up with to explain me not staying more than a few minutes.

"How come you and your friends can't come over here and drink?" Aunt Mattie wanted to know, folding her bat-wing-looking arms.

"Um . . . I don't think they'd be too comfortable over here." My reply must have sounded offensive because Aunt Mattie, Yvonne, and Milton gasped at the same time.

"Humph! I guess your friends think they too good to drink with us?" Aunt Mattie seethed. She glared at me with so much contempt it would take a sling blade to cut through it.

"N-no, that's n-not what I meant," I stammered.

"Well, maybe *you* think your friends is too good to drink with us." Milton caressed his chin as he spoke. I couldn't tell from his tone if he was trying to be sarcastic or funny.

"No, that's not what I meant either. My other friends only drink in real bars or they buy their spirits from the stores. They would never drink homemade liquor. Besides that, they are kind of skittish, so they only like to socialize with a certain type of people. Jook joints and places like bootlegging houses get a little too rowdy for them," I explained.

Aunt Mattie and Yvonne looked at each other then back at me. "They'd probably stop socializing with you if they knew you hung out with people like us," Aunt Mattie growled with one eyebrow raised. "Ain't that right?"

"I don't think so. Um . . . I hate to run, but I'd better get back home. Odell might be coming down with a cold and I need to make sure he's comfortable before I go out tonight," I said, stumbling backward toward the door.

"When we stopped by the store on our way home from the funeral this afternoon, he told us he was going to visit his daddy this evening," Yvonne said.

"That was his plan and I was going to go with him. But since he's not feeling well, I'm making him stay home tonight. Maybe we'll come over for a drink tomorrow," I said as I rushed out the door.

I ran all the way back to my house.

Odell was pacing back and forth when I got inside. He stopped as soon as he saw me. "You back already?" He didn't look or sound sick now.

"You sure recovered fast," I noticed, easing down on the couch.

"Yup! I started feeling better right after I ate that soup you made. I guess it wasn't a cold coming on after all." He sat down next to me. "You could have stayed next door awhile if you wanted to."

"I would have stayed long enough for one drink, but that lady pimp was the only other person there. I don't care for her, so I didn't stay."

"What you got against Aunt Mattie?"

"I don't have anything against that old woman. It's just that she gets on my nerves asking nosy questions and talking about some of the nasty stuff that goes on in her whorehouse. I'd rather not spend too much time being around her unless there's a crowd around. That way, she'd have other people to pick on instead of just me. Um, since we won't be going out together tonight, I'm going to call up a couple of the ladies I work with and see if they want to go out with me for a little while. Do you mind?"

"No, I don't mind. How long will you be gone?"

"Well, since it's Friday, there's no telling. We'll have a few drinks and then probably go get something to eat."

"I do feel so much better. If I'd known you was going to go out, I could have gone to visit my daddy after all."

"Baby, I'm sorry. You can still go, but I've changed my mind about going with you. I know Lonnie will be happy to see you and I know you'll be glad to get out of the house for the night. But you need to skedaddle if you want to get there before him and Ellamae go to bed. You know they don't get back up to answer the door for you or nobody else."

"As soon as I empty my bladder, I'll be on my way."

"And you can stay the whole weekend if you want to. I already told Mama and Daddy I'd go to church with them on Sunday and you know how long-winded Reverend Jessup is, so we'll be there most of the day. After church, they want to have dinner with some of the choir members. I'm not sure I'll go with them to that. But if I do, that'll take up the rest of the day for me. And tomorrow, I think I'll do a few things around the house that I've been putting off."

"You sure you don't mind spending the whole weekend by yourself?"

"Uh-uh! If I run out of things to keep me busy tomorrow, I'll go next door and hang out with Yvonne and Milton. Now, you get going and try to enjoy yourself. And don't you get too close to anybody and give them your germs."

"I won't."

Chapter 35
Odell

BETTY JEAN WAS SO HAPPY TO SEE ME, SHE SHOWERED me with hugs and kisses as soon as I walked through her door. "You sweet thing you," she squealed. "What you doing here? Alline told me you called her at work and said you wasn't coming today on account of you had to go check up on your daddy."

We kissed again. And then I coughed a few times so I could have a few seconds delay before I answered her question. I needed time to line up my lies so I could keep them straight and make them sound believable. "I went by Daddy's house for a little while this evening, and he is doing so much better. Come to find out, he had made other plans to go out with one of his friends and forgot I was coming. I'm sorry I couldn't get here no sooner."

"Oh well. You here now and that's all I care about. I hope you didn't already eat supper. I got some greens and neck bones on the stove." Betty Jean waved me to the couch and we sat down. Before I could get comfortable, she hauled off and kissed me on my neck and poked my crotch. "You sure do feel good, baby. I can't wait to get you into our playroom." She giggled and nodded toward the door to the master bedroom.

"Same here," I said with my voice sounding like a bear growl. She had already poked me enough to give me a hard-on, so I pushed her hand away from my pecker. Then I pulled her into my arms and kissed her long and hard. Joyce was a better kisser. I didn't think about that too much when I was with Betty Jean, though. I wanted to reach up under her skirt and slide her panties off and do my business right on the couch, but I didn't want no audience. I sat up. "Where my boys at?"

"When I told them you couldn't come today, they got real upset. Roy was here when Alline came by and told me you had to cancel, so he offered to take them with him and his kids to Mobile to visit the duck pond and eat at one of them roadside burger places. After they do that, he might visit his brother and spend the night at his house, so they probably won't be back until tomorrow evening or Sunday."

"They took the baby, too?"

"Yeah." Betty Jean nodded and started looking impatient. "I'm happy I get to take a little break. I'm with them boys seven days a week and taking care of them is hard work. But that's something you wouldn't know about. . . ."

"Please don't start up on my case again. It make me feel right shitty," I whined.

"Forget what I just said. Anyway, we done spoiled Leon and he is already a handful. Can you imagine the mess I would have had on my hands if they'd made him stay home?"

"Leon is too little to get close to them ducks, and I don't like him being around a lot of water yet unless he's with me or you."

"I know and I don't like that neither and I tried to keep him home. But he cried up a storm, so Roy let him tag along. Roy's kids is old enough to keep a eye on him so they won't let him get too close to the water myself, eat a bug, or wander off and get lost."

"Is there any way you can get in touch with Roy? Maybe we can drive over to Mobile and pick up the boys. Or maybe he ain't left his house yet."

"They went straight from here to Mobile."

I was disappointed that I wouldn't get to see my boys tonight. But I was pleased that I would at least have a chance to spend some time alone with Betty Jean. We could start working on that baby girl we both been itching to have.

"How long can you stay?" she asked. "Me and you can still do something nice. We could take a long drive or go fishing."

"I'll stay the night and maybe we'll take a drive in the morning."

"The boys will be upset when they find out you came by anyway this weekend and they didn't get to see you." Even though Betty Jean was slightly upset herself, she was still able to show her love by caressing the side of my face and rubbing my chest.

"I know. But tell them we'll do something nice soon. I seen a flyer yesterday advertising a carnival coming through here soon. We can go there and spend a whole day enjoying the rides, playing games, and eating. After that, we can go to a restaurant and have supper."

"That sounds good." Betty Jean stood up and gazed toward the door. "Did you bring anything from the store?"

"Not this time. Some of our vendors is running late with their deliveries, so our inventory is kind of low right now. I have to cut back for a while."

"Well, I hope it ain't too long of a while. The boys keep growing so fast, most of the clothes you already brung them don't even fit no more. And they need socks and underwear real bad." Betty Jean reared back and gave me a dry look. "On top of all that, I'm almost out of flour, meal, and lye soap, too."

"Don't worry about nothing. I'll bring all of that and more next time I come."

Our inventory was low, but not because of our vendors running late. In the last few weeks, I had taken huge amounts of merchandise from the store to Betty Jean, especially things for the boys. *That* was the reason our inventory was low. And somebody had noticed it. Last Monday, that goddamn meddlesome-ass Buddy said something that made me nervous. "We can't seem to keep clothes in stock as long as we used to. I helped load them racks myself just three days ago and they almost empty already," he'd said. "Especially the boy clothes and the women's doodads."

"I noticed that too," I'd mumbled. "And another thing, we can't keep canned goods and a few other items in stock as long as we used to neither. I guess them shoplifters is working overtime."

"That's the same thing I thought. But they so slick, they only do their dirty work when the store is real crowded and me and Sadie too busy to keep our eyes on their thieving tails! If we don't do something to stop them dogs from making us run out of stuff too soon, our customers will start shopping in the white folks' stores and we'll be shining shoes or frying fish, and standing in the bread lines and eating at the soup kitchens."

"Buddy, don't you worry about a thing. I'm going to hire somebody just to walk up and down the aisles on our busy days. That ought to solve the problem."

I was going to hire somebody to help us deal with the shoplifters. But that meant I'd have to come up with a new strategy so I could still take merchandise to Betty Jean. As much as I gave her and the boys, it was never enough. She pestered me for all kinds of beauty products, food, and cute frocks. And every time I turned around, the boys wanted toys and new clothes. One reason I had this problem was because I had spoiled them. Betty Jean had several blouses with the price tags still attached. I would continue to take merchandise, but not enough for somebody to notice. I'd already planned to tell Betty Jean that the MacPhersons had decided to stop carrying certain items, mainly the same things she always requested. That way she wouldn't be expecting all the goodies she'd gotten used to.

I hoped that that would solve the problem, because I needed to lighten up my stress level. If it didn't, I'd just have to come up with a new plan.

Chapter 36
Joyce

BECAUSE I HAD LIED TO YVONNE ABOUT HAVING PLANS to do something with my coworkers this evening, I had to make it look like I went out. After Odell left, I turned off all the lights except the lamp on the nightstand in my bedroom. I was restless and bored. Now I was sorry that I hadn't gone with Odell after all. The house was so quiet inside it was frightening. Outside was too. Suddenly, one of our other neighbor's hound dogs started howling and that frightened me even more. I wasn't superstitious like some folks who believed a howling dog was a sign that somebody was going to die. But it was the last thing I wanted to listen to while I was by myself.

I was tempted to go back and tell Yvonne that the friends I was supposed to go out with had canceled. But just thinking about Aunt Mattie grilling me again about my marriage was enough to squash that temptation. I knew that I couldn't avoid that old crow forever, but the less time I spent in her company, the better.

I got into my nightgown and climbed into bed with the newspaper. Everything on every page was either boring or depressing, but I kept reading. I fell asleep with the newspaper still in my hand. I had a disturbing dream, which was unusual because I rarely had any at all. But Odell had nightmares once or twice a month and he could never remember the details, so we didn't give it much thought. In my dream, a beautiful, light-skinned woman I had never seen before approached me on the street and said she had something to tell me. When I asked her what, I woke up, covered in sweat and confused. I couldn't imagine why a strange woman would be coming to me in my sleep. I dozed back off and had the same dream again, and it ended the same way. I had had other dreams that didn't make much sense. But I'd never had one that included a woman I didn't know. I wasn't going to mention it to Odell or anybody else. Because if it scared me, I knew it would scare them, too. I couldn't get back to sleep, so I finished reading the newspaper.

A few minutes after one a.m. I got up and peeped out the window just in time to see Willie Frank and a thin dark brown woman in a long red wig and short, tight dress stumbling down Yvonne's front porch steps. They stopped abruptly and kissed long and hard before they staggered to Willie Frank's truck, which he had parked in front of our house. When I got back in bed, I fell asleep right away.

I didn't wake up again until somebody pounded on my front door the next morning. I groaned and rolled over so I could see the clock on the nightstand. It was only eight a.m. I was not expecting anybody, so I decided to ignore whoever it was. The pounding stopped suddenly and it got so quiet, I thought for a moment I'd gone deaf. Then somebody started banging on my bedroom window! "Joyce, you all right in there?" It was Mama.

"Coming, Mama!" I hollered as I scrambled out of bed. I stumbled to the window and opened it just high enough to stick my head out. "Mama, do you know what time it is?" I said in a harsh tone, giving her an exasperated look. She had on a brown corduroy duster and a pair of Daddy's shabby house shoes. A thick black hairnet covered the dozens of paper curlers in her hair.

"Do *you* know what time it is?" she barked. "You told me you was coming to the house this morning to help me clean them chitlins I told you and Odell I'd cook for y'all to eat next week on the Fourth of July."

"I forgot. Mama, don't worry about cooking anything for us. Um . . . we invited our new neighbors over for a cookout on the Fourth and they don't eat chitlins." I was getting pretty good at lying. I hadn't even asked Yvonne and Milton to join us for the holiday, but I was going to go over and ask them as soon as I got rid of Mama.

"Well, what am I supposed to do with them chitlins, girl? I ain't got enough room in my icebox to keep them."

"Why don't you cook them for supper this evening for you and Daddy," I suggested.

"Didn't I tell you me and Mac was going to spend a few days in Mobile at Reverend Jessup's retreat? We'll be leaving tonight."

"No, you didn't tell me that. That's nice," I said with a sigh of relief. I was thrilled to hear that my meddlesome parents were going to be out of town for the holiday. Now I wouldn't have to worry about them showing up and embarrassing me and Odell in front of Yvonne and Milton.

We had not introduced them yet and I was not looking
forward to when we did. Last week Buddy told me that
when he told Daddy and Mama during one of their rare
visits to the store that Milton had come in a couple times
smoking a homemade cigarette that had stunk up the
whole store, Mama gasped so hard her eyes crossed.
Daddy shuddered and said, "Get behind me, Satan!" as he
sprayed room freshener in every nook and cranny. That
ominous comment and their reaction told me that my parents had already made up their minds about not liking our
new neighbors. But it was no surprise. As far as they were
concerned, decent, God-fearing people didn't become
bootleggers. I cringed when I thought about what they'd
say when they heard that their best friend, Willie Frank,
was a moonshine-making hillbilly *and* an ex-convict.

"Well, you can cook them chitlins for supper today
yourself. You can still come help me clean them. Unless
you got something else planned for today," Mama whined.

"You can give the chitlins to Buddy or Sadie. I told
Yvonne I'd go downtown with her today to help her pick
out some shorts she wants to wear to our cookout. After
we do that, we're going to go to lunch."

"Humph! Y'all done got thick as thieves already,
huh?"

"Yvonne's a nice woman, Mama. You'll see that when
you meet her and get to know her."

"Well, I ain't in no hurry to meet nobody that sells illegal alcohol. I hope you and Odell don't let them drag
y'all into no scandal and—"

I cut her off with my hand in the air. "Odell and I are
not that stupid and naïve, Mama. Now, you go on back
home and get ready for your trip. I have to get up and get
dressed so I'll be ready when Yvonne gets here."

Half an hour after Mama had left in a huff, I knocked on Yvonne's door.

"Joyce, ain't it kind of early for you to be coming over for a drink?" She was still in her nightgown.

"Um, I didn't come to drink. I was wondering if you wanted to go shopping with me? I'm going to pick up a few things for the holiday. And, if you and Milton don't already have plans for the Fourth, I hope y'all can come to our cookout."

Yvonne yawned. "Who else is coming? Them coworkers you went out with last night?"

"Oh, no. It'll be just the four of us. But if you want to bring a couple of friends, that'll be fine. Just let me know how many so I can make sure we have enough food."

"We didn't have no plans, but I know we'll get a good crowd later in the day after everybody done barbecued and whatnot." Yvonne narrowed her eyes. "Why do you want *me* to go shopping with you today? I figured that's something you do only with people like them ones you went out with last night. . . ."

"Well, not this time."

"Did y'all have fun last night?" I ignored the mild smirk on Yvonne's face.

"Uh-huh."

"Where all did y'all go?"

"Oh, we had supper at that fish shack on Liberty Street, and then we went to visit one of the teachers that just had a baby."

"You must have stayed out late because your lights was still out when I went to bed."

"I did stay out pretty late." I heard footsteps, so I glanced over Yvonne's shoulder. Milton staggered into the room yawning, stretching, and rubbing the side of his head. The living room reminded me of a landfill. One end table was upside down, the footstool Milton usually sat on when we visited was on its side, empty jars and bottles were strewn all over the floor. And the stench of tobacco smoke and snuff was unholy. I sniffed and rubbed my nose. "Well, if you want to go shopping with me, I'm going to be leaving in a couple of hours. We can have lunch at Mosella's too."

"I ain't got no money for Mosella's. Our move set us back a few dollars."

"Don't worry about it. It's my treat. And you can order anything you want," I said quickly and with a sincere smile. That brought a smile to Yvonne's face.

Chapter 37
Joyce

I HAD NO IDEA HOW MUCH I'D REGRET INVITING YVONNE to go shopping. I had never been out in public with a woman as pretty as she was, so I was not prepared for the things that happened to me that day. Before we even got off our block, a handsome, well-dressed man in a shiny black car drove close to the curb and slowed down. I assumed he was going to ask for directions. That was what strange men usually asked when they spoke to me in public. This one rolled down his window, whistled, and yelled, "Stop right there!" Since I was on the outside of the sidewalk, I assumed he was talking to me. I stopped first and then Yvonne did. "Girl, you look so good I'd drink your bathwater!" he whooped. Then he honked his horn.

"You stop that!" I scolded with my hands on my hips. "You ought to be ashamed of yourself, sir!"

"Pffft! I ain't talking to you, you big clumsy ox!" he blasted. My jaw dropped as he continued, looking directly at Yvonne now. "Hey, cutie, can I get your name and address? I sure would like to take you out!"

"My husband wouldn't like that," Yvonne giggled. "Now you go on about your business."

We started walking again and the man drove off. My head started throbbing. This was the first time somebody had insulted me to my face, so I didn't know how to react. I said the first thing that came to my mind. "He's probably got a wife and a bunch of babies at home."

"He wasn't my type anyway." This was not what I had expected Yvonne to say.

"What if a man who is your type comes up to you?"

"What do you mean?"

"Would you cheat on Milton?"

"Well, I ain't cheated on him yet and I don't plan on doing it. But I can't say I won't." We continued walking, and several more men leered at Yvonne and ignored me. "I hope our husbands don't flirt with women like the ones out here today," she grumbled.

"Well, I don't know about yours, but I know my husband doesn't act a fool over women when I'm not around," I stated. I knew I sounded smug, but Yvonne wasn't sharp enough to know that. I hadn't even known her a whole month, but I could tell that she was as dense as she was beautiful.

"I'll say this much, if Milton is pestering other women, he better not let me find out about it," she laughed.

"Would you leave him?"

She gave me a pensive look and shrugged. "That all depends. If he falls in love with another woman and wants to be with her, I ain't going to hold on to him. There is too many other men in the world, so I ain't about to try and keep one that don't want to be kept." Yvonne stopped talking and asked me in a real quiet and serious tone, "Would you leave Odell if he got involved with another woman?"

I stumbled because her question startled me. "That's something I never think about." I paused and took a deep breath. When I started talking again, my voice was so hoarse I didn't even sound like myself. "If he ever decides he wants to be with another woman, I don't know what I'll do," I admitted. Just the thought of Odell cheating on me was so unbearable, I refused to let it stay on my mind more than a few seconds. I wanted to talk about anything but married people cheating on each other. "Um, don't let me forget to pick up some lighter fluid," I mumbled.

We picked up some lighter fluid and a small bag of charcoal at the hardware store on the next block, and then we strolled over to Mosella's for lunch.

I relaxed and forced myself to stop thinking about how all those men had paid so much attention to Yvonne. I got slighted again when the waitress dropped our check onto the table. "You only charged us for one meal," I pointed out.

"I know," the waitress said, giving me a sympathetic look. Then she turned to Yvonne and told her, "The man sitting with the lady in the booth by the door paid for yours."

"Oh." Yvonne sighed, sounding bored. I guess if I had to fight off men as much as she did, I'd be bored by now too.

The waitress lowered her tone to a whisper, leaning closer to Yvonne's ear. "He asked me to get your name and a telephone number if you got one so he can call you up and come take you out."

"Tell him thanks for the meal but he can't take me out because I'm married," Yvonne said firmly. "Joyce, let's get out of here." I paid for my order and we left with me trailing behind her like a lost lamb. "Let's take the bus back home," she said when we reached the bus stop at the end of the block.

"That's fine with me. I don't feel like walking anymore either."

"I don't mind walking. I just don't want to deal with another man trying to get into my bloomers."

Before I could make a comment, another man approached us. This one stopped in front of me, grinning like a fool. "Ma'am, I noticed y'all coming out of Mosella's. I just had to come over here and tell you what a beautiful daughter you got," he swooned. I smiled, but my face felt like somebody had waved a torch in front of it. Then he turned to Yvonne. "I sure would like to get to know you, honey child."

"She ain't my mama!" Yvonne snarled. "And you need to get out of my face because I'm a happy married woman."

"So? I'm a happy married man. But I—"

"Start stepping before I yell rape!" Yvonne threatened.

The man threw up his hands and did a neck roll. "Well, excuse me." He cussed under his breath, and then he put his hands in his pockets and strutted back down the street.

"Can you believe how bold some men can be? I get so sick of ducking and dodging one pass after another! It's nerve-racking!" Yvonne complained. Then she let out a loud sigh and gave me a sorry look. What she said next sent a jolt through me that pierced me to the bone. "Girl, you lucky you don't have to worry about men pestering you all the time like they do me."

She was the one that was lucky. All my life I'd wanted men to pay more attention to me! I couldn't think of anything she could have said that would have made me feel any worse. Stroking her ego was the last thing I wanted to do, so I decided to say something neutral. "You'd better enjoy getting all that attention as long as you can because it won't last forever," I said casually.

The first day I laid eyes on Yvonne, I envied the way she looked. But she had been so nice to me, I hadn't felt any serious resentment toward her. I did now, though. I hated her for being so beautiful—and knowing it. Not only that, she was rubbing it in my face whether she meant to or not. Women who looked like me must have been her worst nightmare. Because of what I'd been through today, I wasn't so sure I still wanted to be friends with her. And then she said something that almost made my jaw drop: "Joyce, that first night you and Odell came to the house and I heard how happy y'all was and how well y'all was doing, I got real jealous of you."

"What?" I couldn't believe my ears. "You're jealous of *me*?"

"Well, I was at first. But now that I know you better, and see how sweet and nice you are, I feel blessed to have a friend like you. Milton feel the same way about Odell and even said he wish he could be more like him. And, I wish I could be more like you."

Chapter 38
Odell

WHEN I GOT HOME SUNDAY EVENING FROM MY VISIT to Betty Jean's house, Joyce was in the kitchen cutting up a chicken in the sink that she was going to fry for our supper. I walked up behind her and wrapped my arms around her waist and kissed the back of her neck. When she giggled and turned around, I kissed her on the mouth. "I was hoping I'd have time to take a bath and splash on some vanilla extract before you got home," she said in a tired tone.

"You don't need it." I kissed her again. She smelled like lard, but that was all right with me. It smelled good on her.

"How was your daddy?"

I let out a long, loud breath and shook my head before I backed to the table and dropped down into the chair facing the sink. "No better, no worse."

Joyce pulled out the chair across from me and sat down with a thud. "And Ellamae?"

"Believe it or not, she wasn't so nasty this time. She even made me a peach cobbler."

"Well, I guess even devils have good days." We laughed at the same time. "I hope they don't expect us to come out there for the holiday on Tuesday."

"They don't," I muttered. There was no way I was going to take Joyce out to my daddy's house until I had actually paid him another visit. That way, if he or Ellamae said something that might make Joyce suspicious about the number of times I did visit, I would be prepared. Daddy's memory lapses had got even worse and Ellamae's was going downhill real fast, and that worked in my favor. The last time I did visit, they didn't remember I'd just seen them three days before.

One of the few things Joyce was real strict about was us being together on holidays, either with her parents or with Daddy and Ellamae. Since I'd started my relationship with Betty Jean, I had only been able to spend a few holidays with her and the boys. I made up for it by being extra nice and generous either before or after those days. This coming weekend, I planned to give her a bottle of the expensive perfume she'd been hounding me to bring her for weeks. We wanted some girl babies to round out our family, so I was going to be extra affectionate on my next visit.

"That's good because I told Yvonne we wanted her and Milton to come over for a cookout."

"Oh? How come I'm just hearing about it?"

"I just asked her yesterday. We went shopping and some things happened that I didn't like. I feel sorry about the way I felt about those things and now I really want to do something nice for her and Milton." Joyce looked away for a moment. When she returned her attention to me, there was a sad expression on her face.

I held my breath for a few seconds and stared into her eyes. "What things?"

Joyce nodded and blinked. "Almost every man we ran into tried to make a move on Yvonne." She told me about the two men who had approached them on the street and the one that had paid for Yvonne's lunch.

I shrugged and gave her a confused look. "And that bothered you?"

"Not that much. What bothered me more was her telling me that I was lucky I didn't have to worry about men pestering me in public."

"Oh. Well, I can see why that'd make you feel bad. In a roundabout way, she was calling you homely—which ain't true!" I reached across the table and grabbed Joyce's hand and kissed it. "You still the most beautiful woman in the world to me. And, I don't want you to be having hard feelings toward Yvonne. She can't help being so pretty. I'd still like to see you and her become real good friends. With them living just one house over, it'd be real uncomfortable for all of us if we didn't get along. Especially after all the collywobbles we went through when the Copelands lived in that house."

Joyce bit her bottom lip, and then a mysterious smile slid across her face. "That's true, but let me finish what I was telling you." She swallowed hard and shifted in her seat. I reached for her other hand and squeezed it as she continued. "She told me they got jealous of us the first night we visited them and talked about how wonderful our marriage is and how well we're doing."

I released Joyce's hands and leaned back in my seat.

"Well, jealousy is one of the worst of the deadly sins. In the Bible some jealous person was always selling somebody into slavery or having them locked up in a dungeon, and doing all kinds of other mean shit to get back at them."

Joyce snickered. "Odell, get a grip. I don't think we have to worry about anything that serious."

"Well, the bottom line is, jealousy can be a dangerous emotion," I insisted.

"They don't feel that way now. She even said they want to be more like us. A compliment like that goes a long way with me. Anyway, I told her about the cookout before we went shopping. Besides that, I had already told Mama we were having them over for the holiday so I have to go through with it—whether I want to or not. I'm going to try and not let petty things like her getting a lot of attention from men bother me too much. And, I don't think she really meant to imply that I'm homely." Joyce exhaled and shook her head. "Besides, we can't overlook the fact that they let us have drinks on the house."

"No, we can't, and I'm glad you feel the way you do because I feel the same way. I'm still feeling a little guilty about the way I treated them on Friday when they asked me to give them a ride home. But we have to keep in mind that Yvonne and Milton is involved in a shady, illegal business which makes them criminals. If we do get closer to them anyway, we should always feed them with long-handled spoons."

It rained all day Tuesday so nobody in our neighborhood had a backyard cookout. But we invited Yvonne and Milton to have supper with us that evening and it turned out to be very pleasant. The only thing was, while Yvonne and Joyce was in the kitchen doing the dishes after we'd eaten the ribs we'd cooked in the oven, Milton asked me for another loan.

"Just a dollar," he whispered, looking toward the doorway. "And please don't tell Joyce because she'll tell Yvonne and I don't want her to know I ain't managing my money right."

"I advise you to start managing your money right, man. It don't look good for a man your age to be so irresponsible. And I don't want you to get too dependent on me."

"Oh, you ain't got to worry about that. I know when to quit." There was a glint in his eye when he grabbed the dollar bill out of my hand.

I knew it wouldn't be long before he hit me up again. But I was not going to let him get too carried away. I knew when to quit too. Even if it ended our friendship.

Chapter 39
Odell

*A*FTER THE FOURTH OF JULY, ME AND JOYCE GOT REAL busy. Wednesday evening, I cut the grass in our front and back yards, pruned our pecan tree, and hand-washed the car. She washed two loads of clothes and hung them on the line in our backyard, and she got down on her hands and knees and scrubbed our kitchen floor. After we'd finished our chores and ate supper, we visited a white couple we'd been friends with for several years. We hadn't seen Yvonne and Milton since they'd eaten dinner with us on Tuesday. But they had people beating a path to their house almost nonstop the rest of the week. Thursday evening Willie Frank pulled up in his pickup truck with several other white folks riding shotgun in the back, including an elderly man they hauled into the house in a wheelbarrow. It seemed like every time Willie Frank visited, so did Aunt Mattie and one or two of her prostitutes.

Milton had made a few comments on this subject during dinner on Tuesday. According to him, Willie Frank felt more comfortable in a colored neighborhood when he wanted to spend his money on a colored woman. "Our house is much more fun than Aunt Mattie's poon palace for Willie Frank to get his ashes hauled. Me and Yvonne treat our guests like friends, not tricks," Milton had said at the same time he was chomping on Joyce's world-beating hush puppies. Later that night when we was alone, Joyce asked me, "What does 'get his ashes hauled' mean?" I giggled and poked her crotch. When I told her that the phrase meant doing "the big nasty," she pinched my hand. "I figured it had something to do with intercourse!" she snapped.

On Thursday when her parents returned from their retreat, we had supper with them. Friday evening I picked Daddy up and we went fishing for a couple of hours and I spent the night at his house. I was so anxious to see Betty Jean and the boys again, I left there after breakfast on Saturday morning.

"I wish you had come over here last night like you usually do on Fridays," Betty Jean said when I entered her house a few minutes past ten a.m. "The boys spent the night with Alline, so you and me could have had a real nice quiet evening."

"I would have come last night, but . . . you know," I said with a hangdog expression on my face that I had been using a lot lately. "Something came up." I had no trouble coming up with a good excuse to tell Betty Jean when I disappointed her. The one I used the most was "something came up" and that was good enough. She rarely asked me for more details, so I rarely told her. She made it easy for me to keep living two lives. It was one of the reasons I still didn't feel too guilty about what I was doing. I was giving Joyce everything I said I would: love and devotion. I had promised her that I would never leave her, and that was one promise I planned to keep. But I had not promised her that I would be faithful. Whenever it felt like guilt was creeping up on me, I looked at the situation from that angle. I was also giving Betty Jean everything I'd promised her: my love and security. I had all the bases covered.

I glanced around the living room, pleased to see it looking so neat and smelling so good. I did a double-take when I noticed a huge picnic basket on the coffee table. There was a folded red-and-white-checked tablecloth on top of it. "What's with this picnic basket?" I lifted the lid and peeped in. My breath caught in my throat when I saw what was inside: several pieces of fried chicken wrapped in wax paper, baked beans, a bowl of potato salad, six bottles of root beer pop, and half a dozen biscuits. I had not been on a picnic since Joyce and I celebrated our fourth wedding anniversary last year. She had packed a basket with *exactly* the same items that day, even down to a red-and-white-checked tablecloth for us to sit on. I didn't believe in bad omens, but this coincidence made me shiver.

I was so caught up in my thoughts, Betty Jean had to pinch my arm to get my attention. "I hate it when you shut down on me like that," she complained.

"I didn't do no such thing."

"Yes, you did just now. You been doing it more and more lately."

"If I did, I didn't mean to. What was we talking about?"

"*I* was talking about the carnival."

"What carnival?"

"See there. You didn't hear a word I said so you must have shut down"

"Okay, maybe I did. I'll try not to do it again."

"I hope you don't because when you get that glazed look in your eyes, I get worried."

"Honey, you ain't got a damn thing to worry about. I love you to death and I'm going to continue doing everything possible to keep you and the boys happy."

"Good. Now, like I was saying, you said we'd go to the carnival when it came through here. Well, it came yesterday and me and the boys been itching to go. They'll be home in a little while."

"I didn't bring enough money for no carnival. Them rides ain't as cheap as they used to be."

"We ain't got to ride on everything," Betty Jean said. "And I made this picnic basket so we ain't even got to spend no money on hot dogs and candy and whatnot."

"I had planned for us to go on a long drive and do some fishing and maybe find a blackberry patch so we can pick enough berries for a few pies."

"Oh, all right. I don't want to go fishing or blackberry picking. We can just take a drive and go on a picnic. But I know it won't be as much fun as the carnival."

The pout on Betty Jean's face was getting to me, but this was one time I couldn't let her have her way. "Look, I know we'd have a lot of fun at the carnival and I'd love to go, but we can't do that because . . . because it's in Lexington this year and that's too close to home," I said.

"Whose home?"

"Mine. Them carnival people changed their route this year. It was supposed to be in Butler County."

"So? It'll take almost a whole hour to drive from here

to Lexington, but I don't mind. And you know how much the boys like to ride around in that car."

I glanced toward the door. I didn't want the boys to bust in and hear what I was about to say to Betty Jean. When I turned back around to face her, I could tell from the tight look on her face that she already knew what I was going to say. But I said it anyway. "We can't go to that carnival, period. Lexington is only five miles from Branson where I live with my wife. Everybody I know will be at that carnival at some point. With our luck, if we show up there today, half of them will too. Come to think of it, any other day it would be the same thing."

"Joyce might even be there, huh?" Betty Jean folded her arms and gave me a look that was so hot, my face felt like I'd stuck it in an oven.

"I doubt that, but people who know her will be. Them students from her school, and her daddy is like a kid when it come to carnivals, so he'll probably be there every day as long as it's in town."

"I'm getting kind of tired of having to sneak around with you, Odell. It ain't fair to me and the boys and . . . it ain't fair to Joyce."

"You let me worry about Joyce. Me and you been doing all right since we met and that's because we don't go to certain places. There is more than enough places in Hartville and other towns where we can go and not worry about running into nobody I know."

"What would you do if we ever run into somebody you know?"

"I ain't sure. I never think about it."

"How come?"

"I ain't thought about that on account of it ain't going to happen. Now let's go get the boys so we can be on our way. After we have our picnic, we'll take a nice long drive. If anybody is still hungry after that, we'll stop off at Po' Sister's Kitchen for supper."

Just as I expected, after our picnic and a long drive to Mobile and back, everybody was hungry again. As usual, there was a long line of hungry people in front of Po' Sister's Kitchen when we got there.

Like Betty Jean always did whenever we ate at this restaurant, she approached the counter and told somebody to send her sister out so we wouldn't have to wait in line. Alline was too busy this time, but she sent a waitress to take care of us. She seated us at a table in the middle of the floor.

"Daddy, I don't like them itty-bitty hush puppies they always give us," Jesse whined before he even sat down.

"And I don't like them chicken feet y'all ordered for us the last time," Daniel complained, pulling out a chair next to me.

"I'm ordering burgers for y'all this time," Betty Jean said, fanning her face with the menu. She and I ordered the buttermilk catfish with fries and a pitcher of grape Kool-Aid. "Odell, this place is really busy today. You sure you want to stay here? We still might have to wait awhile for them to bring us our food."

"I don't mind staying at all. I can't think of no other place I'd rather be."

Right after I said that, Joyce's face flashed in my mind. Everything I did and said now was so routine, I didn't feel as guilty as I used to.

After we put in our orders, the boys got restless. "Jesse, if you don't stop kicking your brother, I'm going to go outside and get a switch," I warned. I lowered my voice when I noticed the people at some of the tables close to ours looking at us. "Leon, stop trying to catch that fly and be still before I get a switch for you, too!" Despite my sons' unruly behavior, I was in my element. I squeezed Betty Jean's hand and stared into her eyes. "Baby, this is one of the best days we ever had. It don't get no better than this."

"I wish you didn't have to leave tomorrow," she said in a low voice with a pout.

"I wish I didn't have to neither. But, you know how it is." I leaned over and kissed her so long, it seemed like every other customer in the place was gawking at us when I pulled away.

Chapter 40
Joyce

SATURDAY EVENING I GOT BORED AND DECIDED TO VISIT Mama and Daddy. I had visited them twice in the last two days and each time I had to listen to complaints about everything in their lives from the greasy food they had eaten at the retreat they'd attended a few days ago to their warnings about me and Odell getting too involved with "them bootleggers" next door.

Within seconds after I entered my parents' living room, I regretted it. "You look like hell," Daddy boomed from the easy chair he occupied facing the couch where Mama sat with her knitting items in her lap.

"Sure enough," she agreed. "What's the matter?"

I let out an exasperated breath. I didn't sit down because I knew this was going to be a very short visit. I stood in front of the door with my hands on my hips. "Nothing is the matter with me," I snapped.

"If your face was any longer, it'd be dragging this floor. Is you and Odell having problems?" Daddy asked with a snort, looking at me from the corner of his suspicious eye.

"Odell and I are doing just fine. The way people keep hinting at us having problems is getting on my nerves."

"Why do they think y'all having problems?" Mama asked, giving me a weary look. "I hope you ain't been mistreating that man after all the fuss you made to marry him. And who is it that's doing the hinting?"

"That's not important. But one woman had the nerve to ask me one night if Odell had left me. My husband is *never* going to leave me!" I insisted. "We haven't had one single argument since we got married. He promised that we'd stay together until we died."

"Whatever you doing, you better keep doing it so Odell won't have no reason to take off," Mama advised, wagging a finger in my direction.

"Amen to that," Daddy added. "I hope you coming to church with us tomorrow. You and Odell ain't been in a while, and Reverend Jessup done asked several times why come that is. I'm sure that if I asked him to, he'd be happy to drop by your house for supper one evening to give you and Odell some spiritual guidance."

I agreed to go to church with Mama and Daddy tomorrow. Not because I wanted to go, but because I didn't want Reverend Jessup to pay us a visit. We already had enough on our plate, so a meddlesome preacher was the last thing we needed.

When I got back home, I did a few chores, listened to the radio for about an hour, and finished reading the book that I had started reading three days ago. The days seemed so much longer when Odell was gone. I couldn't wait for him to come home from his daddy's house. I thought about calling up my coworker Patsy and asking her to drive me out to Lonnie's house so I could surprise Odell. He hated surprises as much as I did, so that idea didn't stay on my mind long. I went to sleep on the living room couch, and that's where I stayed all night.

I still had not seen Yvonne since she'd eaten supper with us on Tuesday. But this afternoon when I got home from church, she was sitting on her front porch steps crying.

"Lord! Yvonne, what's the matter?" I asked as I ran up to her and put my arms around her shoulder. The hurtful things she'd previously said to me didn't even cross my mind. She didn't look like the wild woman I had begun to think she was. She looked like a woman in pain. And nobody knew better than me what that felt like.

"Oh, Joyce! It's a mess!" she said, choking on a sob. She sniffled and wiped her nose with the sleeve of her bright red blouse, which I was pleased to see was not as low-cut as some of her others. "Today is my baby girl's birthday. My babies' birthdays is always depressing for me, so when I got up this morning, the first thing I did was take a drink. Willie Frank drove me to my aunt and uncle's house to visit my babies this morning. But when Aunt Nadine smelled alcohol on my breath, she wouldn't even let me in the house, and told me that it would be better if I stopped coming around at all. She said she'll continue to bring them to see me when she could, but not too often."

"Please tell me you're kidding! Your aunt doesn't want you to see your own children?"

Yvonne shook her head, sniffled some more, and then

words squirted out of her mouth like spit. "I wouldn't kid about something this serious."

"Why? And why do you let her get away with that?"

"See, my kids don't know I'm their real mama."

My whole body tensed up. "What? Who do they think you are all this time?"

"They think I'm their cousin. When my aunt and uncle took them in, my youngest was still in diapers and my oldest had just learned to talk. Aunt Nadine told my babies that their real mama took off with a musician, and got killed in a beer garden brawl somewhere up north."

"My Lord. Let's go in my house," I suggested, shaking my head and rubbing her back at the same time. She trailed behind me like a sheep that had lost its way.

When we got to my living room, I waved her to the couch and then I skittered to the kitchen. I returned with two glasses of elderberry wine and handed the biggest one to her.

"This ain't nothing like the stuff you and Milton serve, but it's just as good." I sat down next to her. We drank at the same time, and then I draped my arm around her shoulder. "I couldn't imagine what it'd be like if I had kids and somebody else was raising them. That would be bad enough. But I couldn't go on if I had some and they thought I was dead. What do they call you?"

"Cousin Yvonne."

"Will you ever tell them who you really are?"

Yvonne nodded. "I will when they get grown. I promised Aunt Nadine and Uncle Sherman that I wouldn't do so until then."

"That's a long time from now. Why would your folks not want your own kids to know who you really are?"

"She's sanctified. And her husband is even worse. He's a deacon in the church they go to and the holiest man I know. He don't even allow my aunt to wear pants or make-up. They believe people that drink and party don't deserve to raise kids."

"I know a lot of folks in Branson that drink and party, but they still have their kids with them and they seem to be doing all right."

"Yeah, but . . . well, there is a real good reason why my kids ain't with me."

"Oh? What is the reason?"

Yvonne took another sip before she answered. "I got in a little trouble when I was too young and foolish to know better and I had to spend a couple of years in jail."

"Oh." I swallowed hard and sucked in some air. This was not what I had expected to hear. I felt bamboozled. I wondered what else Yvonne was hiding from me and Odell. If she had been in jail, there was no telling what kind of deep dark secrets Milton had. "I've never had an ex-con in my house before. . . ."

"Well, you can't say that no more. I don't tell people until I really get to know them. While I was locked up, the state took my children. If my aunt and uncle hadn't took them in, they would have put them in the asylum for orphans. That's the worst place in the world for a colored child to end up."

"My Lord. I'm surprised Willie Frank never blabbed this information to us before now. He already told me he spent time in prison. What about Milton?"

"What about Milton?"

"It doesn't bother him that you spent some time in jail?"

Yvonne let out a loud breath and shook her head. "No,

he don't mind. He was in prison hisself when he met Willie Frank."

Good God! Milton was an ex-con too! I had assumed he had a shady past, so the news about him being a jailbird didn't surprise me at all. "I see. Was it just one time?"

"Uh-huh. Me and Milton ain't been in trouble with the law since. And in case you want to know what we did—"

I held up my hand and shook my head. "It must not have been too bad if they've already turned y'all loose. Most of the colored people I know that go to prison stay there for years and years, or get executed. And that's because they killed somebody or raped a white woman."

"Honest to God, me and Milton would never kill nobody, and he ain't crazy enough to even look at no white woman, let alone rape one. We learned our lesson and even found Jesus."

My jaw dropped. "*Y'all* got religion?" I asked. This news was even more shocking than hearing they'd been in prison.

"Yup. We joined New Hope Baptist Church two years ago, the same one that they use for a school during the week. I attended it from the first to the eighth grade. I didn't learn much, though. But I'm learning a heap of stuff about the Lord."

"Hmmm. I used to feel so sorry for the students that had to go to that dump to learn. Those outside toilets, dog-eared books, and lazy teachers would have made me drop out in a heartbeat!"

"Some of us didn't have no choice."

"Well, that's life." I hunched my shoulders and gave Yvonne a sympathetic look. "The good thing is that's all behind you now. Stay with Jesus, and He'll stay with you. How often do y'all go to church?"

Yvonne blinked and looked embarrassed. "We ain't been since last Easter, but we plan to start going at least a couple of times a month real soon. We want to continue to honor God."

"That's good to hear. Me and Odell don't go as often as we should, but we will in the future. And when we have kids, we'll go *every* Sunday."

Yvonne exhaled and massaged her chest, as if she'd finally removed a heavy load by letting me know more about her past. I didn't feel threatened or concerned about living next door to ex-convicts. She seemed so sorry about whatever it was she'd done that had landed her in jail. And as long as they would "continue to honor God," I truly believed that she and Milton would stay out of trouble. "Thanks for listening to me, Joyce. I feel so much better."

"I know you love your kids and want to spend more time with them. I think you need to have a serious talk with your aunt and uncle and let them know just how much you miss your babies. I hope they don't make you wait until your kids get grown before they tell them who you really are. There is no reason in the world why your children shouldn't know they still have a mama."

"Thanks for saying that, Joyce," Yvonne sniffled. "I'm surprised to hear a woman like you say something like that."

My chest tightened. I hoped she was not going to make another comment that would make me feel bad about myself. I had put that other one she'd made the day we went shopping out of my mind. "What do you mean by that?"

"For one thing, you smarter than any other woman I know. And you real sweet and down to earth for such a

big-boned woman. Exactly what size do you wear anyway, a sixteen?"

"I wear a size fourteen," I sniffed. I sucked in my gut,
even though I had on a girdle that made my stomach look
almost as flat as Yvonne's.

"Oh. I never would have guessed that."

"And at least I'm not fat, I'm just tall." It had been
years since anybody had mentioned my size in my presence. Even though I was comfortable with it now, it was
still a sensitive subject I didn't like to discuss. Especially
with a woman as attractive as Yvonne. Did tiny women
have tiny brains, too? I wondered.

"True. Tall women like you can carry more weight and
still look good. With your long legs and arms, you got a
lot of extra space for the fat to spread out in and not be
too noticeable."

"Do you think there's something wrong with me being
big?" Now my heart was pounding too and I felt hot inside. I braced myself because I had a feeling that whatever else she had to say on the subject probably wouldn't
be flattering. She had all but told me she didn't think I
was attractive. . . .

Yvonne gave me a serious look and shook her head.
"No. It's just that all the other great big women I know is
so bitter because of the way they look, they act cold and
mean and nasty most of the time. They don't even know
how to dress half as sharp as you do. By the way, where
do you buy your frocks? You got a whole lot of style and
you always look real nice."

"I . . . I . . . order a lot of my clothes from catalogs. My
mama makes the rest," I replied. Maybe Yvonne didn't
think I was as unattractive as I'd thought a few seconds

ago. I felt better. "Back to the subject of your kids," I eased in.

She looked confused. "What about my kids?"

"Now don't you take this the wrong way, but Odell is very particular. I know he won't like his children living next door to bootleggers."

"Say what? Girl, y'all ain't even got no children!" Yvonne hollered. Her eyebrows furrowed and her face suddenly got so red, it looked like somebody had spray-painted her.

"No, we don't have any now. But we will have a few someday."

"Humph. Well, none of our guests ever get too rowdy and raise hell the way a lot of folks do in the jook joints and some of the other bootleggers' houses and beer gardens. We ain't never had no fighting and people puking their guts out and yelling and screaming all the time. Me and Milton run one of the most respectable bootlegging houses in Branson!" Yvonne boomed with her lips quivering and her tongue snapping over every word. I was happy to see her so riled up after making that comment about my size.

"I know all that. It's just that for my soon-to-be-born children's sake, I am not going to allow them to spend too much time at your house." I was still slightly hot, but I managed to look as cool as I sounded. "That's a bad environment for real young people."

Yvonne heaved out a sigh and glanced around the room. When she returned her attention to me, she had a misty-eyed look. "You don't want your kids to be friends with me and Milton?"

Despite her opinion of the way I looked, I held up my hand and decided to backpedal. "I didn't say that and it's not what I meant," I said in a gentle tone. "Kids are naturally curious and impulsive. They see something going on in your house that looks like fun, and the next thing you know they'll be trying it out themselves. I really like you and will always be your friend, but I have to draw the line when it comes to raising kids. I'd ball up and die if one of my babies took a shine to that Willie Frank and started chewing tobacco like him!"

Yvonne blinked and nodded. "I can understand you wanting to protect your kids from bad influences. I guess you and Odell won't even drink in your own house no more *if* you ever have any, huh? It's a damn shame that y'all ain't had no luck all these years. . . ."

My chest tightened some more. I felt sad, but I refused to show it. "When me and Odell have ours, we won't drink in front of them. We are going to limit the devilment going on around ours as much as we can."

Yvonne laughed and gave me a dismissive wave. "Joyce, you shouldn't even be thinking about things like that now. Wait until you have some kids. I'm sorry we got on this subject. I can see how bad it's making you feel. But I do know what you mean."

"I'm glad you see things my way. I know you miss not having yours with you, but they are so much better off with your aunt and uncle." I paused long enough to catch my breath. "Too bad you married a man who's involved in bootlegging and socializing with hillbillies and people like Aunt Mattie and a bunch of prostitutes. You'd be much better off if you'd found somebody like Odell."

She gave me a blank stare and took her time responding. "I don't know about that. Odell ain't my type."

I was thrilled to hear her say that. I just hoped she meant it. Not that Odell would *ever* get involved with a woman like Yvonne.

"Milton is the only man I ever really loved. I'm blessed to have him for a husband, praise the Lord. As long as he treat me good, he can associate with anybody he want to. I ain't his mama, so I can't tell him how to live his life," she declared.

"Then you must not want your kids back bad enough." I glanced at her empty glass. "Let me pour you some more wine. You look like you need it."

"Don't bother. I done had enough, and I need to get home and straighten up the house before folks start showing up." Yvonne stood up, and I escorted her to the door.

Chapter 41
Odell

WHEN I PULLED UP IN FRONT OF MY HOUSE SUNDAY night, Joyce was standing on our front porch. Every light was on and the front door was standing wide open. I parked and piled out of the car and ran up the porch steps two at a time. "What's the matter, sugar?" I hollered, grabbing her by the hand.

"Nothing," she said in a weak tone.

I glanced toward the house next door and all the vehicles parked outside. "What you doing standing out here in the dark?"

"I was getting worried about you. It's almost ten o'clock," she said, leading me inside to the couch. I sat down, but she stood in front of me with her arms folded.

"I would have been home a hour ago, but I had to stop by the store." I let out a disgusted groan and shook my head. "I remembered some paperwork I had forgot to finish before I closed up Friday evening."

Joyce's mouth dropped open. "And it couldn't wait until tomorrow when you go back to the store?"

"It could have, but I had promised Mac I'd have it done by Monday morning. What would I do if he decided to pop in tomorrow before I could get it done?"

"Daddy hardly ever goes to the store since he retired, Odell."

"So?"

"So what made you think he'd suddenly decide to show up tomorrow before you could finish your paperwork? Even if he did pop in tomorrow, I doubt if he'd come before noon."

I gave Joyce a weary look and hunched my shoulders. "Baby, come sit down next to me. I missed you." I patted the couch, but Joyce dropped down into my lap. "Now give me some sugar." I kissed her long and hard and squeezed her tittie, the way I always did when I wanted to get her hot.

"I hope you had a good time out there in the sticks," she said before she nibbled on my earlobe.

"Yeah, right. Daddy and Ellamae ain't the most fun-loving people in the world. He slept most of the time I was out there, and she had me doing all kinds of shit around the house. I shucked a whole bushel of corn and washed and walked that lazy hound dog they got. Yesterday, I took Daddy to get his hair cut and when we got back to the house, Ellamae had went to sleep and left a pan of cornbread cooking in the oven. If we hadn't got back when we did, there ain't no telling what might have happened."

"Odell, maybe we should seriously think about moving them closer to us so we can keep an eye on them the way we do with my mama and daddy."

"Pffft! I done told you before that they ain't never leaving that shack alive. Besides, they done paid off the mortgage and moving to a new place where they'd have to pay rent ain't something they'd even think about doing."

"With the few bucks we've saved up, we'd be able to help them with their rent and other expenses. You know I wouldn't mind doing that."

I gasped so hard my heart felt like it rotated in a complete circle. The "few bucks" Joyce thought we had saved up was fewer than she thought. "Baby, our savings is for our old age." I hoped that by the time Joyce and I reached our golden years, my boys would be grown and on their own and Betty Jean would be the only one I'd still be supporting. If Joyce ever got nosy about exactly how much money we had before then, I'd put the blame on our bank. The Great Depression was not as bad as it used to be, but a few banks was still responsible for some folks losing their money. If I had to file a claim against ours just to make my case look good to Joyce, I could drag it out for years. Being colored, no matter what lawyer I hired, I'd be put on a back burner. Me and Joyce would probably die of old age before things got sorted out. I had it all figured out, but I had to stay on my toes. No matter how naïve Joyce was when it came to me, she was still smart in some areas. And I wasn't going to be dumb enough to underestimate her.

"Well, maybe we could move them in with us."

"What's wrong with you? Living with old folks ain't no walk in the park. If Daddy and Ellamae moved in with us, they'd probably drive us crazy in the first month."

"I don't care. I'm thinking about the big picture. Me and you might be in the same boat someday and we'd want our kids to take care of us."

"Let's cross that bridge when we get to it." I gazed in Joyce's eyes and kissed her again. "Baby, let's not talk about nothing like that right now." I glanced toward the kitchen and sniffed. "Do I smell mustard greens cooking?"

"No. When you didn't come home by five or six like you usually do, I made myself a ham sandwich for supper."

"Oh. Well, can I smell some mustard greens?"

"We don't have any and all the stores are closed. I'll go in the kitchen and fix you a sandwich." Joyce stood up, smoothing down the sides of her flowered duster.

"Thanks, baby." I got up and followed her.

"I was going to call up Patsy and ask her to drive me out to your daddy's house this evening," Joyce said as she opened the icebox.

I froze and my stomach started doing flip-flops. "You was going to do what?" I couldn't remember the last time my voice sounded so raspy.

Joyce turned around with a bowl of smoked ham in her hand and set it on the counter. "I didn't do that because I know how much you hate surprises. Besides that, Patsy's husband probably wouldn't have let her out the house at night anyway. That man is so suspicious. For some reason he thinks she's fooling around with another man." Joyce went to the drawer and pulled out a butter knife and a fork. "What do you want on your sandwich?"

"Um, don't worry about it. I ain't as hungry as I thought I was. You feel like having a drink or two?"

"I wouldn't mind," Joyce said, grinning. "But last night I finished off that elderberry wine we had."

I gasped and gave Joyce a stunned look. "Say what? We had a whole bottle when I left the house on Friday."

"Yeah, but Yvonne came over yesterday and we drank almost all of it." Joyce gave me a worn-out look. Then she let out some air and sat down at the table, staring at the wall as she continued talking. "Did you know she and Milton did time in jail?"

I glanced at Joyce, and then I did a double-take. "Say what? No. She told you that?"

"Uh-huh. That's where Milton met Willie Frank."

"Hmmm. What did they do?"

"She didn't say and I didn't ask."

"Well, whatever it was, it couldn't have been too bad if they already out of jail."

"That's what I thought. Anyway, she said a few things I didn't like."

I leaned against the stove. "Again? What was it this time?"

"She was down in the dumps about not having her kids with her, and I think I said the wrong thing about it and upset her even more." Joyce told me some of the things she'd said to Yvonne.

"Them comments would have upset anybody."

"Yeah, you're right. But then she made a remark about my size."

"Listen," I said, pulling out a chair at the table. I sat down and gave her a stern look. "You and Yvonne need to start acting your age. If y'all keep saying stupid shit to one another, sooner or later, one of y'all is going to say something so bad it'll ruin your friendship."

"That might have already happened. I told her you wouldn't want your children being around her and Milton."

My children? I gawked at Joyce like she had just sprouted a mustache. My heart started beating so fast and hard, I thought it was going to beat me into a coma. I swallowed some air and gave her a curious look. There was only one thought on my mind and it chilled me to the bone. Good God! Had she found out about Betty Jean and the boys? If so, why had she not said something before now? My heart calmed down when I told myself that I was letting my imagination run away with me. There was no way in the world I'd still be in one piece if Joyce knew my secret. "What children?"

"The ones I hope we have someday," she said, rolling her neck. She let out a chuckle and pinched my hand, and I breathed a deep sigh of relief. "I only said what I said because she'd made another crack about my size."

"Oh," I mumbled. "Children is a real touchy subject with some folks. Especially you women."

"Tell me about it. And it's getting touchier by the day with me," Joyce whined. I didn't have to read her mind to know what she was going to say next. "I want my own children so bad I don't know what to do. It's unfair that women like Yvonne can have three and I can't have even one. Do you think we'll ever be parents? I know how important it is to you to be a daddy, and I worry about it all the time."

"Yes, I do think we'll have children someday. But it don't do no good for you to fret over it. One of my old bosses and his wife tried to have a baby for ten years. They got so obsessed, they even fixed up a nursery with all kinds of baby knickknacks. There was everything in that room to indicate a baby occupied it, except the baby. That desperate couple finally broke down and adopted a little girl. Then BAM! Six months later, the wife got pregnant! Why? Because they had stopped worrying about it."

"I can't help it. Having a baby is on my mind almost every day, especially when I'm by myself."

"You don't have to be by yourself now that Yvonne and Milton live right next door. They always itching to entertain company."

"If I hadn't been so worried about why you hadn't come home yet, I would have gone over there a couple of hours ago and smoothed things over with Yvonne. I'm sure she told Milton what I said and I regret every word now. I don't like being rude to people—especially ones we live so close to. And I really wish I hadn't made those comments about that grill they work at."

"I know just what you mean. I'm going to be nicer to Milton from now on too." I glanced toward the window then back at Joyce. "Let's do this, baby. Why don't we kill two birds with one stone?"

"What do you mean?"

"We can go get a drink and show Yvonne and Milton some love."

Chapter 42
Odell

MILTON HADN'T PAID BACK THE MONEY HE'D BORrowed last Tuesday, and I wasn't going to remind him about it. But I would if and when he asked for another "loan" before he repaid the last one.

Willie Frank opened the door when we got over there. "Hey, we got two more!" he yelled as he ushered us in. "The folks from next door!"

"The more the merrier," somebody yelled.

The living room had people from wall to wall. There was just enough room on the couch for one more body, so Joyce sat down and I stood in front of her. "What y'all drinking tonight?" Willie Frank asked, looking from me to Joyce. He didn't look drunk, but the alcohol on his breath was so strong, it made my eyes water.

"I'll just have some whiskey," Joyce said, talking loud so she could be heard over all the chatter and music.

Somebody in the back of the room was playing the red piano that Milton had picked up at a garage sale, and somebody else was playing a guitar.

"Pour me the same thing," I told Willie Frank. "Where is Yvonne and Milton?"

"Yvonne is around here somewhere. I dropped Milton off on Morgan Street a while ago so he could get in on some hot crap games. He ain't come home yet."

Just then, Yvonne pushed her way through the crowd and went right up to Joyce. "I'm so pleased to see you ain't mad at me about that stuff I said today."

"Pffft! I forgot all about that conversation, girl." Joyce laughed and waved her hand. And then she tugged on Willie Frank's shirtsleeve. "We can't stay long, so can we get our drinks now?"

Before we got our drinks, the door swung open and Milton strutted in. He greeted some of his guests with smiles and hugs. But there was the strangest expression on his face when he spotted me. I smiled, nodded, and waved. He did the same thing, but he didn't come up to me. Fifteen minutes later, I put my arm around his shoulder and pulled him into a corner. "What you been into, buddy boy?"

"I'm so glad you asked me that. I'm fixing to look into a deal that'll be sweeter than a ton of sugarcane, if I pull it off." He stopped talking and narrowed his eyes. "I can't talk about it right now, though. I'll tell you all about it real soon." He let out a mighty belch and walked away. Every time I peered in his direction, he was looking in mine, staring so hard it made me cringe.

After about twenty minutes, I plowed through the crowd until I found Joyce. She was in the kitchen drinking a glass of water. I was glad she was alone. "We better get going soon so I can get some sleep. I need to be at work a little earlier tomorrow so I can finish up a few things before I open up."

"I thought that was the reason you stopped by the store on your way home this evening," she wailed, looking exasperated.

"It was. And I did finish my paperwork, but I just remembered a few other things I forgot to do."

We left five minutes later. When we got home, we went straight to bed and Joyce started rubbing up and down my rump. Sex was the last thing I wanted tonight. Besides, I'd got myself a pretty good dose before I left Betty Jean's house a few hours ago. I had other things on my mind. I couldn't stop thinking about the way Milton had kept gazing at me and the sugarcane-sweet deal that he was going to talk to me about "real soon." But Joyce wouldn't let up. Even though I was laying there like a log, she slid her hand inside my shorts and started stroking anyway. Well, it didn't take but a few more seconds for me to get aroused. I climbed on top of her so we could get it on and get it over with.

By the time I opened up the store the next morning, I had stopped thinking about Milton and went on about my day. As goofy and meddlesome as Buddy and Sadie was, they kept things under control when I didn't want to be on the main floor. As much as I loved my work, I wanted to do as little as possible. I had been holed up in my office for the past two hours, reading a detective magazine and playing tic-tac-toe on the same pad I used to take notes when I did do some work.

A few minutes after eleven, I went back out to the main floor. I was pleased to see that we had more than a dozen customers. Just as I was about to return to my office and do some more reading and play another game, probably hangman, I scanned the room and spotted Milton lurking at the end of Sadie's counter. "Milton, what you doing here?" I glanced at the clock on the wall and walked up to him. "It's mighty early for you to be shopping. You ain't working today?"

He bit his bottom lip and let out a loud breath. "Naw. I ain't come up in here to buy nothing. I'm here on business," he told me, speaking in a low tone. It wasn't low enough, because Buddy and Sadie heard him and immediately started gawking in our direction. I gave them a stern look, and they returned their attention to their cash registers.

"Oh? What business is that?" I asked, giving Milton a puzzled look.

"Me and you need to conversate about some serious business."

"We do?"

"Yup."

I shrugged. "O . . . kay. What business do we need to conversate about?"

"I think we should go somewhere more private first." Milton pursed his lips and glared at me from the corner of his eye.

"How come we can't talk out here?"

"Trust me, brother man, you don't want nobody else to hear what I got to say."

That was all I needed to hear. I motioned for him to follow me. When we got in my office, I closed the door and sat down in the chair behind my desk. "Can I get you a bottle of pop or a pig foot?"

"Nope. This ain't no social visit. Mind if I sit down?" Before I could answer, he grabbed the metal chair I kept in front of my desk and turned it backward. He straddled it and plopped his butt down with a groan.

Not only was I getting impatient, I was getting annoyed. "I'm real busy, so whatever you got to say, you need to say it fast so I can get back to work."

He caught a glimpse of the magazine and tic-tac-toe pad in front of me. "Uh-huh. I can see how busy you is," he snickered, folding his arms. "I wish my job at Cunningham's was as easy as yours." He blinked and leaned forward. "Odell, I like you and I like Joyce. But sometimes people ain't what they seem to be, even me. Some folks got some serious shit to hide. . . ."

I sighed and scratched the side of my head. "Milton, I know you and Yvonne done spent some time in jail. She told Joyce and Joyce told me. That's your business and I don't know why you'd think it would be a big deal to me. Shit. I ain't never been in jail but I ain't no angel." I cracked up at my own comment. "I don't know why you bothering me with something like this. I—"

Milton held up his hand and cut me off. He gave me a hostile look to boot. "Okay. I'm fixing to get to the point and it ain't got nothing to do with me and Yvonne spending time in jail. It ain't got nothing to do with us at all. This is about *you*."

Chapter 43
Odell

MY BLOOD PRESSURE ROSE SO HIGH AND SO FAST, I thought I was going to drop dead on the spot. "I . . . I ain't got no idea what the hell you . . . you talking about," I stuttered. "I ain't done nothing wrong." As soon as them words slid out of my mouth, I realized what a stupid thing I'd just said. I'd been stealing from my in-laws left and right for years. Other than Betty Jean, nobody else knew about it. Or did they? The thought almost brought me to my knees. I decided to wait until I heard what Milton had to say before I fell apart. Maybe it wasn't nothing serious anyway.

Milton reared back in his seat and coughed. "Where was you at this past weekend?"

"Why?"

"I'm just curious."

"Well, I don't like to tell nobody my personal business, especially if the only reason they want to know is because they 'curious.'"

"You remember Cecil Braxton? That bootlegger that used to run his business out by the railroad tracks?"

I did a double-take and shifted in my seat. "Why you changing the subject all of a sudden?"

"Hold on now. I'm getting to the point."

"You better hurry up and do just that because I ain't got time to be sitting up in here playing games." I let out a disgusted breath and glared at Milton. "Yeah, I remember Cecil. I thought he was dead. I heard he had a stroke."

"He did. But he still as alive as me and you, and doing just fine."

"I'm happy to hear that. The next time you see him, tell him I'm praying for him. So what do Cecil have to do with why you came to talk to me?"

Milton sucked in some air and goggled at me so hard, I flinched. "I was at loose ends this past weekend, so on Saturday I decided to pay a visit to old boy and see how he was doing. His wife is in Selma visiting her sister, and all his other kinfolks live in Huntsville, so he out there in that big old house by hisself. Me and him go way back, so I didn't mind taking the bus out to see him. Him and my daddy used to be running buddies, so he always been like a uncle to me. Anyway, after we had a few beers, I worked on his truck and got it back up and running. It was his idea for us to take a spin. He wanted to pay a visit to Aunt Mattie's house to get him a little booty and some head. He hadn't had none since his stroke." Milton paused and lowered his voice. "Aunt Mattie was so glad to see him back in her house, she gave him a two-for-one deal, so I had me a little fun too."

"Humph!" I grunted, wagging my finger in his face. "You better not let Yvonne find out about it."

Milton howled and snapped his fingers. "Horsefeathers! She just as dense as every other woman. As long as she ain't got nothing to go on, she would *never* get a notion that I was cheating on her." He squinted for a few seconds. Then he started talking real slow. "Anyway, when we left Aunt Mattie's place, Cecil wanted me to drive him somewhere so we could get something to eat. Naturally, I suggested Mosella's, but he didn't want to go there. He told me about a out-of-town place he liked, so we gassed up his truck and got on the road. Guess where we went?"

"I don't know! Shoot!" I hollered.

"That out-of-town restaurant me and Cecil ate at Saturday evening was in Hartville and . . . *so was you.*"

My head started spinning and a lump formed in my throat within a split second. I was a strong man, but for the first time in my life I felt as weak as a sick kitten. "What in the world—"

"Calm down, lover boy. Oops! I meant to call you *Daddy.*"

I gulped so hard I was surprised I didn't swallow my tongue. "What do you know?" I whimpered.

"I know a lot. Me and Cecil was in a booth near the back, but I could still see you sitting at a table in the middle of the floor. By the way, them buttermilk-dipped catfish we ordered was delicious. I noticed that was the same thing you ordered." Milton paused and goggled at me for a few seconds.

His silence and the suspense was torture. "If you seen what I had on my plate, I guess you seen the woman that was sitting at that table with me, huh?"

"Yup! And I seen them three little boys." We stayed silent for about five seconds before Milton spoke again. "At first I thought maybe you was with a cousin or some other relative and her kids. I even thought maybe she was just a friend."

"How do you know she wasn't just a friend?"

"Hah! Don't even go there."

"Don't jump to no conclusions! Let me explain. It wasn't what you thought!" I boomed. I blinked and rubbed my chest, which felt like it was about to explode. I was so frantic I didn't even know what explanation I could come up with that would convince Milton he had misinterpreted what he'd seen.

"Hush up! You think I'm stupid? Odell, that biggest boy could have been your twin!"

"That don't mean nothing! I done seen strangers that could be my twin!"

"On top of that, I seen you haul off and kiss Miss Thing. And, I heard all three of them little boys call you 'Daddy.' Then came the icing on the cake. When Cecil went to use the toilet, I asked our waitress about you, and she told me all kinds of juicy stuff. You got folks over there thinking you a traveling salesman?" Milton laughed and clapped his hands, so I knew he was enjoying watching me squirm like a worm on a fishhook. "Couldn't you come up with a better story than that? I trotted over to the window just in time to see y'all piling into that nice car Joyce's daddy sold to you real cheap. I said to myself, 'That Odell is one lucky son-of-a-gun. He done hooked hisself a piece of prime redbone tail.' Shit! She look better than Yvonne. What's her name and how old is she? And don't lie, I know a *youngblood* when I see one."

The inside of my throat felt like somebody had clawed

it. It hurt to keep talking. "Her name is Betty Jean and she'll be twenty-three in September." My voice was so high-pitched, I sounded like a woman.

"How long you been poking that tender young stuff?" He answered his own question. "Long enough to make three babies, that's how long."

"Milton, I don't want to lose my woman," I said, sounding like a weak old man this time.

"*Which* woman is it you don't want to lose?"

"Joyce. I love her to death. She would leave me in a heartbeat if she knew about Betty Jean and the boys." I was sweating hard and my hands was shaking. "My life wouldn't be worth a defective penny."

Milton smiled. I was in the worst pain I'd ever been in my life and this motherfucker was smiling at me! "Odell, like I done told you more than once before, I really like you. You ain't got to worry about me blowing the whistle on you." I didn't feel no relief, because I had a feeling Milton had something else up his sleeve. I was right. "Now, all you got to do is be nice to me."

"What do you want?" I was glad to hear my voice sounding stronger now. But I was still sweating, and now I was terrified.

"*What you got?*"

"How much do you want?"

"You think I want some hush money?"

"Well, what do you want?"

"Some hush money," he said, grinning. "See, I ain't lucky like you. A spook like me, I have to work real hard just to get by. I got unexpected expenses coming out the woodwork like termites. And, I been losing quite a bit at craps lately. Last night I lost everything but my mind. Two days ago them damn hillbillies upped their prices on their liquor again and didn't give me no warning. On top of that, I had to give Willie Frank and his crew a little extra cash this week so they can pay off them revenuers and keep them happy. If they ever shut down Willie Frank and his brothers and confiscate the still they use to brew their stuff with, I'll be up shit creek and have to find me a new supplier. I really need more money, and you the only one I know I can get it from. . . ."

"Okay. I'm a reasonable man. Just tell me how much you want and let's settle this right here and now."

"I'm a reasonable man myself. First off, I need money to pay my rent. It's already a week late. That'll be twenty bucks, please."

"That's a lot of money."

Milton hunched his shoulders. "I know it is. That's why I want it."

"Is that all you want?"

He shook his head. His short hair reminded me of cockleburs. The grease he'd slathered on it could have passed for molasses shining up his forehead. "Well, since you asked, I wouldn't mind having one of them pinstripe suits y'all sell. A white one. I know I look like a fly in a bowl of buttermilk when I wear that color, but Yvonne and Aunt Mattie's girls love to see me in it. It shows off my bronze skin tone." Milton grinned again.

I nodded. "All right," I mouthed with a heavy sigh. "You'll have to come back after we close this evening to pick out a suit when I'll be here by myself. I'll give you the twenty dollars to pay this month's rent now, and I'll throw in a bonus so you can pay next month's rent too." I took my wallet out of my pocket and pulled out four ten dollar bills. He snatched them so fast, he almost took my hand, too. "Happy?"

"Hell yeah, I'm happy! I'm going to take Yvonne out to supper this evening when we get off work, so I'll have to pick up my suit at another time." He folded the money and slid it into his shirt pocket.

"That's fine." I gave him a hard look and wagged my finger in his face. "Milton, you know blackmail is a serious crime."

His mouth dropped open, and he stood up and reared back on his legs. "Blackmail? Nigger, you crazy!" He waved his arms and shook his head. "This ain't nothing but a business arrangement. I ain't never blackmailed nobody before in my life. Shoot!"

I balled my fist and shook it at him. "On top of that, what you doing is a sin, too! I thought you'd found Jesus."

Milton laughed so hard he got tears in his eyes. He sat back down looking as smug as a tick on a sow's ear. "You a fine one to be talking about sin! You ain't got a leg to stand on!"

He was almost right, because when I stood up, I almost fell so I had to plop back down in my chair. I wagged my finger in his face again. "You can call it whatever you want, but you have to promise me that you'll keep your mouth shut about what you seen in Hartville. Now, I know you know your Bible. If you swear to God that you'll keep your promise, I'll feel a whole lot better."

He licked his finger and used it to cross his heart, which I suspected was even blacker than his hair. "I swear to God I'll keep my promise." He cocked his head to one side and gave me a dry look. His pitch-black eyes reminded me of charcoal. "Let me ask you one thing: Why?"

"Why what?"

"You married to a gold mine, man. Why would you risk all that for a piece of tail?"

I exhaled and my shoulders sagged. He'd asked me a question I had asked myself a thousand times, and none of the answers I came up with made much sense. The one I gave Milton was one of the stupidest ever. "It ain't easy being a man. I didn't go looking for no woman. I was just in the wrong place at the wrong time. Betty Jean came at me like a gangbuster. If she hadn't, none of this would have happened. I wouldn't have never cheated on Joyce on my own."

"Yeah, right. I bet Betty Jean didn't have to put no gun up to your head," he teased.

"No, she didn't. Her weapon was her beauty. I always wanted me a woman that looked like her, but never thought I'd get in this deep with one. All I really wanted was some tail. I don't know nobody in Hartville, so I thought I could get away with it."

"Humph. If a piece of sweet redbone nooky was all you wanted, Aunt Mattie always have two or three working for her at the same time. And, I know where you can find a lot more."

I shook my head and gave Milton the most exasperated look I could come up with. "What's wrong with you? You think I'm stupid enough to fool around with a woman in the same town where people know me and my wife?"

"Hell's bells, man. You went somewhere and got you one where you didn't think nobody would see you, and I seen you. And if it hadn't been me, sooner or later somebody else you know would have caught you."

"Anyway, I thought it would be just a little hanky-panky between me and Betty Jean, but things got out of hand real fast. When she got pregnant the first time, I knew I had to do the right thing. Before I knew it, we had three little boys."

Milton gave me a pitiful look. "You stupid jackass. One baby was bad enough, but you had to stick around and make two more! You better get you some thigh-high boots, because the shit you in is going to get a lot deeper. I wouldn't trade places with you for all the money in the world."

"What do you mean?" I stood up again.

"You ain't just cooked your goose; you done cremated it, my man!"

"You think so?"

"I know so, Odell. But tell me this: How long do you think you can stand all this stress?"

"How do you know I'm stressed?"

"Pffft! You can't hide that from me. I could see it with my eyes closed. When I told you why I came here today, you acted like you seen your own ghost. You lucky it was me that busted you and not a blabbermouth like Yvonne. Or that Buddy or Sadie." Milton gave me another pitiful look. I knew he wasn't feeling sorry for me, so I didn't know what was behind that look. And he was right, I was stressed. But he was the one that was stressing me! The more I gazed at his butt face, the madder I got. It was a good thing for him that I wasn't stupid enough to jump over my desk and wring his neck! "I'm glad we was able to work this thing out as fast as we did. I'm happy and you should be too, because you can go on with your two women. But I advise you to watch your step on account of you walking on real thin ice. If somebody else was to see what I seen, I hope they'll be as reasonable as me."

Milton reached out his hand to me. "You want to shake on our deal?" I gave him the meanest look I could come up with and ignored his hand. "Oh well. I got to get back to work. Thanks for the money. Now, you be cool and have a blessed day." He whistled as he strutted toward the door.

I dropped back down into my chair, but I couldn't sit still. I got up and paced back and forth for about fifteen minutes, recalling everything Milton had said. The whole time I was sweating bullets.

I finally told Buddy, Sadie, and the latest stock boy that I didn't feel well and needed to go home before I got worse.

Chapter 44
Joyce

WHEN I GOT HOME FROM WORK, ODELL WAS ALREADY in bed. I rushed over to him with a wild-eyed look on my face. "Baby, what's the matter? I called the store a little while ago and Sadie told me you got sick a couple of hours ago and had to leave. How come you didn't answer the phone when I called here?" I sat down on the side of the bed and felt his forehead.

"I . . . I must have been using the toilet," he said in a feeble tone. "My bowels have been in a uproar all day. I didn't get much sleep last night, so I could barely keep my eyes open today. That's why I got in this bed as soon as I got home."

"It's my fault. I should not have kept you up half the night trying to make a baby. You stay in bed and I'll make you some tea. You hungry?"

"Uh-uh."

"You say that now, but I'm going to fix some chicken soup. Don't you get out of that bed unless you need to use the toilet again."

Seeing Odell so sick scared me. He was the healthiest man I knew. The whole time we'd been together, he had never been sick enough to leave work and take to his bed. He didn't like doctors, but I was going to do everything I could to get him back up on his feet. I hoped that the only thing wrong with him was a bad case of the runs. I'd been there myself more times than I cared to think about, so I knew how annoying and inconvenient it could be. But it was a condition that wasn't too serious. If he didn't get better by morning, I'd make him stay home and I'd call in sick so I could stay in the house and take care of him. In the meantime, I wanted him to stay in bed.

Odell probably would have done that if Yvonne and Milton hadn't come to the house about twenty minutes after I had given him a bowl of the chicken soup I'd made. Right after they started talking, he stumbled into the living room with the bedspread draped around his shoulders. "I thought I heard company," he said in a weak tone. He stood in the doorway with an expression on his face that scared me. It was the same frightened look I'd seen the day I told him I was pregnant.

"Man, you look terrible," Milton howled. "We heard you wasn't feeling too good." He and Yvonne had already made themselves comfortable on the couch.

"Who told y'all that?" Odell wanted to know, looking at me. I shook my head.

"Sadie told us," Yvonne answered.

"Oh?"

"Uh-huh. We stopped by the store on our way home from work to see if we could get a ride home with you and she told us you'd left already. Sick as a dog. I was so sorry to hear that."

"Thank you, Yvonne," Odell rasped.

"And I wanted to pick out me one of them pinstripe suits today," Milton added, giving Odell a wink.

"Oh," Odell said again, wrapping the bedspread tighter around his body. I could see that he was even weaker than he'd been when I got home, so I hoped Yvonne and Milton wouldn't hang around too long.

"Um, Odell, maybe you should get back in the bed," I advised. I walked up to him and massaged his shoulders. "Did the chicken soup do any good at all?"

"Look like he need something stronger than chicken soup," Milton suggested. He looked Odell up and down and frowned. "You want something a little more medicinal? I can run back home and grab you a bottle of something real sweet. But I have to warn you, them hillbillies aged this batch too long, so it'll kick you like a mule."

"That's all right, Milton, but thanks for asking anyway. I'm already feeling much better." I was glad to see a smile on Odell's face, even though it was a tight one and didn't stay there long. He moaned and flopped down on the arm of the couch.

"What's wrong with you, Odell? It ain't nothing catchy, I hope. Sadie didn't say, but Buddy said something about he'd heard you throwing up in the bathroom."

"I was. And from both ends," Odell rattled. "It must have been something I ate for lunch."

"I think you've been doing too many things and got your system out of whack," I scolded. "My hard-headed daddy had the same problem for years. Like you, he used to run himself ragged. At least once every two or three weeks, he'd have to leave work and go home and stay close to the toilet. But he hasn't had that problem at all since he retired."

"Odell, I think Joyce is right. You been doing *too many things*," Milton threw in gently. "If you change your mind about something to drink, send Joyce over to the house and I'll fix you up. I don't like to see you looking so . . . um . . . distressed."

"I feel the same way," Yvonne added.

I couldn't deny the worried looks on their faces, especially Milton's. It was obvious that they were just as concerned about Odell's well-being as I was. Maybe they were not as crude as I thought they were. . . .

"Thanks," Odell mumbled.

"Y'all hungry? Can I get y'all something? I'm going to fry catfish for supper and y'all welcome to join us," I said, looking from Milton's face to Yvonne's to Odell's.

"That's all right, Joyce. We ate some neck bones at Mosella's on our way home. But thank you for asking. I love catfish," Yvonne chirped. I was in a fairly good mood and was glad she and Milton had come to the house. I had promised myself that I'd forget about all the petty resentment I'd felt toward her recently until I heard what she said next. "Joyce, one thing I can say about you is that you sure know your way around the kitchen. But I never met a large woman that didn't know how to cook up a storm."

"Thanks, Yvonne," I said stupidly with my face burning. By now her references to my size didn't bother me that much, but I was still mildly annoyed, so I had to say something about her that would bring her down a peg or two. "By the way, I can get you some lotion that'll work much better than what you use on your ashy legs now. And, I noticed the other night when you had on that low-cut blouse that you have some stretch marks on the top of your breasts." I stared at her ashy hands and legs and frowned. "Maybe I should get you some of that Corn Huskers brand. It's so strong, it'll even work on alligator skin. Odell, do we have some in stock at the store?"

"I think so," he mumbled, scratching the side of his neck.

"I could use some myself. We'll stop by the store on our way home tomorrow and pick us up a couple of bottles," Milton piped in. "And we can pick up a few other things. Huh, Odell?"

We chatted about a few mundane things for another twenty minutes or so, but nothing of interest to me. I was getting bored and was anxious for them to leave so I could give all my attention to Odell. When he jumped up and made a beeline for the bathroom, it was a good excuse for me to throw out a hint for them to go home. "If y'all don't mind, I'd better check on Odell and make him go back to bed."

"Take your time. It's fun sitting here chit-chatting, so we'll wait on you to get back," Yvonne yipped.

I escorted Odell back to bed and returned to the living room. Another ten minutes dragged by. Yvonne and Milton didn't budge until they heard somebody drive up and park in front of their house.

"That sounds like Willie Frank's truck. He said he was coming back tonight." Yvonne sprung up off the couch like a jack rabbit. "Come on, baby." She grabbed Milton by the hand, and they rushed out the door. I went to the window and parted the curtains. Right after Willie Frank piled out of his truck, another one arrived. I stayed at the window until Odell came up behind me and put his hand on my shoulder.

"Sweet Jesus. I thought they'd never leave," he moaned. I was surprised and delighted to hear how much stronger he sounded now.

"I didn't either. They always seem to come at an inconvenient time. But you have to admit, they are entertaining."

"So is a dancing bear."

"Odell, be nice now. They're not that bad. If we had had something to drink in the house, I wouldn't have gotten bored."

"Well, you can always go over to their house and drink all you want. And with all the activity they got going on, you won't have to worry about them boring you over there," Odell teased.

I gave him a thoughtful look. "That's true. Too bad we can't go next door tonight. I feel like kicking up my heels for a little while, and that Willie Frank is even more entertaining than Yvonne and Milton." I let out a deep sigh and felt Odell's forehead. "How do you feel now?"

"Better still. Not good enough to go drinking next door, though. But why don't you go? After babysitting me, I'm sure a good stiff drink would do you a world of good."

"Odell, you stop talking crazy. I'm not leaving you in this house alone," I insisted.

Chapter 45
Joyce

*A*FTER SUPPER, ODELL TOOK A HOT BATH AND GOT back in the bed. But only because I'd badgered him. He assured me that he was well enough to return to work tomorrow, but he was not in the mood to go next door to have a drink. But I was.

I waited until he was asleep before I scurried out the door. By now even more cars and trucks had arrived. They were parked on both sides of our street, all the way to the end of the block. The music was so loud, I had to pound on the door for about two minutes before somebody opened it. A cute young white man waved me in. There was no room on the couch, and every other seat was occupied. Yvonne was a few feet away, so she grabbed me by the arm and steered me to a corner in the back of the room. "If you want to rest your feet, you'll have to sit on one of them footstools or lard buckets we keep in the pantry," she told me.

"Oh, I don't mind standing. I sit down enough at work and at home. Y'all sure got a nice crowd tonight," I told her as I peered around. "Who's that white boy that opened the door for me? He looks kind of young to be in a place like this."

"Oh, that's Jody, Willie Frank's nephew. He skinny as a lizard and got a baby face, but he turned twenty-four last month." Yvonne leaned closer to me and sniffed. "Either you cooked that catfish or you didn't wash your coochie too good." She gave me a knowing look and whispered, "I have the same problem if I don't use enough soap down there. . . ."

I wondered how many more times she was going to say something unflattering to me. I reminded myself that I had only known Yvonne since last month. I also reminded myself that I was drinking at her house for free, so at least she wasn't stingy. And, Odell really wanted me to develop a strong relationship with her like he planned to do with Milton. I knew he was still feeling guilty about not giving them a ride home after their coworker's funeral.

I didn't have time to respond to Yvonne's comment. It was just as well, because I didn't know how to respond to it anyway. Milton shuffled up to me and gave me a bear hug. "Where is my boy? Is he still feeling like shit?" he asked, giving me an amused look.

"No, he's fine now."

"He going back to work tomorrow?"

"As far as I know. Next to his Daddy's house, and a fishing hole, the store is his home away from home," I replied with a loud, heavy sigh. "It's been a long time since we spent a whole weekend together. Or more than four or five days in a row."

Milton gave me a pensive look. "Being by yourself so much don't bother you?"

"Every now and then it does. If he keeps it up too much longer, I am going to have to put my foot down. As much as I hate to, I'm going to start going fishing with him again, and to his daddy's house. Sometimes he feels like a part-time husband," I laughed.

"Girl, you better do something about that before he ain't no husband at all. I would never let my man spend so much time away from me," Yvonne declared, jabbing Milton's side with her elbow.

What she'd just said bothered me more than the crude fish/coochie comment she'd made. Because of that, I stayed only long enough to have one drink.

Odell was sitting up in bed staring at the wall when I entered the bedroom, unbuttoning my blouse and kicking off my shoes at the same time. "I was hoping you'd still be asleep when I got back," I said dryly. I snatched the flannel nightgown I had left on the bedpost and put it on.

"Why?"

"I didn't want you to know I went out tonight."

"You didn't stay long," he noticed, glancing at the clock on the nightstand. "Did Yvonne say something else you didn't like? Is that why you back home already?"

I exhaled and climbed into bed. "Um, no, she didn't. I didn't stay long because I felt guilty about leaving you by yourself. Besides that, they had too many people over there tonight. And, I didn't like the way some of those men were behaving."

I slid between the sheets, and Odell put his arm around my shoulder and started patting it. "Baby, did one of them drunk jokers try to take advantage of you?" he asked gently.

"Something like that. Even after I told them I was a married woman and would never fool around on my husband!"

"It's a good thing for them I wasn't there. I would have straightened them out."

"I know you would have, honey." Only part of what I was telling Odell was true. Two men had asked me to dance, but only after three other women had turned them down. Neither one of them had shown any romantic interest in me. It did a lot for my ego when I made Odell think that other men found me attractive. What I didn't feel good about was the fact that I had to lie about it. Since we had been married, not a single man had made a pass at me.

"I'm glad to hear that you didn't come home early because Yvonne said something stupid and hurt your feelings again." Odell caressed my chin.

"Well, she did say something I didn't want to hear," I admitted.

"What did she say about you this time?"

"It was something she said about *you*." Odell gulped. He stopped caressing my chin and his body stiffened. "What's the matter?" I gasped, feeling his forehead.

"What did Yvonne have to say about *me*?" he asked in a raspy tone.

"Nothing really that serious. She and Milton both made a few petty, stupid comments. But I said something just as petty and stupid about you myself that I regretted as soon as it left my mouth."

"What was said?" Now Odell's voice sounded hollow and nervous.

"They yip-yapped about how much time you spend away from me. Milton had the nerve to ask if it bothered me. I told him it didn't, but then I said something about you being a part-time husband and how I was going to start going fishing with you, and out to your Daddy's house more often."

"I hope you don't start letting people we don't even know that well give you advice."

"I'm not worried about that happening. They're too ignorant for me to take seriously. There is nothing they could say that I would consider good advice anyway. Especially if it concerns our marriage." I was glad Odell's body felt more relaxed now. "I just want to know one thing and I hope you'll be honest with me like you've always been."

He got stiff again. "What?"

"Do you still love me as much as you did the day we got married?"

"Baby, I couldn't love you no more if I tried."

Chapter 46
Odell

I WAS STILL FEELING PRETTY STRESSED, BUT I MANAGED to fall asleep a few minutes after Joyce. I wished I hadn't. It was one of the roughest nights of my life. I had a nightmare with Milton chasing me down a long dark road, yelling and screaming at me and demanding more money. Me and him was both naked and the only two people in the dream that I could see. But I could hear women screaming on both sides of the road. Finally, one of the women floated out to the road and started running along with me. It was Betty Jean. She was screaming and hollering at me too. Then two more women entered the dream: Joyce and Yvonne. That was enough to wake me up around four in the morning.

I didn't want to face Joyce until I got my bearings back on track, so I snuck out of the house before she woke up.

I made it to the store a hour early, so I sat in my office

and read the Bible that I kept on top of the cabinet that contained the bogus and doctored-up paperwork I kept on file. My daddy told me one time that God answered all prayers when people asked for something, but sometimes he said no. I prayed that God would answer my prayer, which was for me to keep my double life a secret. He'd allowed me to get away with it for over five years, so I saw no reason why He would let things fall apart now.

By nine a.m. when I opened the store, I felt better. But each time I heard a customer enter, I almost jumped out of my skin. All kinds of crazy thoughts started dancing around in my head. The worst one was: What if somebody else from Branson saw me with Betty Jean and the boys? Would I have to pay them off too? Giving Milton two months' rent had really put a dent in my finances, but I was overjoyed that that was all he wanted. I had no idea how I was going to pay Betty Jean's rent and the rest of her expenses for the next two months and still have enough money in my pocket to pay my own bills, and take Joyce out a few times. I had to come up with a plan and I had to come up with one quick. Then it hit me like a thunderbolt. I was in charge of the bookkeeping, so nobody but me knew how much money was coming in and how much was going out. This little problem with Milton could turn out to be a blessing in disguise. My in-laws being so loosey-goosey was going to pay off in a big way for me. After the cashiers turned in their drawers to me at the end of each day, I could do whatever I wanted with that money. It would be like having a great big personal piggy bank. Shit. Mac still didn't trust banks. When I went to his house and handed him that paper bag every Friday evening with the week's earnings, he didn't even count it. He just snatched it out of my hand and tossed it on the coffee table. One week, when I went over the day after I'd dropped off the profits, the paper bag was still laying on the coffee table. And, according to Joyce, he'd even misplaced a few bags among all that junk he and my mother-in-law hoarded. I had advised her to find out where they stashed the money, because if something happened to them before she got that information, she'd have a major problem on her hands trying to find it.

Joyce was going to inherit a lot, but what if she decided she didn't want to stay married to me? What if she got so desperate for a baby, she thought she'd have better luck with a different husband? These were some of the thoughts running through my head while I sat at my desk counting the money I had in my wallet. I was trying to decide how much I was going to give Betty Jean so she could buy the new furniture she'd been begging for all year. I realized I needed to update my backup plan. At ten-thirty a.m., somebody knocked on my door and I opened it right away.

It was Sadie. Standing next to her was Artherine Miller, a bothersome customer who shopped in the store several times a week. And, she complained about something several times a week. "What is it?" I gazed at the Miller woman's angry wrinkled face.

"Odell, I hate to bother you, but Sister Miller got a problem *again*," Sadie told me, rolling her eyes.

I groaned under my breath. "Sister Miller, what's the problem this time?"

"I bought two pounds of hog head cheese here earlier this morning. When me and my husband ate it, we realized right away it was stale and we didn't enjoy it. I want my money back!" Mrs. Miller shouted, waving a receipt in my face.

"I'm sorry to hear that. What did you do with the hog head cheese?"

"We ate it. How you think we found out it was bad?"

"Y'all ate all two pounds?"

"Yeah. Why?"

"If you noticed 'right away' that it was stale, why didn't you stop eating it and bring back what was left so I could take a look at it?"

"That's what I'd like to know," Sadie mumbled.

"We was hungry, that's why we kept eating it!"

I gave Sadie a pleading look. "Give Sister Miller a refund." I turned back to the Miller woman. "Is there anything else I can help you with, ma'am?"

"Well, I been meaning to come talk to y'all about the baloney I got here last Friday. There was a green spot on one of the slices. The only reason I ain't been back to straighten things out is on account of I misplaced that receipt."

I held up my hand. "Um, we can discuss the green baloney when you find that receipt. Now, if you don't mind, I have a lot of work to do. Y'all please excuse me."

I closed my door and sat back down at my desk. There was so many thoughts bouncing around in my head, it started throbbing. After resting for about twenty minutes, I started counting money again. I had lost my place and had to start all over. Two minutes later, somebody knocked on my door again. I assumed the Miller woman had found her receipt and had come back to get another refund. Before I could get up, the door swung open and Milton strutted in like a banty rooster. Something told me this was not going to be a pleasant visit.

"Oh, it's you again," I groaned, dropping the bills to the floor before he could see them. When he started strutting toward me, I scooted the money farther up under my desk with my foot. I stood up with my hands on my hips.

"Yeah, it's me again. I need another favor," he said. He gave me a smug look and held up his hand. "And I swear this will be the last time."

"It better be. What do you need more money for?"

Milton leaned over my desk and whined, "I got a mess on my hands. I got skunked in a crap game we had at the house last night, so I'm in a pickle again. Yvonne will shit a brick if she was to find out I lost the rent money."

"Didn't I give you enough money for two months' rent?"

"You did. That's exactly what I lost. So now I'm right back where I was when I first came to see you. . . ."

I was fit to be tied. I realized that this greedy motherfucker was going to milk me like I was a cow! Somehow I managed to keep my cool. But if I thought I could kill him and get away with it, I would have jumped over my desk and wrung his fucking neck!

"Look, Milton. I ain't a bank, so you need to find another way to get money when you get low. How do I know you won't come back for more?"

"I won't . . . unless I really need to. I don't want to put too much pressure on you. I figure you got enough of that already. You . . . um . . . you do take care of that other woman and them young'ns, right?"

I took my time answering. "I help out as much as I can."

"Good! If I was you, I'd be doing the same thing." He gave me a smug look, and then he had the nerve to smile. His big, dingy teeth reminded me of stale hominy corn. "I really like you, my man, and I enjoy being around you. I hope your class and good manners and whatnot rub off on me. If you give me a job in the store, I can be around you even more. And I'd be able to cut back on my boot-legging hours. I'm so sick of doing that shit so much any-way. Entertaining a house full of drunks every night and doing business with them hillbillies done finally got to me. I do declare, I been waiting on a good opportunity like this all my life."

Chapter 47
Odell

I COULDN'T BELIEVE MY EARS! MILTON WAS THE LAST person I wanted to look at eight hours a day, five days a week. Especially now that I knew what kind of man he really was. If he could blackmail me, there was no telling what else he was capable of doing. I thought about that picnic basket Betty Jean had packed last Saturday and how it had looked exactly like the one Joyce had packed when we'd celebrated our anniversary last year. Now I realized that it had not been just a coincidence; it had been a premonition that something real bad was going to happen to me. "You want me to give *you* a job in this store?"

"Yup. I know you'll pay me good and you know I'm a hardworking man. With me making more money, I'll be able to take care of my finances without no more help from you."

"I don't know if my in-laws would go for me hiring you—"

Milton wasted no time cutting me off. He held up his hand and shook his head. "Uh-uh. Don't even go there. I don't want to hear that shit!"

I let out a loud, heavy sigh and rubbed my eyes. The sight of Milton was making them burn and itch. "The only position I have open right now is stocking shelves. It's only part-time and I can't pay you but thirty cent a hour, the same thing Mac paid me when I stocked shelves. Working part-time, you'll take home about eight dollars a week and—"

He cut me off again. "I'll take it!"

"Hold your horses, Milton," I said with my hand in the air. "It ain't that cut and dry. I need some time to think about this."

He shook his head and glared at me with his eyes looking like slits. "I can start next Monday."

I knew when I was fighting a losing battle. If the corner I'd been backed into got any smaller, I'd blend into the wall. "Okay," I mumbled. "Be here at nine o'clock sharp."

"I'll be here with bells on." Milton winked. Then he clapped his hands and danced a jig. "I can't wait to see Yvonne's face when I tell her I'm going to be working at the famous MacPherson's store! Wahoo!"

"Don't tell her until I tell Joyce first," I pleaded.

"Man, you got Joyce in the bottom of your hip pocket! You can do whatever you want and she won't give you no trouble. Don't you know that by now?"

I nodded real slow because it was true. For how long though? Now Milton had me in the bottom of his hip pocket. But I believed that as long as I kept him, Joyce, and Betty Jean happy, everything would be all right.

"I'll come over to your place this evening after I talk to Joyce about hiring you. Even if she do go along with it, I'd still have to run it by Mac and Millie."

"Wait a minute. You just told me to be here Monday morning at nine o'clock." Milton's eyes darkened. He screwed up his face and wiped his forehead with the back of his hand, which was shaking as hard as mine. That didn't make no sense, because I was the one on the hot seat and had the most to lose.

Now that it had sunk in that I was in one hell of a mess, I was scared to death, to say the least. I tried to keep my voice firm, but it wasn't easy. I wanted to put my fist through the wall and upside Milton's head. But for everybody's sake involved, I had to stay as cool as I could. "Yeah, but I spoke too soon." My tone was more gentle now.

"Bullshit! You trying to tell me you didn't know what you was saying!"

"Man, you can't expect me to be thinking straight when you came out of nowhere with this thing! I just said the first thing that came to my head!"

"Well, you better start using your head for something other than a hat rack."

"Milton, put yourself in my place. You got me over a barrel and I want us to handle this right. Now, like I said, I really do need to make sure it's okay with my wife and my in-laws for me to hire you."

"All right. What *we* going to do if they don't go for it?"

I was so exasperated, I could barely keep on talking. "Look, Milton. I don't know what 'we' going to do if they don't. I'm still just one of Mac and Millie's employees."

"SHIT! I ain't no fool," he shot back. He slapped the top of my desk and for a second I thought he was going to slap me. "You married to their only child and they got you running that damn place, so I know you more than just a employee. Don't tell me you can't get over on your wife and them old geezers!"

"Will you keep your voice down!" I hissed with my hand in the air.

"I guess you done forgot you told me that they said you can hire and fire anybody you want to."

"Yeah, I did tell you that. But you ain't just anybody. You know Mac and Millie is real religious. They have some concerns about me and Joyce being friends with you and Yvonne. And I don't blame them."

"Oh yeah? And what's that supposed to mean?"

"You have a criminal background."

"Don't be bringing up my past. I'm a changed man. I ain't been involved in no criminal activity in years!"

"Oh yeah? Bootlegging is against the law. A lot of people would have a problem with a bootlegger working in a family, Christian-owned store like MacPherson's!" I shuddered and my eyes got big as I peered at Milton with my mouth hanging open. "My preacher would think I done lost my mind."

He gave me a threatening look and puffed out his chest. "Reverend Jessup would probably think the same thing if he found out about you having a outside woman and three babies. Now, I advise you to go up to Joyce as soon as you get home this evening. If you win her over, she'll help you sweeten up Mac and Millie. We straight?"

With my head hanging low, I mumbled, "We straight."

"Good." Milton let out a long, loud sigh and licked his lips. "Well, I'll let you get back to whatever you was doing. I hope when you come to the house this evening, you'll have some good news for me."

"I hope so too. We done here now?"

He gave me a thoughtful look and shook his head. "I want to bring up one more thing."

If my heart started beating any faster and harder, it would leave a tattoo on the inside of my chest. "What? If it's about the pinstripe suit, we ain't got no white ones in stock right now. I put in a new order this morning, but they won't come in until next week."

"I can wait. And what I wanted to talk about was your girl, Billie Jean."

"*Betty* Jean."

"Whatever. She sure is a cutie pie. I been thinking about her ever since I seen her. She must be the finest-looking woman in Hartville. That booty she got on her ought to be served on a platter."

I wanted to gut Milton and hang him out to dry. The thought of this slimy devil trying to get his paws on Betty Jean almost made me puke! "Don't you even think about it!" I shook my fist in his face and gave him the most menacing look I could conjure up. If looks could kill, he would have dropped dead in front of me and that would have been just fine.

"Think about what?" he asked with his eyebrows raised.

"What is it you trying to say now?" I couldn't get any angrier with this jackass if I tried. "If you go near my woman I will—"

Milton wasted no time cutting me off. "Hold still, brother man. Get your mind out the gutter. I wouldn't never go after the woman of my best friend."

"Then where the hell is this conversation going?"

"I admire you for picking a woman that's as easy on the eye as Betty Jean is. All I want to know now is if she got a sister or some friend girls that's as pretty as she is."

"She got a sister and she got several friend girls. But they all married."

"So what? Being married don't mean nothing! That ain't never stopped nobody from creeping," he laughed. "And don't nobody know that better than you, huh?"

"Milton, I have to get back to work." I didn't give him a chance to say anything else. I literally ran to the door and held it open for him. After he left, I read my Bible some more.

Chapter 48
Joyce

WHEN I GOT HOME FROM WORK, YVONNE WAS SWEEP-
ing off her front porch. We waved to each other and five
minutes after I got in the house, she was at my front door.

"It's a shame me and Milton ain't got no phone so I
can call you up sometime instead of having to come
over," she complained.

"Well, phones do come in handy. I don't know what
we'd do without ours. You want to come in?" I was just
being nice. I didn't feel like entertaining her. I still liked
her and she was a lot of fun, but I couldn't ignore the fact
that she was also a source of pain for me. It was no fun
standing in a pretty woman's shadow. It wasn't so bad
when there were other average-looking women around;
like the times I was at her house when there was a crowd.
That way I didn't feel so singled out.

"That's all right. I can't stay. I just wanted to see if

you'd like to go to the shoe store with me on Saturday. One of the waitresses I work with is getting married in a couple of weeks and the only pair of dress shoes I got is so shabby I wouldn't wear them to a dogfight, let alone a wedding."

I hadn't been out in public with Yvonne since that day all those men tried to hit on her. I was still a little irritated about the one that had mistaken me for her mother. And I wasn't ready to get my feelings hurt again so soon by strange men. "Thanks, but I promised Mama I'd help her finish that quilt she started last month."

"Oh. Well, if you change your mind, let me know."

"I'll do that."

When I heard Odell's car pull up a few minutes after six p.m., I ran from the kitchen to the living room window. There was a smile on my face until I spotted Mama and Daddy strutting toward him. Daddy clapped Odell on the back and Mama gave him a hug. I was not in the mood to deal with my parents this evening and I prayed they wouldn't stay long. And because they'd ambushed Odell, I couldn't pretend like I was not in the house. I sighed and went back into the kitchen to check on the supper I had almost finished cooking.

About a minute later, I heard the living room door open. "Whatever it is you cooking in there, I hope you ain't using too much salt!" Mama yelled.

"Pig tails, I bet," Daddy added.

When I returned to the living room a few moments later, Mama and Daddy were on the couch, and Odell had flopped down in the easy chair facing them. My parents looked as bored as they usually did. Odell had already kicked off his shoes and unbuttoned his shirt, but he looked worried. And that worried me.

"Baby, have a seat," he told me, with his voice sounding weak and tired.

"What's the matter?" I was afraid to hear his answer. I remained standing in the middle of the floor with my hands on my hips.

Odell blew out some air and rubbed the back of his neck. "Nothing is the matter. I, uh, got something to run by all of y'all and I'm glad everybody is here so I won't have to say it but one time."

"Odell, what's going on?" I demanded, folding my arms and shifting my weight from one foot to the other.

"Y'all know I need to hire another boy to help stock the shelves." He stopped and gave me a hopeful look. Mama and Daddy had curious expressions on their faces, and the rest of their bodies looked as stiff as statues.

"What's going on here, boy?" Daddy peered at Odell from the corner of his eye. "Get to the point," he ordered.

"I'm getting to it," Odell said, looking at me with both his eyebrows raised. "Joyce, you know how we been trying to be better friends with our new neighbors."

"So? What do they have to do with you needing to hire another stock boy?" I wanted to know.

"Milton said he would like to take the job."

"That bootlegger next door?" Mama and Daddy said at the same time. Mama looked horrified. Daddy looked amused. Odell still looked worried. I didn't know how to react.

"Did he lose his job at that grill?" I asked.

"No, he said he can keep that and still work for us part-time," Odell replied.

"Pffft! Naw, naw! That scalawag ain't working in our store part-time, or no other time. He'd give the place such a bad name, the customers that done kept us in business all these years would run us out of town on a rail," Daddy howled. "How can you even fix your lips to spew out them words, boy?"

"What's wrong with you, Odell Watson? You ought to be ashamed of yourself," Mama scolded.

"Milton and Yvonne are really nice people in their own way. I feel kind of sorry for them," I said, more for Odell's benefit than mine. I was convinced that it was going to be harder for him to develop a good relationship with Milton than me with Yvonne. Milton was a little more of an ignoramus than she was, so more work had to be done on him to lift him up to our level.

"Well, I don't feel sorry for them fools, and you can tell them just what I said," Daddy boomed. "When did this come up?"

"Milton came by the store today," Odell went on. "Him and Yvonne is having a rough time paying their rent and could use a little more income."

"Didn't they think about that before they moved to this neighborhood?" Mama barked.

"I guess they didn't," Daddy added. "That ain't our problem! Don't even think about putting no bootlegger on our payroll. Shoot!"

Odell looked relieved. I was glad when he laughed and shook his head. "I kind of figured this is what y'all would say and I told him so. But he still wanted me to run it by y'all. I'll let him know as soon as I see him again."

"Odell, tell him in a nice way," I suggested. "Or do you want me to tell him?"

"I don't care which one of y'all tell him. If I wasn't superstitious about going up in a bootlegger's house, I'd go

over there right now and tell him myself." Right after
Mama said that, somebody pounded on our door. I was so
anxious to see who it was, I literally ran to open it.

It was Milton. There was a smile on his face that was
as wide as a crocodile's.

"Oops! I didn't know y'all had company. I can come
back later," he said when he saw Mama and Daddy sitting
on the couch frowning like pallbearers.

"Naw, you come on in," Odell invited. "You ain't met
my in-laws yet."

"Uh, I done spoke to Mr. MacPherson in the store a
time or two." Milton stumbled over his words and was
just as clumsy with his feet when he walked into the
house. He almost tripped over one of my area rugs. When
he got close to the couch, Daddy reached his hand up and
shook Milton's. Milton, with that stupid grin still on his
face, nodded at Mama. "I met you before too, Mrs. Mac-
Pherson. One day I came in the store to buy some baloney
and you gave me a complimentary pig foot. I guess y'all
don't remember me."

"I remember you. Right after you gobbled up that pig
foot, you had the nerve to ask for another one," Mama
sniffed.

"That was because it tasted so good." Milton put his
hands in his pockets. "Um, I ain't going to stay but a hot
minute. Yvonne sent me over here to see if Joyce had
some baking powder she can borrow so she can make
some hush puppies to go with them collard greens she
cooking for supper this evening."

"I'll go get it," Odell said before I could. He leaped up
out of his seat and headed toward the kitchen with Milton
on his heels.

"Do that Yvonne gal even know how to cook worth a

dime?" Mama asked in a low voice as soon as they were out of earshot.

"She must. Didn't you notice the size of that boy's belly?" Daddy brought up.

"He could have a tumor for all you know," Mama pointed out.

"I don't know about that. But one thing I do know is that wife of his gets around like a spinning top. I seen her in Mosella's the last time I was there. She was acting like a floozy with some white joker."

"Daddy, how did you know it was Yvonne? Have you ever met her?" I asked.

"Girl, I ain't met a lot of the colored folks in this town, but I know who is who."

"That white guy you saw her with was probably their best friend, Willie Frank; the man they buy their alcohol from," I explained. "He's a real nice guy."

"Humph! I bet he ain't nice enough to take no colored people around his kinfolks," Mama said sharply.

"Mama and Daddy, for your information, Willie Frank's relatives are not racists. I met his nephew and he seems real sweet. And Yvonne and Milton go visit with Willie Frank and his folks at their house all the time."

It didn't matter what I said, my parents continued to mean-mouth Yvonne and Milton. Despite the few "mean" thoughts I'd had about them myself, I still defended them some more. "Once you get to know them, they're not so bad."

"Maybe they ain't. But I advise you and Odell not to never let your guard down with them two buggers. You don't know what they capable of doing. There is a heap of bootleggers in prison," Daddy said with a firm nod.

"And even more in the cemeteries," Mama threw in.

I gave them an exasperated look. Knowing how they felt, I knew that I would never tell them that Yvonne and Milton had already done jail time. But the statements they'd just made sounded so ominous, a chill that felt like a bolt of lightning shot up my spine.

A couple of minutes had passed and Odell and Milton were still in the kitchen. I had no idea what was taking them so long. The baking powder was on the counter where it always was.

Chapter 49
Odell

"*M*ILTON, I TRIED TO TELL YOU THAT THEY WOULDN'T go for me giving you a job," I said in a low voice through clenched teeth. "How many more times do I have to tell you that?"

"You want me to talk to Mac?"

My mouth dropped open. "What good would that do?"

Milton scratched his chin and gave me a disgusted look. Now that I knew how greedy and evil he was, I realized he was as ugly on the inside as he was on the outside. His flat, pie-shaped face reminded me of a gnome I'd seen in one of them *Weird Tales* horror magazines I used to read when I was younger. "This ain't good, man. I could sure use some extra money. I would love to have me a car."

I gasped. "I'm sure everybody else that ain't got no car would love to have one," I snapped. "Now, you just going

to have to be satisfied with what I done gave you already.
I thought that was going to be all you wanted. I gave you
everything you asked for and then some. That was all I
could spare. You telling me now you need even more?"

Milton heaved out a loud breath and gave me a look
that was so intense, it made me tremble. I moved a few
steps away from him. "Well, like you told me yesterday, I
spoke too soon. I do need more. . . ."

My jaw dropped. "And you call yourself my friend?"

His liver-colored lips quivered, and for a second I
thought he was going to bust out laughing. "Yeah, I'm
your friend. That's why I'm willing to work with you."

I waved my hands in the air. "Okay, tell me what else
you want. And I want it to be the last thing you ask me
for, because I can't do no more! I'm done!"

His eyes suddenly lit up and he rubbed his hands together. "But I ain't 'done' and we both know that where
there is a will, there is a way."

I slapped the side of my head, which felt so heavy I
was surprised I was still able to hold it up. "Why don't
you tell me what that way is? All I know is, you can't get
blood from a turnip."

"You can milk a cow dry, but once they get motivated
again, they will produce more milk. The way your jaw is
twitching, I can tell you know exactly what I mean."

Just when I was about to open my mouth again, Joyce
yelled from the living room, "Odell, you can't find the
baking powder?"

"Um, yeah, baby. I got it," I yelled back. I snatched the
can of baking powder off the counter and handed it to
Milton. "We better get back out there."

"We ain't finished talking yet," he hissed.

"We is for now!"

"Then you better come over tonight so we can finish. Unless you want me to come by the store again tomorrow."

"That's another thing. I don't want you coming back to the store no time soon. And I don't want you coming there too often. Buddy and Sadie will start putting bugs in Mac's ear."

"Pffft! Why would them old fools do that? They know me and you is friends and neighbors."

"It is real suspicious for me and you to hole up in my office with the door shut when we ain't never done it before. We did that two days in a row and it got Buddy and Sadie's attention. How many more times do you think we can meet like that before their long tongues start wagging?"

"Well, we gots to talk *somewhere*."

"I'll come over tonight. Now will you go on back home?" I ushered Milton out the back door and returned to the living room. I was glad to see that Mac and Millie had left.

"I thought they was staying for supper?" I said. Joyce was sitting on the couch, and I sat down next to her.

"They decided to go to Mosella's instead." She gave me a curious look. "What was Milton talking about in there?"

I shrugged. "Nothing important. He was telling me about how Willie Frank almost got busted by the revenuers the other day."

"I thought he paid them off so they'd leave him alone."

"Well, they done got greedy and now they want more money."

Joyce blinked and touched my thigh. "Well, if he asks

you for more loans, I don't mind as long as he pays you back. Did you tell him you couldn't hire him?"

"Yeah. He was all right with it. I told him I'd come over for a little while this evening. You want to go with me?"

Joyce took her time responding. "I think I'll stay home tonight. I don't want to wear out my welcome. Besides, I have a bushel basket of clothes to iron."

Within minutes after Joyce and I had eaten supper, I eased out of the house and headed next door. Milton let me in and wasted no time getting in my face. "Come on. Let's go somewhere so we can talk," he growled. He steered me toward the kitchen, clutching my arm like he thought I was going to try to escape.

There was a small crowd milling about. Yvonne and Willie Frank were huddled in a corner and didn't notice me. "If you don't mind, can I have a drink first?" I stopped abruptly and pried Milton's fingers off my arm.

"You can get all you want after we talk," he insisted. I followed him into the kitchen, but there was a woman at the sink rinsing out jars. "Let's go in the bedroom."

I followed Milton back down the narrow hall and into the bedroom directly across from the bathroom. When we got inside, he clicked on a lamp. Just like the ones in the living room, it didn't have a shade neither. He closed and locked the door and turned to me with his hands on his hips.

"I got a solution to our problem. It came to me a little while ago." Milton rubbed his nose and snorted. There was actually a gleam in his eyes. "You told me you'd pay me thirty cent a hour to stock shelves, right?"

"Yeah, and I told you that I can't hire you now."

"But you can still pay me thirty cent a hour."

"Excuse me?"

Milton put his hand on my shoulder. "If you was going to pay me when you thought you could hire me, that mean you got the money to pay me. The only difference is, I won't be working. That would be a much sweeter deal."

I threw up my hands and headed back toward the door. He followed me, walking so close he stepped on my heels. I stopped and whirled around. "You must think I'm crazy!"

"If you make me blow the whistle on you when I'm giving you a chance to stop me, you crazier than me!" he yelled, stabbing my chest with his finger.

I grabbed Milton by his shoulders. I pushed him up against the wall and held him in place. I couldn't tell which one of us was breathing and snorting the loudest. "Do you honestly think I'd be willing to put you on the MacPherson's payroll and you don't work there?"

"Turn me loose, Odell!" His breath was so hot, I was scared I'd get scorched. I released him and moved to the side, huffing and puffing like a bull. "Don't you never come in my house and manhandle me again. It'd make things a whole lot worse than they already is," he warned.

"All right. I'm sorry. I just lost it," I apologized.

"You give me my money under the table in cash and ain't nobody got to know nothing."

I stared at the floor, which was where I thought my stomach had dropped to. When I looked back at Milton, that stupid, crocodile grin I had come to hate was on his face. "And how long do you expect me to pay you off, man?"

He shrugged. "As long as you want to."

"And what will happen when I don't want to?"

"You can answer that question yourself."

Chapter 50
Odell

*L*AST NIGHT AFTER TWO DRINKS AND LISTENING TO A few more minutes of Milton's rigmarole, I agreed to pay him off every Wednesday, starting this week. That bastard! I cursed the day I met his greedy, lowdown black ass!

The day after our conversation at his house, he showed up at my door a few minutes after I got home from work with a stupid look on his face. "Today is Wednesday, so you know what I come for," he snickered, looking over my shoulder. "Where Joyce at?"

"Don't worry about her. She went to a tent revival with her mama and daddy so she'll be gone for a while. Come on in." I didn't waste no time pulling out my wallet, disappointed to see that I didn't have exact change. All I had on me was two tens and some loose change. "Can you break this?" I waved one of the bills in his face. "I didn't have time to check my money before I left the store. I meant to get a few dollars from Joyce before she left but I forgot."

"Nope, I can't break no ten-spot. I ain't got nothing on me but some pocket change." He grabbed the money and slid it into his back pocket. "It's cool, so don't worry about it. I wouldn't cheat you. Next week all you need to pay me is six bucks."

"Fine," I mumbled. "Listen, man. It'll look suspicious for you to suddenly start coming over here every Wednesday. Sooner or later, Joyce will start asking questions."

He shrugged. "No problem. Then you'll need to bring my money to me. Just don't hand it to me in front of Yvonne. And just to show you how fair I am, if you pay late I ain't going to charge you interest. Just don't make being late no habit." Milton sniffled and gave me a smug look. "You mind if I sit down and stay a few minutes? I had a real hard day." I couldn't believe how casual he was acting. I didn't want to do or say nothing that would make him mad. Paying him off wasn't enough. I had to be "nice" to him too, so he wouldn't raise the stakes.

"Yeah, but I have to go somewhere in a little while," I told him as I waved him to the couch. I sat down at the opposite end with my arms folded, tapping my foot impatiently.

"I won't stay long. I just wanted to chat for a little bit."

"What about?"

"You really love your babies, don't you?"

"Of course I do. I hope to have some more. I just pray that me and Joyce have a few someday. It would mean the world to her, and to me. But, after all this time, I don't know if she's able to get pregnant again or not. I'd never say that to her though. The miscarriage she had a few years ago was real rough on her. She bled for almost a whole week. What do you care? I thought all you cared about was money."

Milton focused on the wall for a moment, and then he turned to me with the saddest face I'd ever seen. I thought he was about to cry. If one of us had something to cry about it was me! But I refused to let him see me squirm any more than he already had. "I can understand you having a attitude, but things could be a whole lot worse for you. I could have been a sure enough asshole and took your money and told Joyce about you and Betty Jean anyway."

"You might still do that!" I seethed. I got up and stood in front of him. "But I'm telling you now, if you do, you'll curse the day you was born!"

Milton's eyes got as big as walnuts and he stood up. "I could take that as a threat!"

"You can take it for whatever you want."

"Humph! Well, I know you don't mean it as no threat. I don't know you that well, but I can tell that you too sissified to be the violent type. I picked up on that the first time I met you." The self-satisfied smirk on his face was off the charts. I couldn't get no madder if I tried. On top of everything else, this low-down dog was hinting that I was a *pantywaist*! It was one of the worst things you could call a man—colored or white. I didn't react to his comment—which was a straight-up lie. I was scared that if I did he'd harp on it until I snapped. And if that happened, all hell would break loose and I wouldn't settle down until one of us was dead. He sat back down and crossed his legs. I stayed in the same spot. "You know me and you can't act no different now," he continued. The smirk was still on his face.

"Milton, what the hell do you mean by that?"

"We can't stop being buddy-buddy and have Joyce, Yvonne, Willie Frank, and everybody else asking a bunch of nosy questions. I want you to keep coming to the house for drinks, and I'll keep coming here now and then for supper and just to say hello. Since we had to skip that Fourth of July cookout, it would be nice if we could do one before it get too cold," Milton babbled, holding up his hand. "I heard you know how to cook some mean ribs." The thought of this monkey taking my money and eating my food made my blood boil. If he didn't leave in the next couple of minutes, I was not going to be responsible for my actions.

"Joyce said something about having a barbecue toward the end of next month. Summer school will be out then and she'll have a couple of weeks of free time on her hands until regular school starts back up."

"Good! Just let us know when." He stood up and stretched. "Your couch is so comfy, I would have stretched out and took me a nap—if you didn't have to go somewhere. In the meantime, I'd better skedaddle so you can go wherever it is you got to go. When you get there, have fun." He winked and made a obscene gesture with his fingers.

"You . . . you won't let me down, will you?" I asked, walking him to the door.

"Let you down how?"

"With the arrangement we made, I ain't never got to worry about you blabbing my business, right?"

"Not as long as you keep up your end of the deal. And by the way, if you ever need to use me as a alibi, I'm game."

"Why would I need to use you?"

"Pffft!" Milton dipped his head and crowed like the beast he was. "Brother, your daddy got one foot in the grave and the other one on a banana peel. When he go to meet his maker, where you going to tell Joyce you going when you need to go to Hartville? That day I seen you in that restaurant with your other woman and them kids, Joyce had told us that you was with your daddy. It don't take no genius to figure out that's what you got her believing a lot of other times, too. And that fish story you keep using was fishy from the get-go to me."

"I do go fishing a lot!"

"I'm sure you do. But now that the jig is up, I got a feeling you wasn't fishing all them times you claim you was. After your daddy is gone, you can tell Joyce you going fishing with me and Willie Frank. We go at least twice a month, and some days we stay five or six hours. That's more than enough time for you to sneak over to Hartville to play house and get a quickie."

I gave Milton a doubtful look and shook my head. "I don't want Willie Frank to know nothing about my business in Hartville."

"Well, unless you tell him, or he catches you too, he won't. What I'm trying to tell you is that I do go fishing. Sometime I go by myself. If you want Joyce to think you with me, just let me know."

"You must be the last person in the world I'd expect to want to help me keep the wool over Joyce's eyes. Why did you even bring it up?"

"Eight dollars a week is a good enough reason for me. If Joyce was to find out some other way that you been playing her for a fool all these years, you won't have no reason to keep paying me, and then I'll be back to having the same financial problems I had before. Now, like I said, anytime you want to use me for a alibi, just let me know." He opened the door and before he darted out, he had the nerve to give me a playful punch on my shoulder.

I hadn't planned to visit Betty Jean again until the weekend, but it had been a couple of weeks since I'd seen her on a weekday. Five minutes after I got rid of Milton, I splashed some cold water on my face to calm my nerves, and then I stumbled out to my car and shot off toward the highway. I was so worked up I needed to see her, especially since she was the cause of the pickle I was in. I wasn't going to tell her what was going on. But she knew something was wrong the minute I walked in her door and didn't kiss or grope her the way I usually did.

"Odell, what's the matter?"

"Where the boys at?"

"They outside playing with the kids that live down the road. Sit down before you fall down and tell me why you looking like you seen a haint." We sat down on the couch.

"Uh, it ain't nothing for you to worry about." I swallowed hard and started raking my fingers through her hair.

"If it's something for you to worry about, it's something for me to worry about. Now tell me what it is."

"Um . . . I had to hit somebody today and I feel real bad about it."

Betty Jean reared back and gave me a skeptical look. "*You*? You didn't even want to squash them ants that almost ruined our picnic last Saturday! Who did you hit and why?"

"A customer was trying to steal some gum and I caught him in the act. We tussled and he swung at me." My lie was as flimsy as it could be, but it was the best I could come up with. "And I hit him back."

"If you was defending yourself, why do you feel bad about it? Did you hurt him?"

I shook my head. "I just busted his lip. But he wasn't no more than fifteen or sixteen. I ain't never hit a kid and that's why I feel bad about it. I know his mama. She is the frantic type, so she'll probably come to the store and raise hell."

"So let her! Did anybody see what happened?"

"Yeah, the cashiers and a couple of other customers."

Betty Jean laughed. "I thought something real serious had happened. You really had me scared for a minute. The next time you come here in such a funk, I hope it's because of something we really need to worry about. The way you was looking a few minutes ago, I thought maybe somebody in Branson had found out about me."

"Baby, they don't know and they never will. I got everything under control."

"Well, I hope you keep it under control. You the only person me and the boys can always count on. If I was to lose you, my life would never be the same again."

"I feel the same way, sugar." I pulled Betty Jean into my arms and gave her the most passionate kiss I ever gave any other woman—including Joyce.

Eight dollars a week was a lot of money to give Milton. But it was a small price to pay to keep everybody happy. I was prepared to do it until I died, unless he died first.

ONE HOUSE OVER

Mary Monroe

ABOUT THIS GUIDE

The suggested questions that follow are included to
enhance your group's reading of this book.

DISCUSSION QUESTIONS

1. Joyce was a smart woman, but she was also a desperate woman. She couldn't wait to get married so her meddlesome parents would stop badgering her to find a husband. By the time she turned thirty she was willing to marry *any* man—whether she loved him or not—because she wanted children and didn't want to grow old alone. Do you think it's a bad idea for anyone to get married for these reasons?

2. Despite her intelligence, Joyce was naïve enough to believe *everything* Odell told her because she was hopelessly in love with him. She even got pregnant on purpose so she would at least have part of him in case he ended their relationship. Have you ever been this crazy in love?

3. If you answered yes to the question above, are you still a fool when it comes to love? If not you, do you have any close acquaintances who are as lovestruck as Joyce? If so, do you ever try to talk some sense into their heads?

4. Joyce was well-to-do and meek. She was the perfect prey for down-on-his-luck Odell. If you have ever been as easy to exploit as Joyce, did it lead to a bad experience? If so, did you learn from it, or were you gullible enough to make the same mistakes more than one time? With the same mate or new ones?

5. Odell wanted security and a wife. Joyce was not the physical type of woman he'd always wanted to settle down with, but he loved her anyway. The fact that she was going to inherit a small fortune someday sweetened the pot. Were you surprised when he cheated on her the month after their wedding?

6. It was love at first sight the moment Betty Jean saw Odell. She used every trick in the book to get him into her bed as fast as she could—which was only a couple of hours after they'd met. Do you think if he had not been in "the wrong place at the wrong time" (the excuse he blamed for his predicament), he would have never cheated on Joyce?

7. Odell hadn't planned on having a serious relationship with Betty Jean until he got her pregnant. Do you think that if Joyce hadn't lost her baby, he might not have gotten so involved with Betty Jean and had two more children with her?

8. Joyce's parents were meddlesome, but they meant well. Do you think she would have been a stronger and more realistic woman if she had moved away from home when she was much younger?

9. Betty Jean was attracted to Odell because he was tall, dark, well-built, very handsome, and he had a great personality. Joyce was attracted to him for the same reasons. Are a person's looks important to you? If your answer is no, would you consider an

out-of-shape partner with plain features if they had a great personality?

10. Yvonne and Milton had criminal backgrounds and they did whatever they had to do to get what they wanted. They were jealous of Joyce and Odell and started plotting ways to use them. Do you know any people who are "best friends" and "worst enemies" at the same time? Have you ever been in this situation?

11. To support his mistress and their children, Odell embezzled money from the business he managed for his in-laws. Do you blame Joyce's parents for being so trusting and nonchalant about money?

12. Odell had a good thing going until Milton accidentally discovered his relationship with Betty Jean and decided to blackmail him. Would Odell have been better off if he had not agreed to pay Milton, told Joyce about Betty Jean himself, and put some of the blame on Joyce for his affair because she hadn't been able to give him children?

13. Odell thought that paying Milton off would be a one-time thing. Milton came back the next day and asked for more money *and* a job. Blackmail usually ends badly for everyone involved. Do you think Odell dug a deeper hole for himself by agreeing to Milton's new demands?